(Law)
ZET

(L̲aw)
ZE⁻

William Janvesup

AN

APPEAL

To all that Doubt, or Difbelieve

The Truths of the GOSPEL,

WHETHER

They be DEISTS, ARIANS, SOCINIANS,
Or *Nominal* Chriftians.

IN WHICH

The true Grounds and Reafons of the whole
Chriftian FAITH and LIFE are plainly and
fully demonftrated.

By *WILLIAM LAW*, M. A.

To which are added,

Some Animadverfions upon Dr. *Trap*'s
Late REPLY.

The SECOND EDITION.

LONDON:

Printed for W. INNYS, and J. RICHARDSON,
in *Pater Nofter Row.*

M DCC LVI.

CHAP. I.

Of Creation in general. Of the Origin of the Soul. Whence Will and Thought are in the Creature. Why the Will is free. The Origin of Evil solely from the Creature. This World not a first, immediate Creation of God. How the World comes to be in its present State. The first Perfection of Man. All Things prove a Trinity in God. Man hath the triune Nature of God in Him. Arianism *and* Deism *confuted by Nature. That Life is uniform through all Creatures. That there is but one kind of Death to be found in all Nature. The fallen Soul hath the Nature of Hell in it. Regeneration is a real Birth of a Divine Life in the Soul. That there is but one Salvation possible in Nature. This Salvation only to be had from* Jesus Christ. *All the Deists Faith and Hope prov'd to be false.*

1. IT has been an Opinion commonly received, tho' without any Foundation in the Light of Nature, or Scripture, that God created this whole visible World, and all Things in it,

B *out*

out of Nothing. Nay, that the Souls of Men,
and the higheſt Orders of Beings, were created
in the ſame Manner. The Scripture is very deciſive againſt this Original of the Souls of Men.
For *Moſes* ſaith, God *breathed into Man (Spi-*
ràculum Vitarum) the Breath of Lives, and
Man became a Living Soul. Here the Notion
of a Soul created *out of Nothing,* is in the
plaineſt, ſtrongeſt Manner rejeɗed, by the
firſt Written Word of God ; and no *Jew* or
Chriſtian can have the leaſt Excuſe for falling
into ſuch an Error ; here the higheſt and moſt
Divine Original is not darkly, but openly,
abſolutely, and in the ſtrongeſt Form of Expreſſion aſcribed to the Soul ; it came forth as
a Breath of Life, or Lives, out from the Mouth
of God, and therefore did not come out of the
Womb of *Nothing,* but is what it is, and has
what it has in itſelf, from, and out of the firſt
and higheſt of all Beings.

For to ſay that God breathed forth into Man
the Breath of Lives, by which He became a
Living Soul, is direɗly ſaying, that *That* which
was Life, Light, and Spirit in the living God,
was breathed forth from Him to become the
Life, Light and Spirit of a Creature. The
Soul therefore being declared to be an Ef-
fluence from God, a *Breath* of God, muſt
have

have the *Nature* and *Likeness* of God in it, and is, and can be nothing else, but something, or so much of the *Divine Nature*, become creaturely existing, or breathed forth from God, to stand before Him in the *Form* of a Creature.

When the Animals of this World were to be created, it was only said, Let the Earth, the Air, the Water bring forth Creatures after their kinds; but when Man was to be brought forth, it was said, *Let us make Man in our own Image and Likeness.* Is not this directly saying, Let Man have his Beginning and Being out of us, that He may be so related to us in his Soul and Spirit, as the Animals of this World are related to the Elements from which they are produced. Let Him so come forth from us, be so breathed out of us, that our tri-une, divine Nature may be manifested in Him, that he may stand before us as a creaturely Image, Likeness, and Representative of that which we are in ourselves.

Now, from this original Doctrine of the Creation of Man, known to all the first Inhabitants of the World, and published in the Front of the first Written Word of God; these great Truths have been more or less declared to all the Nations of the World. *First*, That all Mankind are the *created Offspring* of the One

God.

God. *Secondly*, That in all Men there is a Spirit or Breath of Lives, that did not begin to be *out of Nothing*, or was created out of No-thing; but came from the true God into Man, as his *own Breath* of Life breathed into Him. *Thirdly*, That therefore there is in all Men, wherever difperfed over the Earth, a *divine*, *immortal, never-ending* Spirit, that can have nothing of Death in it, but *muft* live for-ever, becaufe it is the Breath of the *everliving* God. *Fourthly*, That by this immortal Breath, or Spirit of God in Man, all Mankind ftand in the fame Nearnefs of Relation to God, are all equally his Children, are all under the fame Neceffity of paying the fame Homage of Love and Obedience to Him, all fitted to receive the fame Bleffing and Happinefs from Him, all created for the fame eternal Enjoyment of his Love and Prefence with them, all equally called to worfhip and adore Him in Spirit and Truth, all equally capable of feeking and finding Him, of having a Bleffed Union and Communion with Him.

Thefe great Truths, the firft Pillars of all true and Spiritual Religion, on which the Holy and Divine Lives of the antient Patriarchs was fupported, by which they worfhipped God in a true and right Faith; thefe Truths, I fay,

were

were moſt *eminently* and *plainly* declared in the expreſs Letter of the *Moſaic* Writings, here quoted. And no Writer, whether *Jewiſh* or *Chriſtian*, has ſo plainly, ſo fully, ſo deeply laid open the true Ground, and Neceſſity of an *Eternal, never-ceaſing Relation* between God, and all the Human Nature ; no one has ſo inconteſtably aſſerted the *Immortality* of the Soul, or Spirit of Man ; or ſo deeply laid open, and proved the Neceſſity of *one* Religion, *common* to all Human Nature, as the Legiſlator of the *Jewiſh Theocracy* has done. *Life and Immortality are* indeed juſtly ſaid to be *brought to Light by the Goſpel* ; not only becauſe they there ſtand in a new Degree of Light, largely explained, and much appeal'd to, and abſolutely promiſed by the Son of God Himſelf, but chiefly becauſe the precious *Means* and *Myſteries* of obtaining a *bleſſed* Life, and a *bleſſed* Immortality, were only revealed, or brought to Light by the Goſpel.

But the inconteſtable *Ground* and *Reaſon* of an immortal Life, and eternal Relation between God, and the whole Human Nature, and which lays all Mankind under the ſame Obligations to the ſame true Worſhip of God, is moſt fully ſet forth by *Moſes*, who alone tells us the *true Fact* ; *How*, and *Why* Man is im-

mortal

mortal in his Nature, *viz.* becaufe the Beginning of his Life was a Breath, breathed into Him from God ; and for this End, that he might be a living Image and Likenefs of God, created to partake of the Nature and Immortality of God.

This is the *great Doctrine* of the *Jewifh* Legiflator, and which juftly places Him amongft the *greateft Preachers* of true Religion. St. *Paul* ufed a very powerful Argument to perfuade the *Athenians* to own the true God, and the true Religion, when he told them, " that " God made the World and all Things there- "'in ; that He giveth Life and Breath, and " all Things ; that he hath made of *one* " *Blood*, all Nations of Men to dwell on the " Earth ; that they fhould *all feek* the Lord, " if haply they might feel after, and find " Him, feeing He is not far from any of us, " *becaufe in Him we live, move, and have our* " *Being* *." And yet this Doctrine, which St. *Paul* preaches to the *Athenians*, is nothing elfe, but that *fame Divine* and *Heavenly* Inftruction, which He had learnt from *Mofes*, which *Mofes* openly and plainly taught all the *Jews*. The *Jewifh* Theocracy therefore was by no means an *Intimation* to that People, that

---

* Acts xvii. 24.

that they had no Concern with the true God, but as Children of *this World*, under his temporal Protection or Punishment; for their Lawgiver left them *no room* for such a Thought, because He had as plainly taught them their *eternal Nature* and *eternal Relation*, which they had to God in common with all Mankind; as St. *Paul* did to the *Athenians*, who only set before them that *very Doctrine* that *Moses* taught all the *Jews*. The great End of the *Jewish* Theocracy was to shew, both to *Jew* and *Gentile*, the absolute, uncontroulable Power of the one God, by such a *Covenanted Interposition* of his Providence, that all the World might know, that the *one God*, from whom both *Jew* and *Gentile* were fallen away, by departing from the Faith and Religion of their First Fathers, was the only God, from whom all Mankind could receive either Blessing or Cursing.

This was the great Thing intended to be proclaimed to all the World by *this Theocracy*, viz. that only the God of *Israel* had Power to save or destroy, to punish or reward, according to his Pleasure; and that therefore all the Gods of the Heathens, were mere Vanity.

If therefore any *Jews*, by *reason* of those extraordinary Temporal Blessings and Cursings

which

which they received under their Theocracy, grew *grofsly ignorant*, or dully fenfelefs of their eternal Nature, and eternal Relation to God, and of that *one true Religion*, which by Nature they were obliged to obferve in common with all Mankind ; if they took God only to be their *local* or *tutelary* Deity, and themfelves to be only Animals of this World ; fuch a Groffnefs of Belief was no more to be charged upon their great Lawgiver, *Mofes*, than if they had believed, that a Golden Calf was their true God. But to return to the Creation.

2. It is the fame Impoffibility for a Thing to be created *out of* Nothing, as to be created *by* Nothing *. It is no more a Part, or Prerogative of God's Omnipotence to create a Being out of Nothing, than to make a Thing to be, without any one *Quality* of Being in it ; or to make, that there fhould be *Three*, where there is neither *Two*, nor *One*. Every Creature is nothing elfe, but *Nature* put into a *certain Form* of Exiftence ; and therefore a Creature not form'd *out of* Nature, is a Contradiction. A *Circle*, or a *Square* cannot be made *out of Nothing*, nor cou'd any Power bring them into Exiftence ; but becaufe there is an *Extenfion* in Nature, that can be put into the *Form* of a

Circle,

* See *Spirit of Prayer*, Part II. Page 58, &c.
Way to divine Knowledge, Page 247, &c.

Circle, or a Square: But if dead Figures cannot by any Power be made *out of Nothing*, who fees not the Impoſſibility of making Living Creatures, Angels, and the Souls of Men out of Nothing?

3. *Thinking*, and *Willing* are Eternal, they never began to be. Nothing can think, or will *now*, in which there was not Will and Thought from *all Eternity*. For it is as poſſible for Thought *in General* to begin to be, as for *That* which thinks in a particular Creature to *begin* to be of a *Thinking* Nature: therefore the Soul, which is a *Thinking*, *Willing* Being is come forth, or created *out of* That which hath *Willed* and *Thought* in God, from all Eternity. The *created* Soul is a Creature of *Time*, and had its Beginning on the *Sixth* Day of the Creation ; but the *Eſſences* of the Soul, which were, then form'd into a Creature, and into a State of Diſtinction from God, had been in God from all Eternity, or they could not have been *breathed* forth from God into the Form of a living Creature.

And herein lies the true Ground and Depth of the *uncontroulable Freedom* of our Will and Thoughts: They muſt have a *Self-motion*, and *Self-direction*, becauſe they came out of the *Self-exiſtent* God. They are eternal, divine

Powers,

Powers, that never began *to be*, and therefore cannot begin to be in Subjection to any Thing. That which *thinks* and *wills* in the Soul, is That *very same* unbeginning Breath which *thought* and *willed* in God, before it was breathed into the Form of an human Soul; and therefore it is, that Will and Thought cannot be bounded or conftrained.

Herein alfo appears the high Dignity, and never-ceafing Perpetuity of our Nature. The *Effences* of our Souls can never ceafe to be, becaufe they never began to be: and nothing can live eternally, but that which hath lived from all Eternity. The Effences of our Soul were a Breath in God before they became a Living Soul, they lived in God before they lived in the created Soul, and therefore the Soul is a Partaker of the Eternity of God, and can never ceafe to be. Here, O Man, behold the great Original, and the high State of thy Birth; Here let all that is within thee praife thy God, who has brought Thee into fo high a State of Being, who has given Thee Powers as eternal, and boundlefs at his own Attributes, that there might be no End or Limits of thy Happinefs in Him. Thou begannefl as *Time* began, but as Time was in Eternity before it became *Days* and *Years*, fo Thou waft in God

before

before Thou waſt brought into the Creation :
And as Time is neither a *Part* of Eternity,
nor *broken* off from it, yet come *out of it*; ſo
thou art not a Part of God, nor broken off
from Him, yet born out of Him. Thou
ſhould'ſt only will that which God willeth,
only love that which He loveth, co-operate,
and unite with Him in the whole Form of
thy Life ; becauſe all that Thou art, all that
Thou haſt, is only a Spark of his own Life
and Spirit derived into Thee. If thou deſireſt,
inclineſt, and turneſt to God, as the *Flowers*
of the Field deſire, and turn towards the Sun,
all the Bleſſings of the Deity will ſpring up in
Thee; Father, Son, and Holy Ghoſt, will make
their Abode with Thee. If thou turneſt in
towards thyſelf, to live to thyſelf, to be happy
in the Workings of an *own Will*, to be rich in
the Sharpneſs and Acuteneſs of thy *own Reaſon*, thou chuſeſt to be a *Weed*, and canſt only
have ſuch a Life, Spirit and Bleſſing from
God, as a *Thiſtle* has from the *Sun*. But to
return.

. 4. To ſuppoſe a *Willing, Underſtanding* Being, created *out of Nothing*, is a great Abſur-
dity. For as *Thinking* and *Willing* muſt have
always been from all Eternity, or they could
never have been either in Eternity, or Time;
ſo,

fo, wherever they are found in any particular, finite Beings, they muft of all Neceffity, be direct Communications, or Propagations of *that Thinking and Willing*, which never could begin to be.

The Creation therefore of a Soul, is not the Creation of Thinking and Willing, or the making That to *be*, and to *think*, which before had Nothing of Being, or Thought; but it is the Bringing the *Powers* of Thinking and Willing out of their *Eternal State* in the One God, into a *Beginning State* of a Self-confcious Life, diftinct from God. And this is God's omnipotent, creating Ability, that He can make the *Powers* of his *own Nature* become Creatural, Living, Perfonal Images of what He is in Himfelf, in a State of *diftinct Perfonality* from Him: So that the Creature is one, in its finite, limited State, as God is one, and yet hath nothing in it, but that which was in God before it came into it : For the Creature, be it what it will, high or low, can be Nothing elfe, but a limited Participation of the Nature of the Creator. Nothing can be in the Creature, but what came from the Creator, and the Creator can give nothing to the Creature, but that which it hath in itfelf to give. And if Beings could be created out of
Nothing,

Nothing, the Whole Creation could be no more a Proof of the Being of God, than if it had sprung up of itself out of Nothing: For if they are brought into Being out of Nothing, then they can have *Nothing of God* in *them*; and so can bear *no Testimony* of God; but are as good a Proof, that there is no God, as that there is one. But if they have *any Thing* of God in them, then they cannot be said to be created out of Nothing.

5. That the Souls of Men were not created out of Nothing, but are born out of an *Eternal Original*, is plain from hence ; from that *Delight* in, and *Desire* of *Eternal Existence*, which is so strong and natural to the Soul of Man. For nothing can delight in, or desire Eternity, or so much as form a *Notion* of it, or *think* upon it, or any way reach after it, but that alone which is generated from it, and come out of it. For it is a Self-evident Truth, that Nothing can look higher, or further back, than into its *own Original* ; and therefore, Nothing can look or reach back into Eternity, but that which came out of it. This is as certain, as that a *Line* reaches, and can reach no further back, than to that *Point* from whence it arose.

Our

Our bodily Eyes are born out of the *firma-mental Light* of this World, and therefore they can look no further than the *Firmament :* But our Thoughts know no Bounds ; therefore they are come out of that which is boundlefs. The Eyes of our Minds can look as eafily backwards into that Eternity which always hath been, as into that which ever fhall be ; and therefore it is plain, that *That* which *Thinks* and *Wills* in us, which fo eafily, fo delightfully, fo naturally penetrates into all Eternity, 'has always had an Eternal Exiftence, and is only a Ray or Spark of the Divine Nature, brought out into the Form of a Creature, or a limited, perfonal Exiftence, by the Creating Power of God.

6. Again. Every Soul fhrinks back, and is frighted at the very Thought of falling into Nothing. Now this undeniably proves, that the Soul was not created *out of* Nothing. For it is an Eternal Truth, fpoken by all Nature, that every-Thing ftrongly afpires after, and cannot be eafy, till it finds and enjoys that Original out of which it arofe. If the Soul therefore was brought forth out of Nothing, all its *Being* would be a *Burden* to it ; it would want to be diffolved, and to be deliver'd from every kind and Degree of *Senfibility* ; and nothing

thing could be fo fweet and agreeable to it, as
to think of falling back into That *Nothingnefs,*
out of which it was called forth by its Creation.
Thus is the Eternal, immortal, divine Nature
of the Soul, which the *Schools* prove with fo
much Difficulty one of the moft obvious, felf-
evident Truths in all Nature. For Nothing
but that which is Eternal in its own Nature,
can have the leaft Thought about Eternity.

If a *Beaft* had not the *Nature* of the Earth
in it, Nothing that is on the Earth, or fprings
out of it, could be in the leaft Degree agreeable to it, or defired by it. If the Soul had
not the *Nature* of Eternity in it, Nothing that
is eternal could give it the *fmalleft* Pleafure, or
be able to make *any kind* of Impreffion upon
it. For as Nothing can tafte, or relifh, or enter
into the agreeable Senfations of this World,
but that which hath the *Nature* of this World
in it ; fo Nothing can tafte, or relifh, or look
into Eternity with any kind of Pleafure, but
that which hath the *Nature* of Eternity in it.

7. If the Soul was not born, or created *out
of* God, it could have no *Happinefs* in God,
no *Defire,* nor any *Poffibility* of enjoying Him.
If it had *nothing of God in it*, it muft ftand
in the *utmoft Diftance* of Contrariety to him,
and be utterly incapable of living, moving,
and

and having its Being in God: For every Thing
muſt have the *Nature* of That, out of which
it was created, and muſt live, and have its
Being in that *Root or Ground* from whence
it ſprung. If therefore there was nothing of
God in the Soul, nothing that is in God could
do the Soul any Good, or have *any kind* of
Communication with it ; but the *Gulph* of
Separation between God and the Soul, wou'd
be even greater than that which is between
Heaven and Hell.

8. But let us rejoice, that our Soul is a *Think-*
ing, Willing Being, full of Thoughts, Cares,
Longings, and Deſires of Eternity ; for *this is*
our *full Proof,* that our Deſcent is from God
Himſelf, that we are born *out of* Him,
breathed forth *from him* ; that our Soul is of
an Eternal Nature, made a Thinking, Willing,
Underſtanding Creature *out of* That which
hath *Will'd* and *Thought* in God from all Eternity ; and therefore muſt, for ever and ever,
be a Partaker of the Eternity of God.

And here you may behold the ſure Ground
of the abſolute Impoſſibility of the *Annihila-*
tion of the Soul. Its Eſſences never began to
be, and therefore can never ceaſe to be ; they
had an *Eternal Reality* before they were in,
or became a diſtinct Soul, and therefore they
must

muft have the fame Eternal Reality in it. It
was the *Eternal Breath* of God before it came
into Man, and therefore the Eternity of God
muft be *infeparable* from it. It is no more a
Property of the divine Omnipotence to be *able*
to annihilate a Soul, than to be able to make
an *Eternal Truth* become a *Fiction* of Yefter-
day: And to think it a Leffening of the
Power of God, to fay, that he cannot annihilate the Soul, is as abfurd, as to fay, that it is
a Leffening of the *Light* of the *Sun*, if it cannot *deftroy*, or *darken* its own Rays of Light.

O, dear Reader, ftay a while in this important Place, and learn to know thyfelf: All
thy Senfes make Thee to know and feel, that
thou ftandeft in the *Vanity* of *Time*; but every
Motion, Stirring, Imagination, and Thought
of thy Mind, whether in *fanfying*, *fearing*, or
loving Everlafting Life, is the fame *infallible*
Proof, that Thou ftandeft in the *Midft of E-
ternity*, art an Offspring and Inhabitant of it,
and muft be for ever infeparable from it. Afk
when the *firft Thought* fprung up, find out the
Birth-Day of Truth, and then thou wilt have
found out, when the Effences of thy Soul firft
began to be. Were not the Effences of thy
Soul as old, as *Unbeginning*, as *unchangeable*,
as *Everlafting* as Truth itfelf, Truth would be

at the *same Diftance* from Thee, as abfolutely
unfit for Thee, as utterly unable to have *any
Communion* with Thee, as to be the *Food* of a
Worm.

The *Ox* could not feed upon the *Grafs,* or
receive any Delight or Nourifhment from it,
unlefs Grafs and the Ox had *one and the fame*
Earthly Nature and Original : Thy Mind
could receive no Truth, feel no Delight and
Satisfaction in the Certainty, Beauty, and Harmony of it, unlefs Truth and the Mind ftood
both in the fame Place, had *one and the fame*
unchangeable Nature, Unbeginning Original.
If there will come a Time, when *Thought itfelf* fhall ceafe, when all the Relations and
Connections of Truth fhall be *unty'd* ; then,
but not till then, fhall the Knot, or Band of
thy Soul's Life be unloofed. It is a Spark of
the Deity, and therefore has the Unbeginning,
Unending Life of God in it. It knows nothing of Youth, or Age, becaufe it is born
Eternal. It is a Life that muft burn for ever,
either as a Flame of Light and Love in the
Glory of the Divine Majefty, or as a miferable
Firebrand in that God, which is a *Confuming
Fire.*

9. It is impoffible, that this World, in the State
and Condition it is now in, fhould have been

an *immediate* and *Original* Creation of God :
This is as impoffible, as that God fhould create Evil, either *Natural*, or *Moral*. That this
World hath Evil in all its Parts ; that its Matter is in a corrupt, diforder'd State, full of
Groffnefs, Difeafe, Impurity, Wrath, Death
and Darknefs, is as evident, as that there is
Light, Beauty, Order and Harmony every
where to be found in it. Therefore it is as
impoffible, that this outward State and Condition of Things, fhould be a *firft* and *immediate* Work of God, as that there fhould be
Good and Evil in God Himfelf. All Storms
and Tempefts, every Fiercenefs of Heat, every
Wrath of Cold proves with the *fame Certainty*,
that outward Nature is not a *firft Work of*
God, as the *Selfifhnefs, Envy, Pride, Wrath*,
and *Malice* of Devils, and Men proves, that
they are not in the *firft State* of their Creation.
As no Kind or Degree of *Moral Evil* could
poffibly have its Caufe in, or from God, fo
there cannot be the leaft Shadow of *Imperfection* and *Diforder* in outward Nature, but
what muft have fprung up in the *fame manner*,
and from the *fame Caufes*, as Sicknefs and corrupt Flefh is come into the Human Body,
namely, from the Sin of the Creature. Storms,
Tempefts, Gravel, Stone, four and dead Earth

are

are the *same Things*, the *same Diseases*, the *same Effects* of Sin, produced in the *same manner* in the outward Body of Nature, as corrupt Flesh, *Fevers, Dropsies, Plagues, Gravel, Stone,* and *Gout*, are produced in the outward Body of Man. For That, and That only which produces Stone in the *Body of Man*, did produce Stone in the *outward Nature*, as shall plainly appear by and by. For Nature within, and without Man, is *one* and the *same*, and has but one and the same way of Working; a *Stone* in the Body, and a Stone out of the Body of Man, proceeds from one and the *same Disorder* of Nature.

When therefore you see a *diseased, gouty, leprous, asthmatical, scorbutick* Man, you can with the utmost Certainty say, this is not that Human Body which God *first* created in Paradise; so, when you see the Disorders of *Heat* and *Cold*, the *poisonous Earth, unfruitful Seasons*, and *malignant Qualities* of outward Nature, you can with the same Certainty affirm, this State of Nature is not a *first* Creation of God, but *that same* must have happened to it, which has happened to the Body of Man. For *dark, sour, hard, dead Earth*, can no more be a first, immediate Creation of God, than a *Wrathful Devil*, as such, can be created by Him.

For

For dark, four, dead Earth is as diforder'd in its kind, as the Devils are, and has as certainly . loft its *firft* heavenly Condition and Nature, as the Devils have loft theirs. But now, as in Man, the *little World*, there is Excellency and Perfection enough to prove, that Human Nature is the Work of an all-perfect Being, yet, fo much Impurity and Difeafe of corrupt Flefh and Blood, as undeniably fhews, that Sin has almoft quite fpoiled the Work of God. So, in the *great World*, the Footfteps of an infinite Wifdom in the Order and Harmony of the Whole, fufficiently appears; yet, the Diforders, Tumults, and Evils of Nature, plainly demonftrate, that the prefent Condition of this World is only the *Remains* or *Ruins*, firft, of a *Heaven* fpoil'd by the Fall of Angels, and then of a *Paradife* loft by the Sin of Man. So that Man, and the World in which He lives, lie both in the *fame State* of Diforder and Impurity, have both the *fame Marks* of Life and Death in them, both bring forth the fame fort of Evils, both want a Redeemer, and have need of the fame kind of Death and Refurrection, before they can come to their firft State of Purity and Perfection.

10. That this outward World was not created *out of Nothing*, is plainly taught by St. *Paul*,

who

who declares, *Rom.* i. 20. that the Creation of
the World is out of the *Invisible Things of God*;
so that the outward Condition and Frame of
Visible Nature, is a plain Manifestation of that
Spiritual World from whence it is descended.
For as every *Outside* necessarily supposes an *In-
side*, and as temporal *Light* and Darkness
must be the Product of Eternal Light and
Darkness, so this outward, visible State of
Things necessarily supposes some inward, invisible State, from whence it is come into this
Degree of Outwardness. Thus all that is on
Earth is only a Change or Alteration of *something* that was in Heaven: And Heaven itself
is Nothing else but the *first glorious Out-birth*,
the *Majestick Manifestation*, the *beatific Visi-
bility* of the One God in Trinity. And thus
we find out, how this temporal Nature is related to God; it is only a *gross Out-birth* of
that which is an *Eternal Nature*, or a *blessed
Heaven*, and stands only in such a Degree of
Distance from it, as *Water* does to *Air*; and
this is the Reason why the *last Fire* will, and
must turn this gross, Temporal Nature into its
first, heavenly State. But to suppose the gross
Matter of this World to be made *out of* Nothing, or to be a Grossness that has proceeded
from Nothing, or compacted Nothing, is more
absurd

abfurd, than to fuppofe *Ice* that has *congeal'd*
Nothing, a *Yard* that is not made up of *Inches*,
or a *Pound* that is not the Product of *Ounces*.

11. And indeed to fuppofe this, or any other
material World to be made out of Nothing,
has all the fame Abfurdities in it, as the fuppofing *Angels* and Spirits, to be created out
of Nothing.

All the Qualities of all Beings are Eternal;
no *real Quality* or *Power* can appear in any
Creature, but what has its *eternal Root*, or
generating Caufe in the Creator. If a Quality
could *begin* to be in a Creature, which did not
always exift in the Creator, it would be no
Abfurdity to fay, that a Thing might begin to
be, without any Caufe either of its Beginning,
or Being. All Qualities, Properties, or whatever can be affirmed of God, are *felf-exiftent*,
and *neceffary exiftent*. Self and neceffary Exiftence is not a *particular* Attribute of God, but
is the *general Nature* of every Thing that can
be affirmed of God. All Qualities and Properties are *felf-exiftent* in God : Now, they cannot
change their Nature when they are deriv'd, or
form'd into Creatures, but muft have the *fame
Self-birth*, and neceffary Exiftence in the Creature, which they had in the Creator. The
Creature *begins* to be, when, and as it pleafed

God;

God ; but the *Qualities* which are become *Creaturely*, and which conftitute the Creature, are *felf-exiftent*, juft as the fame Qualities are in God. Thus, *Thinking*, *Willing*, and *Defire* can have no *outward Maker*, their Maker is *in themfelves*, they are felf-exiftent Powers *wherever* they are, whether in God, or in the Creature, and as they form themfelves in God, fo they form themfelves in the Creature. But now, if no Quality can *begin* to be, if all the Qualities and Powers of Creatures muft be *eternal* and *neceffary* exiftent in God, before they can have any Exiftence in any Creature ; then it undeniably follows, that every created Thing muft have its whole Nature *from*, and *out of* the Divine Nature.

All Qualities are not only good, but *infinitely perfect*, as they are in God ; and it is *abfolute-ly* impoffible, that they fhould have any *Evil* or *Defect* in them, as they are in the One God, who is the great and *Univerfal All*. Be-caufe, where *all Properties* are, there muft ne-ceffarily be an *all poffible Perfection* : And that which muft *always* have *All* in itfelf, muft, by an *abfolute* Neceffity, be *always all perfect*. But the fame Qualities, thus infinitely good and perfect in God, may become *imperfect* and *evil* in the Creature ; becaufe in the Creature, being limited and finite, they may be *divided*

and

and *separated* from one another by the Creature itself. Thus *Strength* and *Fire* in the Divine Nature, are Nothing elfe but the *Strength* and *Flame of Love*, and never can be any thing elfe; but in the Creature, *Strength* and *Fire* may be feparated from *Love*, and then they are become an *Evil*, they are Wrath and Darknefs, and all Mifchief : And thus that fame *Strength* and *Quality*, which in Creatures making a right Ufe of their *own Will*, or *Self-motion*, becomes their *Goodnefs* and *Perfection*, doth in Creatures making a wrong Ufe of their Will, become their evil and mifchievous Nature : And it is a Truth that deferves well to be confidered, that there is *no Goodnefs* in any Creature, from the higheft to the loweft, but in its *continuing* to be fuch an *Union of Qualities* and *Powers*, as God has brought together in its Creation.

In the higheft Order of created Beings, this is their ftanding in their *firft Perfection*, this is their *Fulfilling* the whole Will or Law of God, this is their *Piety*, their *Song* of Praife, their *Eternal Adoration* of their great Creator. On the other hand, there is no Evil, no Guilt, no Deformity in any Creature, but in its *dividing* and *feparating* itfelf from fomething which God had given to be in Union with it. This, and This alone, is the *Whole Nature* of all

Good

Good, and all Evil in the Creature, both in the *moral* and *natural* World, in Spiritual and Material Things. For Inftance, *dark, fiery Wrath* in the Soul, is not only very like, but it is the very felf-fame Thing in the Soul which a *Wrathful Poifon* is in the Flefh. Now, the Qualities of *Poifon* are in themfelves, all of them *good Qualities*, and neceffary to *every* Life; but they are become a *Poifonous Evil*, becaufe they are *feparated* from fome other Qualities. Thus alfo the Qualities of *Fire* and *Strength* that conftitute an *Evil Wrath* in the Soul, are in themfelves very *good Qualities*, and neceffary to every good Life; but they are become an evil Wrath, becaufe feparated from fome other Qualities with which they fhould be united.

The Qualities of the *Devil* and all fallen Angels, are good Qualities; they are the *very fame* which they received from their infinitely perfect Creator, the very fame which *are*, and *muft be* in all heavenly Angels; but they are an hellifh, abominable Malignity in them *now*, becaufe they have, by their *own Self-motion*, feparated them from the *Light* and *Love* which fhould have kept them glorious Angels.

And here may be feen at once, in the cleareft Light, the *true Origin* of all Evil in the Creation, without the leaft Imputation upon the

the Creator. God could not *poffibly* create a
Creature to be an *infinite All*, like Himfelf :
God could not bring any Creature into Exiftence, but by deriving into it the *felf-exiftent,
felf-generating, felf-moving* Qualities of his own
Nature : For the Qualities muft be in the
Creature, *that* which they were in the Creator,
only in a State of Limitation ; and therefore,
every Creature muft be *finite*, and muft have a
Self-motion, and fo muft be capable of moving
right and wrong, of uniting or dividing from
what it will, or of falling from that State in
which it ought to ftand : But as every Quality,
in every Creature, both within and without itfelf, is equally *good*, and equally *n ceffary* to the
Perfection of the Creature, fince there is nothing that is evil in it, nor can become evil to
the Creature, but *from* itfelf, by its *feparating
That* from itfelf, with which it can, and ought
to be united, it plainly follows, that *Evil* can no
more be charged upon God, than *Darknefs* can
be charged upon the *Sun* ; becaufe every Quality is *equally good,* every Quality of Fire is as
good as every Quality of Light, and only becomes an Evil to that Creature, who, by his
own Self-motion, has feparated Fire from the
Light in his own Nature.

12. If a delicious, fragrant *Fruit* had a Power of separating itself from that rich *Spirit*, fine *Taste*, *Smell*, and *Colour* which it receives from the Virtue of the *Sun*, and the Spirit of the *Air*; or if it could in the *Beginning* of its Growth, turn away from the *Sun*, and receive no Virtue from it, then it would stand in its own first Birth of *Wrath*, *Sourness*, *Bitterness*, and *Astringency*, just as the *Devils* do, who have *turned back* into their own dark Root, and rejected the *Light* and *Spirit* of God: So that the hellish Nature of a Devil is Nothing else, but its own *first Forms* of Life, withdrawn, or separated from the heavenly Light and Love; just as the *Sourness*, *Astringency*, and *Bitterness* of a Fruit, are Nothing else but the *first Forms* of its own vegetable Life before it has reached the Virtue of the *Sun*, and the Spirit of the *Air*.

And as a *Fruit*, if it had a *Sensibility* of itself, would be full of Torment, as soon as it was shut up in the *first Forms* of its Life, in its own *Astringency*, *Sourness*, and Stinging *Bitterness*: So the Angels, when they had *turned back* into these very same *first Forms* of their own Life, and broke off from the Heavenly Light and Love of God, they became their own Hell. No *Hell* was *made* for them, no

new

new Qualities came into them, no *Vengeance* or
Pains from the God of Love fell upon them;
hey only ftood in that State of *Divifion* and
Separation from the Son, and Holy Spirit of
God, which, by their own Motion, they had
made for themfelves. They had nothing in
them, but what they had from God, the *firft
Forms* of an Heavenly Life, Nothing but what
the moft heavenly Beings have, and muft have,
to all Eternity ; but they had them in a
State of Self-torment, becaufe they *had feparated them* from that *Birth* of Light and Love,
which alone could make them glorious Sons,
and blefled Images of the Holy Trinity.

The fame ftrong *Defire*, fiery *Wrath*, and
Stinging *Motion* is in Holy Angels, that is in
Devils, juft as the fame *Sournefs*, *Aftringency*,
and biting *Bitternefs* is in a full ripened Fruit,
which was there before it received the Riches
of the Light and Spirit of the *Air*. In a
ripened Fruit, its firft Sournefs, Aftringency,
and Bitternefs is not *loft*, nor *deftroyed*, but becomes the *real Caufe* of all its rich *Spirit*, fine
Tafte, fragrant *Smell*, and beautiful *Colour* ;
take away the *working*, *contending* Nature of
thefe *firft Qualities*, and you *annihilate* the Spirit, Tafte, Smell, and Virtue of the Fruit, and
there

there would be nothing left for the *Sun* and *Spirit* of the Air to enrich.

Juſt in the ſame manner, that which in a Devil is an evil *Selfiſhneſs*, a wrathful *Fire*, a Stinging *Motion*, is in an Holy Angel, the *everlaſting Kindling* of a divine Life, the *ſtrong Birth* of an Heavenly Love, it is a *real Cauſe* of an ever-ſpringing, ever-triumphing Joyful-neſs, an ever-increaſing Senſibility of Bliſs.

Take away the *working, contending* Nature of theſe firſt Qualities; which in a Devil, are only a *Serpentine Selfiſhn ſs*, *Wrath*, *Fire*, and Stinging *Motion* ; take away theſe, I ſay, from Holy Angels, and you leave them neither *Light*, nor *Love*, nor heavenly Glory, Nothing for the Birth of the Son, and Holy Spirit of God to riſe up in.

So that here you may ſee this glorious Truth, that the Love and Goodneſs of God is as *plain* and *undeniable* in having given to the fallen An-gels, thoſe *very Qualities* and Powers which are now *their Hell*, as in giving the firſt Sour-neſs, Aſtringency and Bitterneſs to *Fruits*, which alone makes them capable of their de-licious Spirit, Taſte, Colour, and Smell.

13. And thus you ſee the uniform Life of all the Creatures of God ; how they are all raiſed, enriched, and bleſſed by the *ſame Life* of God,

derived

derived into different Kingdoms of Creatures.
For the Beginnings and Progress of a perfect
Life in Fruits, and the Beginnings and Progress
of a perfect Life in Angels, are not only like
to one another, but are the very same Thing,
or the working of the very *same Qualities*,
only in different Kingdoms. *Astringency* in a
Fruit, is the very same Quality, and does the
same Work in a Fruit, that *attracting Desire*
does in a Spiritual Being ; it is the same *Beginner*, *Former*, and *Supporter* of a Creaturely
Life in the one, as in the other. No Creature
in Heaven, or Earth, can *begin* to be, but by
this *Astringency*, or *Desire*, being made the
Ground of it : And yet this Astringency kept
from the Virtue of the *Sun*, can only produce
a *poisonous Fruit*, and this *astringent Desire* in
an Angel, turned from the Light of God, can
only make a *Devil*. The biting, stinging Bitterness of a Fruit, if you could add *Thought* to
it, would be the very *gnawing Envy* of the
Devil : And the envious Motion in the Devil's
Nature, would be Nothing else but that Stinging Bitterness which is in a Fruit, if you cou'd
take Thought from the Devil's Motion.

14. From this Attraction, Astringency, or
Desire, which is *one* and the *same* Quality in
every individual Thing, which is the *first Form*

of Being and Life, the very *Ground* of every
Creature, from the higheſt Angel to the loweſt
Vegetable, we are led by an unerring Thread
to the *firſt Deſire,* or that Deſire which is in
the *Divine Nature.* For as this Attraction, or
aſtringent Deſire is in Spiritual and corporeal
Things, one and the ſame Quality, working
in the ſame Manner, ſo is it *one* and the *ſame*
Quality with that *firſt, unbeginning Deſire,*
which is in the Divine Nature.

That there is an attracting Deſire in the Divine Nature, is undeniable, becauſe *Attraction*
is eſſential to all Bodies ; and *Deſire,* which is
the ſame Quality, is abſolutely inſeparable from
all intelligible Beings ; therefore, that which is
neceſſarily exiſtent in the Creature, upon the
Suppoſition of its Creation, muſt neceſſarily be
in the Creator ; becauſe no inherent, operative
Quality can be in the Creature, unleſs the ſame
kind of Quality had always been in the Creator : Therefore, Attraction or Deſire, which
are inſeparable from every created Being and
Life, are only various *Participations* of the
Divine Deſire ; or *Emanations* from it, form'd
into different Kingdoms of Creatures, and
working in all of them according to their
reſpective Natures.

In

In *Vegetables*, it is that Attraction, or Defire, which brings every growing Thing to its
higheft Perfection : In Angels, it is that bleffed
Hunger, by which they are fill'd with the
Divine Nature : In Devils, it is turn'd into
that Serpentine Selfifhnefs, or crooked Defire,
which makes them a Hell and Torment to
themfelves.

15. On the other hand, as we thus prove *a
pofteriori*, from a View of the Creature, that
there muft be an *attracting* Defire in the Divine Nature; fo we can prove *a priori* alfo,
from a Confideration of God, that there muft
be an *attracting Defire* in every Thing that ever
was, or can be created by God: For nothing can
come into Being, but becaufe God *wills* and
defires it; therefore the *Defire* of God is the
Creator, the Original of every Thing. The
Creating *Will*, or *Defire* of God, is not a *diftant*, or *feparate* Thing, as when a Man wills
or defires fomething to be done, or removed
at a Diftance from him; but it is an Omni-
prefent, working Will and Defire, which is itfelf, the Beginning and Forming of the Thing
defir'd. Our own Will, and defirous Imagination, when they work and create in us a *fettled
Averfion*, or *fix'd Love* of any thing, refemble
in fome Degree, the Creating Power of God,

D which

which makes Things out of itſelf, or its own
working Deſire. And our Will, and working
Imagination could not have the Power that it
has now even after the Fall, but becauſe it is a
Product, or Spark of that *firſt* Divine Will or
Deſire which is omnipotent.

16. Here therefore we have plainly found
the true Original, or *firſt Source* of all Things.
The *Deſire* in God is the firſt *Former, Generator,* and *Creator* of all Things; they are all
the *Births* of this omnipotent, working Deſire; for every Thing that comes into Being,
muſt have the Nature of that Power that
form'd it, and therefore the Nature of every
Creature muſt ſtand in an *attractive Deſire,* that
is, every Thing muſt be a *Created, attractive
Power*; becauſe it is the *Birth,* or *Product* of
a Deſire, or attractive Power, and could neither come into, nor continue in Being, but
becauſe it was generated not only *by,* but *out
of* an attracting Deſire. And herein lies the
Band, or *Knot* of all created Being and Life.

17. *Will* or *Deſire* in the Deity, is juſtly conſidered as God the *Father,* who from Eternity
to Eternity, *wills* or *generates* only the *Son,*
from which eternal Generating, the Holy Spirit eternally proceeds: 'And this is the infinite
Perfection

Perfection or Fullnefs of Beatitude of the Life of the Tri-une God.

Now, as the unbeginning, eternal Defire is in God, fo is the created Defire in the Creature; it ftands in the *fame Tendency*, hath the Nature of the Divine Defire, becaufe it is a *Branch* out of it, or created from it. In the Deity, the Eternal Will or Defire, is a *Defiring*, or *Generating* the Son, whence the Holy Spirit proceeds; the Defire that is come out of God into the *Form* of a Creature, has the *fame Tendency*, it is a Defire of the Son and Holy Spirit. And every created Thing in Heaven and Earth attains its Perfection, by its Gaining in fome Degree, the *Birth* of the Son and Holy Spirit of God in it : For all Attraction and Defire in the Creature, *generates* in them as it did in God ; and fo the Birth of the Son and Holy Spirit of God arifes in *fome Degree*, or other, in all Creatures that are in their proper State of Perfection.

18. And here lies the Ground of that plain, and moft fundamental Doctrine of Scripture, that the Father is the *Creator*, the Son the *Regenerator*, and the Holy Spirit the *Sanctifier*. For what is this but faying in the plaineft manner, that as there are *Three* in God, fo there muft be *Three* in the Creature, that as

the

the *Three* ftand related to one another in God,
fo muft they ftand in the fame Relation in the
Creature. For if a threefold Life of God muft
have diftinct Shares in the Creation, Bleffing,
and Perfection of Man, is it not a Demonftration, that the Life of Man muft ftand in
the fame threefold State, and have fuch a Trinity in it, as has its true Likenefs to that Trinity which is in God?

That which *generates* in God, muft generate
in the Creature; and that which is *generated*
in God, muft be generated in the Creature;
and that which *proceeds* from this Generation in
the Deity, muft *proceed* from this Generation
in the Creature: And therefore, the fame *threefold Life* muft be in the Creature in the fame
manner as it is in God. For a Creature that
can only exift, and be bleffed by the *diftinct
Operation* of a Tri-une God upon it, muft have
the fame Tri-une Nature that is anfwerable
to it. And herein lies our true, and eafy, and
found, and edifying Knowledge and Belief of
the Myftery of a Trinity in Unity: And this
is all that the Scripture teaches us concerning it. It is not a Doctrine that requires
learned or nice Speculations, in order to be
rightly apprehended by us. But when with
the Scriptures, we believe the Father to be our
Creator,

Creator, the Son our *Regenerator,* and the Holy Spirit the *Sanctifier* ; then we are learned enough in this Myſtery, and begin to know the Tri-une God in the ſame Manner in *Time,* that we ſhall know him in *Eternity.*

And the Reaſon why this great Myſtery of a Trinity in the Deity is thus reveal'd to us, and the Neceſſity of a Baptiſm in the Name of Father, Son, and Holy Spirit, laid upon us, is this ; it is to ſhew us, that the Divine, Tri-une Life of God is loſt in us, and that nothing leſs than a Birth from the Son and Holy Spirit of God in us, can reſtore us to our firſt Likeneſs to that Tri-une God, who at firſt created us. This I have fully ſhewn in the little *Treatiſe* upon *Regeneration.*

19. When Man was created in his Original Perfection, the Holy Trinity was his *Creator ;* the *Breath of Lives,* which *became a Living Soul,* was the Breath of the *Tri-une* God : But when Man began to *will,* and *deſire,* that is, to *generate* contrary to the Deity, then the Life of the Tri-une God *extinguiſhed* in him.

The *Deſire* in Man being turn'd from God, loſt the *Birth* of the Son, and the *Proceeding* of the Holy Spirit ; and ſo fell into, or under the Light and Spirit of this World : That is, of a Paradiſical Man, enjoying Union and

Communion

Communion with Father, Son, and Holy
Ghoft, and living on Earth in fuch Enjoyment
of God, as the *Angels* live in Heaven, he became an Earthly Creature, fubject to the Do-
minion of this outward World, capable of all
its evil Influences, fubject to its Vanity and
Mortality; and as to his outward Life, ftood
only in the higheft Rank of *Animals*. This
and This alone, is the true *Nature* and *Degree* of the *Fall* of Man; it was neither more
nor lefs than this. It was a Falling out of *one
World*, or Kingdom, into *another*, it was
changing the Life, Light and Spirit of God,
for the Light and Spirit of this World. Thus
it was that *Adam* died the very Day of his
Tranfgreffion, he died to all the Influences and
Operations of the Kingdom of God upon
him, as we die to the Influences of this
World, when the Soul leaves the Body; and,
on the other hand, all the Influences, Operations and Powers of the Elements of this Life
became opened in him, as they are in every
Animal at its Birth into this World.

All other Accounts of that Fall, which *only*
fuppofe the Lofs of fome Moral Perfection, or
Natural Acutenefs of his Rational Powers, are
not only fenfelefs Fictions, but are an exprefs
Denial of the Old and New Teftament Account

count of it; for the Old Teftament exprefsly
fays, that *Adam* was *to die* the *Day* of his
Tranfgreffion, and therefore it is certain, that
He then did die, and that the Fall was his
lofing his firft Life: And to fay that he did
not die to that firft Life in which he was
created, is the fame Denial of Scripture, as to
fay, that he did not eat of the forbidden Tree.

Again, the fame Scripture affures us, that
after the *Fall,* his *Eyes were opened*; I fuppofe
this is a Proof, that before the *Fall,* they were
fhut. And what is this, but faying in the
plaineft manner, that before the Fall, the *Life,*
Light and *Spirit* of this World, were *fhut* out
of him? and that the Opening of his Eyes,
was only another way of faying, that the Life
and Light of this World were opened in him?

If an *Angel,* or any Inhabitant of Heaven,
was to be fent of a Meffage into this World,
it muft be fuppofed, that neither the Darknefs,
nor Light of this World could act according
to their Nature upon him; and therefore, tho'
he was here, he muft be faid not to have
the *opened Eyes* of this World: But if this
Heavenly Meffenger fhould be taken with our
Manner of Life, fhould be in Doubts about returning to Heaven, and long to have fuch
Flefh and Blood as ours is, as earneftly as

Adam

Adam long'd to eat of the earthly Tree; and if by this Longing, he fhould actually obtain that which he defir'd; muft it not then be faid of him, when he had got this new Nature, *his Eyes were opened*, to fee *Light* and *Dark-nefs*; and that only for this Reafon, becaufe the Heavenly Life was departed from him, and the Earthly Life of this World was opened in Him? And thus it was that *Adam* died, and thus his Eyes were opened.

Again, when his Eyes were thus opened, or the Light and Life of this World thus open'd in him, he was immediately afham'd and fhock'd at the Sight of his own Body, and wanted to *hide* it from himfelf, and from the Sight of the Sun. Now, how could this have happened to him, if his Body had not under-gone fome very extraordinary Change, from a State of Glory and Perfection, to a lamentable Degree of Vilenefs and Impurity?

All the Terror at his fallen State, feems to arife from the fad Condition, in which he faw and felt his outward Body. This made him afham'd of himfelf; this made him tremble, at hearing the Voice of God; this made him creep behind the Trees, and endeavour to hide and cover his Body with Leaves.

And is not all this the fame Thing, as if

Adam

Adam had faid, *All my Sin, my Guilt, my Mifery, and Shame, is publifhed before Heaven and Earth, by this fad State and Condition in which my Body now appears.*

But now, what was this fad State and Condition of his Body? What did *Adam* fee in the Manner and Form of it that fill'd him with fuch Confufion? Why, he only faw that he was fallen from his Paradifical Glory, to have the fame grofs Flefh and Blood as the Beafts and Animals of this World have; which was, to bring forth an Offspring in the fame earthly Manner, as they did. He could fee, and be afhamed of no other Deformity in his Body; but that which he had in common with the Animals of this World; and therefore there was nothing elfe in his outward Form that He could be afhamed of; and yet it was his *outward Form* that fill'd him with Confufion. And is not this the greateft of all Proofs, that before his Fall, his Body had not *this Nature* and Condition of the Beafts in it? Is it not the fame Thing, as if he had faid, *this Body which now makes me afham'd, and which I want to hide, tho' it be only with thin Leaves, becaufe it brings me down amongft the Animals of this World, is not that firft Body of Glory into which God*

at

at firſt breathed the Breath of Lives, and in which I became a Living Soul.

Again, if *Adam*'s Body had been of the ſame kind of Fleſh and Blood as ours is now, only in a better State of Health and Vigour, How could he have been created Immortal? If he was not created Immortal, how can it be ſaid, that Sin alone brought Mortality, or Death into Human Nature? But if he had Immortality in his firſt created State, then he muſt have ſuch a Body as none of the Elements, or Elementary Things of this World could act upon; for there is no Death in any Creature of this World, but what is brought upon it by that Strife and Deſtruction which the four Elements bring upon one another. But if Sin alone gave the Elements, and all Elementary Things their firſt Power of acting upon the Body of *Adam*; then it is plain, that before his Sin, he had not, could not have a Body of *ſuch Fleſh* and *Blood* as we now have, but that he ſtood, as to the *State, Nature,* and *Condition* of his outward Body, at as great a Diſtance and Difference from the Animals of this World, as Heaven does from Earth, and was created with Fleſh and Blood as much exalted above, and ſuperior to the Nature and Power of all the Elements, as the Beaſts of this World are under them.

And

And herein plainly appears the true Senfe of that faying, *God made not Death*, that is, he made not *That* which is *mortal*, or *dying* in the Human Nature, but Sin alone form'd and produced *That* in Man, which could, and muft die like the Bodies of Beafts. *Death*, and the *Grave*, and the *Refurrection*, are all three, ftanding Proofs, that the Body of *beftial* Flefh and Blood, which we now have, at the Sight of which *Adam* was afhamed, which muft die, which can rot in the Grave, which muft not be feen after the Refurrection, was not that firft Body, in which *Adam* appeared before God in Paradife: For if it is an undeniable Truth of Scripture, that this *Flefh and Blood cannot enter into the Kingdom of God*; it muft be a Truth of the fame Certainty, that *this Flefh* and *Blood* could not by God Himfelf be brought into Paradife ; but that it muft have the *fame Original* with every other polluted Thing that is an Abomination in his Sight, or incapable of entring into the Kingdom of God.

20. That the Gofpel alfo plainly fhews, that Man was created in the Dignity and glorious Enjoyment of the Tri-une Life of God, and that his Fall, was a falling into the earthly Life of the Light and Spirit of this World, I have fufficiently proved from the greateft Articles

ticles of our Chriftian Faith, concerning the Neceffity, Nature, and Manner of our Redemption, in the Book of *Chriftian Regeneration*. I have there fhewn, that Baptifm in the Name of the Father, Son, and Holy Ghoft, fignifies Nothing but our being born again into this Tri-une Life of God.——That the Neceffity of being born again of the *Word* or Son of God, of being born of the *Spirit*, or receiving Him as a Sanctifier of our new rais'd Nature, plainly proves that what we loft by the Fall, was this Tri-une Life of God: He that denies this, denies the whole of the Chriftian Redemption *.

21. It has been already obferved, that when Man was created in his Original Perfection, the Holy Trinity was his Creator; but when Man was fallen, or had loft his firft Divine Life, then there began a new Language of a *Redeeming* Religion. Father, Son, and Holy Ghoft were now to be confidered, not as creating every Man as they created the Firft, but as *differently* concerned in raifing the fallen Race of Mankind, to that firft Likenefs of the Holy Trinity in which their firft Father was created: Hence it is, that the Scriptures fpeak of the Father, as *Drawing*, and *Calling* Men;

becaufe

* See *Spirit of Prayer*, Part II. Page 63, &c. Page 91. *Way to divine Knowledge*, Page 39—53.

becaufe the *Defire* which is from the Father's Nature, muft be the firft Mover, Stirrer, and Beginner. This Defire muft be moved and brought into an *anguifhing State*, and have the Agitation of a Fire that is *kindling* ; and then Men are truly *drawn* by the *Father.*

The Son of God is now confidered as the *Regenerator* or Raifer of a new Birth in us ; becaufe he enters a fecond Time into the Life of the Soul, that his own Nature and Likenefs may be again generated in it, and that he may be *That* to the Soul in its State, *which* he is to the Father in the Deity.

The Holy Ghoft is reprefented as the *Sanctifier*, or Finifher of the Divine Life reftored in us ; becaufe as in the Deity, the Holy Ghoft proceeds from the Father and the Son, as the amiable, bleffed *Finifher* of the Tri-une Life of God ; fo the fallen Nature of Man cannot be raifed out of its unholy State, cannot be bleffed and fanctified with its true Degree of the Divine Life, till the Holy Spirit arifes up in it.

Since then the Tri-une God, or the three Perfons in the one God, muft have this Difference of Shares, muft reach out this different Help to the Raifing up of fallen Man, it is undeniable, that the firft created Man ftood

in

In the Image and *real Likeneſs* of the one God,
not only repreſenting, but *really having* in his
Birth and Life, the Birth and Life of the Holy
Trinity. God the Father, Son, and Holy
Ghoſt had *ſuch* a Unity in Trinity *in Man*, as
they had in the Deity itſelf : How elſe could
Man be the Image and Likeneſs of the Holy
Trinity, if it was not ſuch a Birth in Man, as
it was in itſelf ? Or, how could the Holy Tri-
nity dwell and operate in Man, each Perſon
according to its reſpective Nature, unleſs there
was the ſame threefold Life in Man as there is
in God ? How could the Holy Trinity be an
Object of Man's Worſhip and Adoration, if
the Holy Trinity had not produced itſelf in
Man ? The Creature is only to own and worſhip its Creator ; therefore Father, Son, and
Holy Ghoſt muſt have each of them their
Creaturely Offspring, or *Product* in Man, if
Man is to worſhip Father, Son, and Holy
Spirit. If therefore you deny *Angels*, and the
Souls of perfect Men to have the tri-une Na-
ture, or Life of God in them : If you deny
that Father, Son, and Holy Spirit, have ſuch
Union and Relation in the Soul, as they have
out of it, you are guilty of as great Hereſy and
Apoſtacy from the Goſpel, as if you denied
the Father to be the Creator or Him that

calleth

calleth and *draweth*, the Son to be the Re-
deemer, or Him that regenerateth, and the
Holy Spirit to be Him that fanctifieth Human
Nature.

22. Again: Confider this great Truth,
which will much illuftrate this Matter; you
can be an *Inhabitant* of no World, or a *Partaker* of its Life, but by its being inwardly
the *Birth* of your own Life, or by having the
Nature and *Condition* of that World *born* in
you. As thus, *Hell* muft be *inwardly born* in
the Soul, it muft *arife* up within it, as it does
without it, before the Soul can become an
Inhabitant of it.

Again: That which is the Life of this outward World, *viz.* its *Fire,* and *Light,* and
Air, muft have fuch a *State* and *Birth* within
you, as they have without you, before you can
be an Inhabitant or Partaker of the Life of
this World; that is, Fire muft be in you, muft
be the *fame Fire,* have the fame *Place* and
Nature within you, have the fame Relation
to the *Light* and *Air* that is within you, as
it has without you, or elfe the Fire of the
outward World, cannot keep up, or have *any*
Communion with your own Life.

The Light of this World can fignify nothing
to you, cannot reach or enrich you with its

Powers and Virtues, if the fame Light is not arifen in the *fame Manner* in the kindling of your own Life, as it arifes in the outward World.

The *Air* alfo of this World can do you no Good, can be no *Blower* up and Preferver of your Life, but becaufe it has the *fame Birth* in you, that it has in outward Nature. And therefore it muft be a Truth of the greateft Certainty, that fo it muft of all Neceffity be, with Refpect to the *Kingdom of God*, or that *Life* which is to be had in the *Beatifick Prefence* of God; it muft, by an abfolute Neceffity, have the *fame Birth* within you, as it has without you, before you can enter into it, or become an Inhabitant of it : If you are to live, and be eternally bleffed in the *tri-une Life*, or Beatifick Prefence of God, that Tri-une Life, muft, of the utmoft Neceffity, firft make itfelf *creaturely* in you; it muft *be* and *arife* in you, as it does without you, before you can poffibly enter into any Communion with it.

Now is there any Thing more plain and Scriptural, more eafy to be conceived, more pious to be believed, and more impoffible to be denied, than all this? And yet this is all that I have faid, in two Propofitions in the Treatife

upon

upon *Christian Regeneration :* It is there said,
" Man was created by God *after his own Image,*
" and *in his own Likeness,* a Living Mirror of
" the Divine Nature ; where *Father, Son, and*
" *Holy Ghost* each brought forth their own
" Nature in a Creaturely Manner." Now,
what is this, but saying, That the Holy Trinity brought forth a Creature in its own Likenefs, ftanding in a creaturely Birth of the divine, tri-une Life ? If it did not ftand thus,
how could it have a Likenefs of the Holy Trinity ? Or how could it have its *Form* or *Crea-*
tion from the Holy Trinity ? Or how could it
without this tri-une Life in itfelf, enter into,
or be a Partaker of the tri-une Life or Prefence
of God ? In the next Propofition it is faid ;
" In it, that is, in this created Image of the
" Holy Trinity, the Father's Nature genera-
" ted the Divine *Word,* or *Son* of God, and
" the Holy Ghoft proceeded from them both
" as an amiable, moving Life of both. This
" was the *Likenefs* or *Image* of God, in which
" the firft Man was created, a true Offspring
" of God, in whom the Divine Birth fprung
" up as in the Deity, where Father, Son, and
" Holy Ghoft, faw themfelves in a creaturely
" manner."

E   Now,

Now, what is this, but faying in the plaineft Manner, only thus much, that the tri-une,
creaturely Life ftood in the *fame Birth* and
Generation of its threefold Life, as the Deity
doth, whofe Image, Likenefs, and Offspring
it is? And can it poffibly be otherwife; for if
the Creature cometh from the Father, Son,
and Holy Ghoft, as their *created Image* and
Likenefs, muft not That which it hath from
the Father, be of the *Nature* of the Father,
That which it hath from the Son, be of the
Nature of the Son, and That which it hath
from the Holy Ghoft, be of the *Nature* of
the Holy Ghoft? And muft they not therefore ftand in the Creature in fuch Relation to
one another, as they do in the Creator? If
it is the Nature of the Father to *generate*, if it
is the Nature of the Son to be *generated*, if it is
the Nature of the Holy Ghoft to *proceed* from
both, muft not That which you have from
the Father generate in you, That which you
have from the Son be *generated* in you, and
that which you have from the Holy Ghoft,
proceed from both in you? All which is only
faying this plain and obvious Truth, that That
Being, or *created Life*, which you have from
Father, Son, and Holy Ghoft, muft ftand in
fuch a *tri-une Relation* within you as it does
without

without you ; that having this threefold Likenefs of God, you may be capable of entring
into an Enjoyment of his *tri-une, beatifick*
Life or Prefence.

For, confider again this Inftance, with regard to the Life of this World. The *Fire*,
and *Light*, and *Air*, of outward Nature, muft
become *creaturely* in you ; that is, you muft
have a Fire that is your *own creaturely* Fire,
you muft have a Light that is generated by,
or from your *own Fire*, a *Breath* that proceeds from your *own Fire* and *Light*, as the
Air of outward Nature proceeds from its Fire
and Light : You muft have all this *Nature*
and *Birth* of Fire, and Light, and Air in your
own creaturely Being, or you cannot poffibly
live in, or have a Life from the Fire, and
Light, and Air of *outward Nature :* No Omnipotence can make you a *Partaker* of the
Life of this outward World, without having
the Life of this outward World *born in* your
own creaturely Being. And therefore, no
Omnipotence can make you a *Partaker* of
the Beatifick Life or Prefence of the Holy
Trinity, unlefs that Life ftands in the *fame tri-
une State* within you, as it does without you.

The Nature of this World muft become
creatural in you, before you can live, or have

a Share

a Share in the Life of this World ; the tri-une
Nature of God muſt breathe forth itſelf to
ſtand creaturely in you, before you can live,
or have a Share in the Beatifick Life or Preſence of the tri-une God.

Now, is not all this ſtrictly according to the
very outward *Letter*, and inward *Truth* of the
moſt important Articles of the Chriſtian Religion ? For what elſe can be meant by the
Neceſſity of our being born again of the *Word*,
or Son of God, being born of the *Spirit* of
God, in order to our Entrance into the Kingdom of Heaven ? Is not this ſaying, that the
tri-une Life of God muſt firſt have *its Birth* in
us, before we can enter into the tri-une, beatifick Life, or Preſence of God ? What elſe is
taught us by that *new Birth* ſought for by a
Baptiſm, in the Name of the Father, Son,
and Holy Ghoſt ? Does it not plainly tell us,
that the tri-une Nature of the Deity is *That*
which wants to be born in us, and that our
Redemption conſiſts in Nothing elſe but in the
Bringing forth this new Birth in us, and that,
being thus born again in the *Likeneſs* of the
Holy Trinity, we may be capable of its threefold Bleſſing and Happineſs ? The New Teſtament tells us of the Impoſſibility of our being
redeemed, but by the Son of God, of the Impoſſibility

poffibility of our being made *holy*, but by the
Holy Spirit of God : Now, how could we
want any diftinct Thing *particularly* from the
Son of God, any diftinct Thing, *particularly*
from the Holy Ghoft, in order to raife and
repair our fallen Nature, how could *this Particularity* be thus *abfolutely neceffary*, but becaufe the holy *threefold Life* of the Deity muft
ftand *within* us, in the Birth of our own Life,
as it does without us, that fo we may be capable of living in God, and God in us.

Search to Eternity, why no *Devil*, or *Beaft*
can poffibly be a *Partaker* of the Kingdom of
Heaven, and there can only this *one Reafon* be
affign'd for it, becaufe neither of them have
the *tri-une*, *holy Life* of God in them : For
every created Thing does, and muft, and can
only want, feek, unite with, and enjoy That
outwardly, which is of the *fame Nature* with
itfelf. Remove a *Devil* where you will, he is
ftill in Hell, and always at the *famé Diftance*
from Heaven ; he can touch, or tafte, or
reach Nothing but what is in Hell. Carry a
Beaft where you pleafe, either to *Court*, or to
Church, he is yet at the *fame infinite Diftance*
from the Joys and Fears either of *Church*, or
Court, as the Beafts that never faw any Thing
elfe but their own Kind : And all this is
grounded folely on this Eternal Truth ; name-

ly,

ly, That no Being can rife *higher* than its *own* Life reaches. The *Circle* of the *Birth* of Life in every Creature is its neceffary *Circumference*, and it cannot poffibly reach any farther; and therefore it is a joyful Truth, that Beings created to *worfhip* and *adore* the Holy Trinity, and to enter into the beatifick Life and Prefence of the tri-une God, muft, of all Neceffity, have the *fame tri-une Life* in their own Creaturely Being. And now, what can be fo glorious, fo edifying, fo ravifhing, as this Knowledge of God and ourfelves? The very Thought of our ftanding in this *Likenefs* and *Relation* to the Infinite Creator and *Being* of all Beings, is enough to kindle the Divine Life within us, and melt us into a continual Love and Adoration: For how can we enough love and adore that Holy Trinity which has created us in its own Likenefs, that we might live in an Eternal Union and Communion with it? Will any one call this an *irreverend* Familiarity, or *bold* Looking into the Holy Trinity, which is nothing elfe but a thankful Adoration of it, as our Glorious Father and Creator? It is our beft and only Acknowledgment of the greateft Truths of the Holy Scriptures; it is the Scripture Doctrine of the Trinity kept in its own mplicity, feparated from *Scholaftick Speculations,*

tions, where the three in God, are only diftinguifhed by that threefold Share that they have
in the Creation and Redemption of Man.
When we thus know the Trinity in ourfelves,
and adore its high Original in the Deity, we
are poffeffed· of a Truth of the greateft Moment, that enlightents the Mind with the moft
folid and edifying Knowledge, and opens to us
the fulleft Underftanding of all that concerns
the Creation, Fall, and Redemption of Man.

Without this Knowledge, all the Scripture
will be ufed as a *dead Letter,* and form'd only
into a *figurative, hiftorical* Syftem of Things,
that has no Ground in Nature ; and learned
Divines can only be learned in the Explication
of Phrafes, and verbal Diftinctions.

The firft Chapters of *Genefis* will be a Knot
that cannot be unty'd ; the Myfteries of the
Gofpel will be only called *faederal Rites,* and
their inward Ground reproached as enthufi-
aftick Dreams ; but when it is known, that
the *tri-une Nature* of God was brought forth
in the *Creation* of Man, that it was loft in his
Fall, that it is *reftored* in his *Redemption,* a
never-failing Light arifes in all Scripture, from
Genefis to the *Revelations.* Every Thing that
is faid of God, as Father, Regenerator, or
Sanctifier of Man ; every Thing that is faid of

E 4   Jefus

Jesus Christ, as Redeeming, forming, dwelling in, and quickening ; and of the Holy Spirit, as moving and sanctifying us : Every Thing that is said of the Holy Sacraments, or promised in and by them, has its deep and inward Ground *fully discovered* ; and the whole Christian Religion is built upon a *Rock*, and that Rock is *Nature*, and God will appear to be doing every Good to us, that the God of all Nature can possibly do. The Doctrine of the Holy Trinity is wholly practical ; it is revealed to us, to discover our high Original, and the Greatness of our Fall, to shew us the deep and profound Operation of the tri-une God in the Recovery of the Divine Life in our Souls; that by the Means of this Mystery thus discovered, our Piety may be rightly directed, our *Faith* and *Prayer* have their proper Objects, that the Workings and Aspirings of our own Hearts may co-operate, and correspond with that tri-une Life in the Deity, which is always desiring to manifest itself in us ; for as every Thing that is in us, whether it be Heaven, or Hell, rises up in us by a *Birth*, and is generated in us by the Will-spirit of our Souls, which kindles itself either in Heaven, or Hell ; so this Mystery, of a tri-une Deity manifesting itself, as a *Father* creating, as a *Son*, or *Word*, regenerating,

regenerating, as a *Holy Spirit* fanctifying us, is not to entertain our Speculation with dry, metaphyfical Diftinctions of the Deity, but to fhew us from what a Height and Depth we are fallen, and to excite fuch a Prayer and Faith, fuch a Hungring and Thirfting after this triune Fountain of all Good, as may help to generate and bring forth in us that firft Image of the Holy Trinity in which we were created, and which muft be born in us before we can enter into the State of the Bleffed : Here we may fee the Reafon, why the Learned World has had fo many fruitlefs Difputes about this Myftery, and why it has been fo often a Stone of Stumbling to Philofophers and Criticks ; it is becaufe they began to reafon about that, which never was propofed to *their Reafon*, and which no more belongs to human Learning and Philofophy, than *Light* belongs to our *Ears*, or Sounds to our *Eyes*. No Perfon has any *Fitnefs*, nor any *Pretence*, nor any *Ground* from Scripture, to think, or fay any Thing of the Trinity, till fuch Time as he ftands in the State of the Penitent Returning *Prodigal*, weary of his own finful, fhameful Nature ; and defiring to renounce the World, the Flefh, and the Devil, and then is he *firft* permitted

to

to be baptized *into the Name of the Father,
Son, and Holy Ghost :* This is the *first Time*
the Gospel *teaches,* or calls any one to the Acknowledgment of the Holy Trinity. Now,
as this Knowledge is first given in Baptism,
and there only as a Signification of a tri-une
Life of the Deity, which must be regenerated
in the Soul; so the Scriptures say Nothing af-
terwards to this Baptized Penitent concerning
the Trinity, but only with Regard to *Regeneration,* every where only shewing him how
Father, Son, and Holy Ghost, all equally divine, must draw, awaken, quicken, enlighten,
move, guide, cleanse, and sanctify the new-born
Christian : Is it not therefore undeniably plain,
that all abstract Speculations of this Mystery,
how it is in itself, how it is to be *ideally* conceived, or Scholastically expressed by us, are a
Wandring from that true Light, in which the
Trinity of God is set before us, which is only
revealed as a Key, or Direction to the true
Depths of that Regeneration, which is to be
sought for from the tri-une Deity ? But to go
on in a farther Account of the Creation.

23. Now, as all Creatures, whether intellectual, animate, or inanimate, are Products,
or Emanations of the *Divine Desire,* created
out

-*out of* the Father, who from Eternity to Eternity generates the Son, whence the Holy Spirit eternally proceeds; fo every intelligent, created Being, not fallen from its State, ftands in the *fame Birth*, or *generating Defire*, it generates in its Degree, as God the Father generates eternally the Son, and is bleffed and perfected in the Divine Life, by having the Holy Spirit arife up in it.

Hence it is, that thofe Angels which ftood, and continued in the *fame Will* and *Defire* in which they came out from God, willing and defiring as God from all Eternity had *will'd* and *defir'd*, were by the Rifing up of the Holy Spirit in them, *confirm'd* and *eftablifhed* in the Divine Life, and fo became eternally and infeparably united with the ever-bleffed tri-une Deity.

On the other hand, thofe Angels which did not keep their *Will* and *Defire* in its firft created *Tendency*, but raifed up an *own Will* and *Defire*, which own Will and Defire was their *direct, full* chufing and defiring to *be*, and *do* fomething which they could not be, and do in God, and is therefore properly called their afpiring to be *above* God, or to be without any *Dependance* upon him; thefe Angels, by thus going *backwards* with their Will and Defire

out of, or *from* God and the *Divine Truth;*
could only find, or generate *That* which had
the *utmost Contrariety* to God and the Divine
Birth, and fo became under a Neceffity of
finding themfelves in an Eternal *State*, *Spirit*
and *Life* that was *directly contrary* to all that
is good, holy, amiable, bleffed and divine.

   Now, the *Will* and *Defire* in every Creature
is *generating*, and *efficacious*, ftrictly according to
the State and Nature of that Creature *; therefore, Eternal Beings in an Eternal State, muft
have an Eternal Power, and Efficacy in the
Working of their Wills and Defires : When
therefore thofe Angels, with all the Strength
of their Eternal Defires, turn'd away from,
and contrary to God and the Divine Birth, they
could become Nothing elfe, but Beings eternally feparated and broken off from all that was
God and Goodnefs: For Eternal Beings that
ftood only in an eternal State, acting with all
their Vigour, not doubting, but ftrongly willing, could not do any thing that had only a
Temporal Nature and *Effect*, becaufe they ftood
not in fuch a Nature or fuch a World, and
therefore what they will'd and generated with
all their Nature, (which was a Contrariety to
God) that became the Eternal State of their
                                        Nature.

* See *Way to divine Knowledge*, Page 139——160.

Nature. And this is the Birth and Origin of Hellish Beings.

God had done all to them and for them, that he had done to and for the Angels that stood ; he had given them the same holy *Beginning* of their Lives, had brought them forth out of himself in the *same Tendency*, that which was the Nature of other Angels, was theirs; he could not make any established, fix'd, and unchangeable Angels, because the Life of every Thing must be a *Birth*, and *willing* Beings must have a *Birth* of their *Wills* ; he could not make them *fix'd*, because every Thing that comes from God, must *so* come from him, *as* it was in him, a *self-exiſtent* and *self-moving* Power, and therefore no Goodness of God could hinder their having a *Self-motion*, because they were, and could be Nothing else but Creatures brought forth *by*, and *out* of his own *self-exiſtent* and *self-moving* Nature.

God is all Good, and every Thing that comes out from him, as his Creature, Product, or Offspring, must come forth in *that State* of Goodness, which it had in Him ; and every Creature, however high in its Birth from God, must in the Beginning of its Life, have a *Power* of joining with or departing from God, because the Beginning of its Life is nothing
else

elfe but the Beginning of its *own Self-motion* as
a Creature ; and therefore no Creature can have
its State or Condition *fix'd*, till it gives itfelf
up either wholly unto God, or turns *wholly*
from him ; for if it is an Intelligent Creature,
it can only be fo, by having the Intelligent
Will of God derived into it, or made creaturely
in it ; but the Intelligent Will brought into
a creaturely Form, muft be *That* which it was
in the Creator, and therefore muft be the fame
felf-exiftent and *felf-moving* Power that it was
before it became creaturely in any Angel or
Spirit. And thus the Caufe and Origin of
Evil, where-ever it is, is abfolutely and eternally feparated from God.

24. Again : As all Intelligent Beings can no
way attain their Happinefs and Perfection, but
by ftanding with their Will and Defire united
to God, in the *fame Tendency* in which the Father eternally generateth the Son, from whence
the Holy Spirit proceedeth as the Finifher of
the tri-une, beatifick Life, fo the fame Thing
is manifeftly proved to us by the loweft kind
of Beings that are in this vifible World ; for
all *Vegetables*, by their Attraction or Aftringency, which is *their Defire*, and is an *Out-birth*
of the Divine Defire, reach their utmoft Perfection by the *fame Progrefs*, that is, by getting
a Birth

a Birth of the *Light* and *Spirit* of this outward World into them, and so become infallible, tho' remote Proofs that no Life can be
brought to its proper Perfection in the Creature,
till the Image of the *tri-une Life* of God, is,
according to the State and Capacity of the
Creature, form'd in it: Look where you will,
every Thing proclaims and proves this great
Truth. The Christian Doctrine of the Salvation of Mankind by a Birth of the Son, and
Holy Spirit of God in them, is not only written in Scripture, but in the *whole State* and
Frame of Nature, and of every Life in this
World; for every perfect Fruit openly declares,
that it can have no Goodness in it, till the
Light and *Spirit* of this World has done that
to it and in it, which the Light and Spirit of
God must do to the Soul of Man, and therefore
is a full Proof, that it is as absolutely necessary
for every Human Creature to desire, believe,
and receive the Birth of the Son and Holy
Spirit of God to save it from its own Wrath
and Darkness, as it is necessary for every Fruit
of the Earth to be raised and regenerated from
its own Bitterness and Sourness, by receiving
the Light and Spirit of this World into it.

25. Some Learned Men, willing to discover the Image of the Holy Trinity in the Creation,

ation, have obferved *three Properties* both in Body and Spirit, which they fuppofed to be a proper Likenefs of the Trinity. But all this is Nothing to the Matter.

For as the Holy Trinity is a *threefold Life* in God, fo the Image of the Trinity is only found in a *threefold Life* in the Creature ; for it is the *whole Birth*, or Generation of the Thing itfelf, whether it be corporeal or fpiritual, that ftands in fuch a *threefold State* as the Holy Trinity doth, that is the *proper Likenefs* or Image of the Trinity. As there is one infinitely perfect Deity, becaufe this one Deity is Father, Son, and Holy Spirit, fo every Creature that is an original Production of the Deity, or in its proper State of Perfection, ftands in its whole Being, or generating as the Deity doth, and neither hath, nor ever can have any Perfection, but becaufe the Tri-une Nature of God is manifefted and brought forth in it ; for Perfection of Life *in* God, and a Perfection of Life *deriv'd* from God, muft ftand in the fame threefold State, and that which is a Life from the Deity, muft have a Life of the Trinity in it.

26. Take away *Attraction*, or *Defire* from the Creature of this World, and you annihilate the Creature ; for where there is no
Attraction

Attraction or Defire, there can be no Nature or
Being ; and therefore Attraction or Defire
fhews the Work of the Creator in every Thing,
or what is meant by the *divine Fiat,* or Creating Power. Now, what is it which this *Attraction* or *Defire* wants, hungers, draws and
reaches after ? Nothing elfe but the *Light* and
Spirit of this World. What is the *true, deep,*
and *infallible* Ground of this ? Why does this
Defire *thus* work in every Life of this World ?
It's becaufe the Eternal Will in the Deity, is a
Defiring or *Generating* the Son, from whence
the Holy Spirit of God proceeds : And therefore Attraction, which is an *Out-birth* of the
Divine Defire, ftands in a perpetual Defiring of
the Light and Spirit of this World, becaufe they
are the two *Out-births* of the Light and Holy
Spirit of God. What rational Mind can help
being charm'd with this wonderful Harmony
and Relation betwixt God, Nature, and Creature ?

27. And now, my dear Reader, if you are
either *Arian,* or *Deift,* be fo no longer : The
Ground is dug up from under you, and neither Opinion has any Thing left to ftand upon ;
you may wrangle and wreft the Doctrine of
Scripture, becaufe it is only taught in Words;
but the Veil is now taken off from Nature,

and every *Plant* and *Fruit* will teach you with
the Clearneſs of a Noon-day Sun, theſe two
great Truths; *Firſt*, That Father, Son, and
Holy Spirit are one Being, one Life, one God:
Secondly, That the Soul, which is dead to the
Paradiſical Life, muſt be made alive again by
the Birth of the Son and Holy Spirit of God in
it, in the ſame Manner as a *dead Seed* is, and
only can be brought to Life in this World, by
the Light and Spirit of this World.

If you are an *Arian*, don't content yourſelf
with the Numbers that are with you, or with
a Learned Name or two that are on your
Side: *Arianiſm* has never yet been recommended by the Genius and Learning of a *Ba-
ronious*, or *Bellarmin*; and nothing but a poor,
groping, purblind Philoſophy, that is not able
to look either at God, Nature, or Creature, hath
ever led any Man into it: For it is a Truth
proclaimed by all Nature and Creature, that
there is a *threefold Life* in God, and every
Thing that is, whether it be *happy*, or *miſerable*, perfect or imperfect, is only ſo, becauſe
it has, or has not the *tri-une Nature* of God
in it.

A *beginning* Fruit is like a *Poiſon*; a *Seed*,
for a while, is ſhut up in a *hard Death*. Why
are they both at *firſt* in this State? It is becauſe

cauſe each of them ſtands *as yet* only in that *firſt Birth* of Nature, which is but a *Beginning Manifeſtation* of the Deity. Let the Light of the Sun, and the Spirit of this World be born in them, and then the ſour, aſtringent Fruit, and the *dead Seed* becomes a perfect, vegetable Life, and is in its kind perfect, for this *one only* Reaſon, becauſe the tri-une Life of the Deity is truly manifeſted in it.

28. If you are a *Deiſt*, made ſo, either by the diſorderly State *of your own* Heart, or by Prejudices taken from the Corruptions and Diviſions of Chriſtians, or from a Diſlike of the Language of Scripture, or from an Opinion of the Sufficiency of a Religion of Human Reaſon, or from whatever elſe it may be, look well to yourſelf, Chriſtianity is no Fiction of Enthuſiaſm, or Invention of Prieſts.

If you can ſhew, that the Goſpel propoſes to bring Men into the Kingdom of Heaven by any other Method, than that, which *Nature* requires to make any Creature a living Member of this World, then I will acknowledge the Goſpel not to be founded in Nature.

But if what the Goſpel ſaith of the abſolute Neceſſity, that the fallen Soul be born again of the Son and Holy Spirit of God, is the very ſame which all temporal Nature ſaith of every

Thing

Thing that is to enter into the Life of this World, *viz.* that it cannot partake of the Life of this World, till the Light and Spirit of this World is born in it; then does not all Nature in this World, and every Life in it, declare, that the Chriftian Method of Salvation is as *neceffary* to raife fallen Man, as the Sun and Spirit of this World is, to bring a Creature alive into it ?

Now, as there is but one God, fo there is but *one Nature*, as unalterable as that God from whom it arifes, and whofe Manifeftation it is; fo alfo there is but *one Religion* founded in Nature, and but one Salvation *poffible* in Nature. Revealed Religion is nothing elfe but a Revelation of the *Myfteries* of Nature, for God cannot reveal, or require any Thing by a fpoken or written Word, but that which he reveals and requires by *Nature*; for *Nature* is his great *Book* of Revelation, and he that can only read its Capital Letters, will have found fo many Demonftrations of the Truth of the written Revelation of God *.

But to fhew, that there is but one Salvation *poffible* in Nature, and that Poffibility folely contained in the Chriftian Method : Look from the Top to the Bottom of all Creatures, from the higheft to the loweft Beings, and

you

* *Spirit of Love,* Part II. Page 134—149.

you will find, that *Death* has but *one Nature*
in all Worlds, and in all Creatures : Look at
Life in an Angel, and Life in a *Vegetable*, and
you will find, that *Life* has but *one* and the
same Form, one and the same Ground in the
whole Scale of Beings : No Omnipotence of
God can make that to be Life, which is not
Life, or that to be Death, which is not Death,
according to Nature ; and the Reafon is, becaufe Nature is nothing elfe but God's own
outward Manifeſtation of what he inwardly is,
and can do ; and therefore no Revelation from
God can teach, or require any Thing but that
which is taught and required by God in, and
through Nature. The Myfteries of Religion
therefore, are no higher, nor deeper than the
Myfteries of Nature, and all the *Rites*, *Laws*,
Ceremonies, *Types*, *Inſtitutions* and *Ordinances*
given by God from *Adam* to the Apoftles, are
only typical of fomething that is to be done,
or inſtrumental to the doing of that, which the
unchangeable Working of Nature requires to be
done. As fure therefore as there is but one and
the fame Thing that is *Death*, and one and the
fame Thing that is *Life* throughout all Nature,
whether temporal or eternal, fo fure is it, that
there is but one Way to Life or Salvation for
fallen Man. And this Way, let it be what it
F 3 will,

will, muſt and can be only that, which has its
Reaſon and *Foundation* in that one Univerſal
Nature, which is the one unchangeable Manifeſtation of the Deity. For if there is but *one Thing*
that is Life, and one thing that is Death throughout all Nature, from the higheſt *Angel* to the
hardeſt *Flint* upon Earth, then it muſt be
plain, that the *Life* which is to be raiſed or
reſtored by Religion, muſt, and can only be
reſtored according to Nature: And therefore,
true Religion can only be the Religion of Nature, and Divine Revelation can do nothing
elſe, but reveal and manifeſt the Demands
and Workings of Nature.

29. Now, the one great Doctrine of the
Chriſtian Religion, and which includes all the
reſt, is this, that *Adam*, by his Sin, *died* to
the Kingdom of Heaven, or that the *Divine
Life* extinguiſhed in him ; That he cannot be
redeemed, or reſtored to this firſt *Divine Life*,
but by having it kindled or regenerated in him
by the Son and Holy Spirit of God : Now,
that which is here called *Death*, his loſing the
Light and Spirit of the Kingdom of Heaven,
and that which is here made neceſſary to make
him *alive* again to the Kingdom of Heaven, is
that *very ſame* which is called, and is *Death*
and *Life* throughout all Nature, both temporal
al : And therefore, the Chriſtian Religion

ligion requiring this Method of raising Man to
a Divine Life, has its infallible Proof from all
Nature*. Confider Death, or the Deadness
that is in a *hard Flint*, and you will fee what is
the *Eternal Death* of a fallen *Angel:* The
Flint is dead, or in a State of Death, becaufe
its *Fire* is bound, compacted, fhut up, and
imprifoned ; this is its Chains and Bands of
Death : A *Steel* ftruck againft a *Flint* will
fhew you, that every Particle of the Flint
confifts of this *compacted Fire.*

Now, a fallen Angel is in no other State of
Death, knows no other Death than this : It is
in its whole Spiritual, Intelligent Being, nothing
elfe, but that *very fame* which the Flint is, in
its infenfible Materiality, *viz.* an imprifon'd
compacted, darkened Fire-fpirit, fhut up, and
ty'd in its own Chains of Darknefs, as the Fire
of the Flint ; and you fhall fee by and by,
that the Flint is chang'd from its firft State into
its prefent Hardnefs of Death, in the fame
Manner, and by the fame Means, as the Heavenly Angel is become a fiery Serpent in the
State of Eternal Death.

Now, look at every Death that can be
found betwixt that of a fallen Angel, and that
of a hard Flint, and you will find that Death
enters no where, into no kind of Vegetable,

Plant,

* *Spirit of Love,* Part II. Page 117, &c.

Plant, or Animal, but as it has entered into the *Angel*, and the *Flint*, and ftands in the fame manner in every Thing where-ever it is.

Now, that a fallen Angel, is nothing elfe but a Fire-fpirit *imprifon'd* in the fame manner as a Flint is an imprifon'd Fire, is plain from the Scripture Account of them; not only becaufe all the wrathful Properties of a Fire *without Light*, are afcrib'd to them as their effential Qualities, but becaufe the *Place* of their Habitation, or the *State* of their Life, is a *Fire of Hell*. For how could it be poffible, that a *hellifh Fire* fhould be the Eternal *State* of their Life, unlefs their *Nature* was fuch a Fire? Muft not their painful Condition arife from *their Nature*, and their Mifery be only a Senfibility of themfelves, of that which they have made themfelves to be? Therefore, if Fire *fhut up* in Darknefs, is the Nature of Hell, it can only be fo, becaufe fuch a darkened Fire is the *very Nature* of a fallen Angel. Or how again could the Human Soul, which has withftood its Salvation in this Life, be faid to fall into *Eternal Death*, or the Fire of Hell, if the Soul itfelf did not become *that Fire* of Hell? For when you fay the Soul enters into Hell, you fay neither more nor lefs, than if you had faid, that Hell enters into the Soul;

therefore,

therefore, the State of Hell, and the State of
the Soul in Hell, is one and the same Thing.
If therefore Hell is a State of Fire shut up,
and imprison'd from all Communion with
Light, then the same dark, imprison'd Fire
must be the Nature of the fallen Angel and
lost Soul; and thus, what your Eyes see to be
the *Death* or *Deadness* of a Flint, is that same
Thing, or that *same State* of the Thing, which
the Scripture assures you, to be the *Eternal
Death* of a fallen Angel, and a lost Soul.
Here also you may see a plain Proof of what
I have elsewhere declared concerning the fallen Soul; that considered *without* its Redeemer
in it, or the *in-spoken Word* of Life given to
Adam at his Fall, it is in itself, as a fallen Soul,
the *same dark, fiery* Spirit, as the Devils are;
and that the Reason why Men wholly given up
to Wickedness, and who have *suppressed* the
Redeeming Power of God in their Souls, do
not become *fully sensible* of this State of their
Souls, is this, because the Soul, while it is in
this Flesh and *Blood*, is capable of being *sof-
tened, asswaged,* and *comforted* in some Degree
or other, by the Influences of the *Sun* and
Spirit of this World, as all other Creatures
and Beings are. And if it was not thus, how
could it be a plain, constant Doctrine of Scripture,

·ture; that when the *Unredeemed Soul* departs this Life, it is incapable of any thing but Hell ? Is not this directly saying, that Hell, or the Senfibility of Hell was only hid and fuppreffed in fuch a Soul, by the Life and Light of this World fhining upon it ?

Now what I have faid of the fad Condition of the Soul at the *Fall*, that it loft the Divine Life, or the Birth of the Son and Holy Spirit of God in it, and fo became of the *fame dark, fiery* Nature, as the Devils, is not poffible to be denied, without denying the moft univerfally received Doctrine of Scripture.

Is it not a fundamental Doctrine of Scripture, that *Adam* and all his Pofterity had been *left* in a State of *Eternal Death*, or Damnation, unlefs Jefus Chrift had become their Redeemer, and taken them out of their natural State ? But how can you believe, or own they had been *left* in this State, without believing and owning that they were *in* it ? Or, how can you with the Scripture believe, that by the Fall they became *Heirs* of Eternal Death and Damnation with the Devils, unlefs you believe and affirm, that by the Fall they became a hellifh, diabolical Nature ? Or how can you hold, that by the Fall they *wanted to be* delivered from the State of the Devils, and yet

not

not allow, that by the Fall, they got the Nature of the Devils? Can any Thing be more absurd and inconsistent? Is it not the same Thing as saying, that God made them Heirs of Eternal Death and Hell, before they were by Nature fit for it, or before they had extinguished in themselves the Divine Life which was at first brought forth in them?

Again: It is a Scripture Doctrine of the utmost Certainty and Importance, that those Souls which have *totally* resisted and withstood all that God has done in them and for them by his Son Jesus Christ, will, at their Departure from the Body, be incapable of any Thing but *Eternal Death*, or a hellish Condition. Now, how can you possibly hold this Doctrine of Scripture, without holding at the same Time, that the Soul was in that State by the Fall, before it had received its Redeemer, as it is then in, when it has *refused* to receive him; for all that you can say of a lost Soul is only this, that it has *lost* its Redeemer, and therefore is only in the Condition of that Soul which has *not received* him: And therefore, if a lost Soul is only an unredeemed Soul, it must be plain, that the Soul, *before* it had received its Redeemer, was in the miserable Condition, and had the miserable Nature of a Lost Soul; and

therefore,

therefore, the only Difference between the fallen Soul, and the loft Soul is this, they are both in the *fame need* of a Saviour, both have the *fame miferable* Nature, becaufe they have him *not*; but the one has the Offer of him, and the other has refufed to accept of Him: But his final Refufal of him, has only left him in Poffeffion of that *fallen State* of a hellifh Condition, which it had before a Saviour was given to it; and therefore, it is a Truth of the utmoft Certainty, that *Adam*, by his Fall, died to the Divine Life, and that by this Death, his Soul became of the *fame Nature* and *Condition* with the fallen Angels; and that therefore *that new Birth* or Regeneration, which he is to obtain by his Redeemer Jefus Chrift, is nothing elfe but the bringing back his Soul into the Kingdom of Heaven, by a *Birth* of the Son and Holy Spirit of God brought forth in it, that fo the Life of the tri-une God may be in him *again*, as it was at his *Creation*, when his Soul was firft breathed forth from the tri-une God. Is there any Thing more great, more glorious, or more confiftent than thefe Truths? Or is there any Poffibility of denying any Part of them, without giving up the whole? Or is there any Reafon, why a Chriftian fhould be loth to believe this, and this alone, to be the

true

true State of that Regeneration which is fo abfolutely required by the Gofpel? Is it an unreafonable or uncomfortable Thing to be told, that our Regeneration is a true and real Regaining that heavenly, divine, immortal Life which at firſt came forth from God, and which alone can enter into the Kingdom of Heaven?

Say that *Adam* did not die a real Death at his Tranfgreſſion, that he did not loſe a divine, immortal Life, Light and Spirit, that he did not then firſt become a mere earthly, mortal, Diabolical Animal in the true and proper Senſe of the Words, but that theſe Things could only be affimed of him in a figurative Form of Speech; fay this, and then tell me what Reality you have left in any Article of our Salvation?

But if all theſe Things muſt be faid of fallen Man according to the ſtricteſt Truth of the Expreſſion, then the Gofpel Regeneration, by a Birth of the Son and Holy Spirit of God, ariſing a *ſecond Time* in the Soul of Man, muſt mean ſuch a real Birth of a new, heavenly Life, as the proper Senſe of the Words denote.

30. But to return now to my Argumentation with the Deiſt.

I have

I have plainly ſhewn you, that there is, and
can be but one kind of Death through all
Nature, whether temporal or eternal ; and
this I have done, by ſhewing that *Eternal
Death* in an *Angel*, is the ſame Thing, and
has the ſame Nature, as the hard Death that is
in a ſenſeleſs Flint. But if it be a certain
Truth, that Death has but *one Way* of entring
into, or poſſeſſing any Being from the higheſt
of ſpiritual to the loweſt of material Creatures,
then, tho' nothing elſe could be offered, it
muſt be an infallible Conſequence, that *Life*
has but one Way of being *kindled* throughout
all Nature, and that therefore there can be
but *one true* Religion, and that only can be it,
which hath the *one only way* of kindling the
heavenly Life in the Soul.

Now, look where you will, the Birth or
kindling of Life through all Nature ſhews
you, that the Way of Goſpel Regeneration,
or Raiſing the Divine Life again in the fallen
Soul, is that one and the ſame Way, by which
every kind of Life is, and muſt be raiſed,
wherever it is found. The Goſpel ſaith, unleſs
the fallen Soul be born again from above, be
born again of the Word, or Son, and the Spirit of God, it cannot ſee, or enter into the
Kingdom of Heaven: Now here it ſays a Truth,

as

as much confirm'd and ratify'd by all Nature, as when it is faid, except a Creature hath the Light and Spirit of this World born in it, it cannot become a living Animal of this World: Or, except a *Seed* have the Light and Spirit of this World incorporated in it, it cannot become a *Vegetable* of this World, either as Plant, Fruit, or Flower. Afk now wherein lies the abfolute Impoffibility, that the fallen Soul fhould be raifed to its Divine Life, without a *Birth* of the *Son* and Holy *Spirit* of God in it, and the true Ground of this Impoffibility is only this, becaufe a *Seed* fhut up in its own cold hardnefs, cannot poffibly be raifed into its higheft Vegetable Life, but by a *Birth* of the *Light* and *Spirit* of this World rifing up in it.

On the other hand, afk why a *Seed* cannot poffibly become a Vegetable Life, till the Light and Spirit of this World has been incorporated, or generated in it; and the only true Ground of it is, becaufe a fallen Soul can only be raifed to a Divine Life, or become a Plant of the Kingdom of Heaven, by receiving the Birth of the Light and Spirit of God into it. For the true Reafon, why Life is in *fuch a Form,* and rifes in *fuch* a Manner in the loweft Creature living, is becaufe it does, and muft arife

in

in the *same manner*, and ſtand in the *ſame Form* in the higheſt of Living Creatures : For Nature does, and muſt always act and generate in *one* and the *ſame unchangeable* Manner, becauſe it is nothing elſe but the *Manifeſtation* of one unchangeable God.

It is *one* and the *ſame* Operation of Light and Spirit, that turns Fire into every Degree and kind of Life that can be found either in temporal or eternal Nature : It is one and the ſame Operation of Light and Spirit, that upon one State of Fire, raiſes only a *vegetable* Life, upon another State of Fire, raiſes an *animal* Life, upon another State of Fire, raiſes an *intellectual* and *angelical* Life.

There is no State or Form of Death in any Creature, but where ſome kind of Fire is ſhut up from Light and Spirit, nor is there any kind of Life but what is kindled by the ſame Operation of Light and Spirit upon ſome ſort of Fire.

A *Fruit* muſt firſt ſtand in a *poiſonous, ſour, aſtringent, bitter,* and *fiery* Agitation of all its Parts, before the Light and Spirit of this World can be generated in it. And thus Light and Spirit operate upon one ſort of Fire in the Production of a vegetable Life.

An

An *Animal* muft be conceived in the fame manner, it muft begin in the *fame Poifon*, and when Nature is in its *fiery Strife*, the Light and Spirit of this World kindles up the true animal Life.

Thus alfo there is but one kind, or State of Death that can fall upon any Creature, which is nothing elfe, but its *lofing the Birth* of Light and Spirit in itfelf, by which it becomes an imprifon'd, dark Fire. In an Animal, Vegetable, or mere Matter, it is a fenfelefs State of imprifon'd Fire; in an Angel, or intellectual Being, as the Soul of Man, it is a *felf-tormenting, felf-generating, fiery* Worm, that cannot lofe its Senfibility, but is in a State of Eternal *Death*, becaufe it is feparated *eternally* from that Light and Spirit, which alone can raife a divine Life in any intellectual Creature.

And thus it is plain, beyond all Poffibility of Doubt, that there is neither *Life* nor *Death* to be found in any Part of the Creation but what fets its infallible Seal to this Gofpel Truth, that fallen Man cannot enter into the Kingdom of Heaven any other Way, than by being born again of the Son and Holy Spirit of God.

31. And here, my Friend, you may with Certainty fee what a poor, groundlefs *Fiction*,

G   . your

your Religion of *Human Reason* is; its Infig-
nificancy and Emptineſs is ſhewn you by every
Thing you can look upon.

Salvation is a *Birth of Life*, but Reaſon can
no more bring forth *this Birth*, than it can
kindle Life in a *Plant*, or *Animal*: You
might as well write the Word, *Flame*, upon
the out-fide of a *Flint*, and then expect that
its impriſon'd Fire ſhould be *kindled* by it, as
to imagine, that any *Images*, or *Ideal Speculations* of Reaſon painted in your Brain, ſhould
raiſe your Soul out of its State of Death, and
kindle the Divine Life in it. No: Wou'd you
have Fire from a *Flint*; its Houſe of Death
muſt be *ſhaken*, and its Chains of Darkneſs
broken off by the Strokes of a *Steel* upon it.
This muſt of all Neceſſity be done to your
Soul, its *impriſon'd Fire* muſt be awakened by
the *ſharp Strokes* of Steel, or no true Light of
Life can ariſe in it: All Nature and Creature
tells you, that the Heavenly Life muſt begin
in you from the ſame Cauſes, and the ſame
Operation as every earthly Life, whether vegetable, or animal, does in this World *.

Now, look where you will, all Life muſt
be generated in this Manner: Firſt, an *Attraction*, or an *aſtringing* Deſire, muſt work
'f into an *anguiſhing Agitation*, or *painful
Strife* ;

* *Way to divine Knowledge*, Page 162, &c.

Strife; this Attraction become reſtleſs, and highly agitated, is that *firſt Poiſon*, or Strife of the *Properties* of Nature, which is and muſt be the *Beginning* of every *Vegetable* or *Animal* Life; it is by this *Strife*, or inward *Agitation*, that it reaches and gets a *Birth* of the Light and Spirit of this World into it, and ſo becomes a Living Member, either of the animal or vegetable World.

Now, this muſt be your Proceſs, a *Deſire* brought into an *anguiſhing State*; or the *bitter Sorrows* and *fiery Agitations* of Repentance, muſt be the *Beginning* of a Divine Life in your Soul; 'tis by this awakened Fire, or inward Agitation, that it becomes capable of being re-generated, or turned into an heavenly Life, by the Light and Holy Spirit of God.

Nothing is, or can poſſibly be Salvation, but this regenerated Life of the Soul: How vain and abſurd would it be, to talk of a Crea-ture's being made a Member of a vegetable or animal Kingdom, through an *outward Grace* or *Favour*? or by any *outward Thing* of any kind? For does not Senſe, Reaſon, and all Nature force you to confeſs, that it is abſo-lutely impoſſible for *any Thing* to become a *Living Member* of the animal or vegetable Kingdom, but by having the animal or vege-

table

table Life *raifed* or brought forth in it ? There-fore, does not Senfe and Reafon, and all Na-ture join with the Gofpel in affirming, that no Man can enter into the Kingdom of Hea-ven, till the *Heavenly Life*, or that which is the Life in Heaven, *be born* in him ?

The Gofpel fays to the fallen, earthly Man, that he muft be *born again from above*, before he can fee, enter into, or become a Living Member of the Kingdom that is above.

Now, he that underftands this to be a *figu-rative Saying*, that requires no *real Birth* of a *real Life* that is only above, but that an earthly Man may enter into the Life of Heaven, by only carrying this figurative Saying along with him, is as abfurd, as ignorant, and offends as much againft Senfe, Reafon, and all Na-ture, as he who holds, that it is a *figurative Expreffion*, when we fay that nothing can enter into the vegetable Kingdom, till it has the *vegetable Life* in it, or be a Member of the Animal Kingdom, till it hath the Animal Life born in it *.

And if fome Learned Men will fay, that it is *Religious Enthufiafm* to place our Salvation, or Capacity for the Kingdom of Heaven in the *inward Life* or *Birth* of *Heaven* derived into our Souls, they are only as learned as thofe

who

* *Way to divine Knowledge*, Page 159.

who fhould call it *Philofophical Enthufiafm* to place the true Nature of a Vegetable, or Animal, in its getting the *inward, real Birth* of a Vegetable and Animal Life. But to return to the Deift.

You act as if God was a Being that had an *arbitrary, difcretionary* Will, or Wifdom, like that of a great Prince over his Subjects, who will reward Mankind according as their Services appeared to him. And fo you fancy, that your Religion of Reafon may appear as valuable as a Religion that confifts of Forms, and Modes, Ordinances, and Doctrines of Revelalion; but your Idea of the laft Judgment is a Fiction of Reafon that knows nothing rightly of God. God's laft rewarding, is only his laft feparating every Thing into its own Eternal Place; it is only putting an end to all temporary Nature, to the Mixture of Good and Evil that is in Time, and leaving every Thing to be *That* in *Eternity*, which it has made itfelf to be in *Time*. Thus it is that our Works follow us, and thus God rewards every Man according to his Deeds *.

During the Time of this World, God may be confidered as the good Hufbandman; he fows the Seed, the End of the World is the Harveft, the Angels are the Reapers; if you

G 3 are

* *Way to divine Knowledge*, Page 169—183.

are *Wheat*, you are to be gathered into the Barn, if you are *Tares*, it fignifies nothing, *whence*, or *how*, or by what *Means* you are become fo ; Tares are to be rejected, becaufe they are Tares, and Wheat to be gathered by the Angels, becaufe it is Wheat : This is the Mercy, and Goodnefs, and Difcretionary Juftice of God that you are to expect at the laft Day. If you are not Wheat, that is, if the heavenly Life, or the Kingdom of God, is not grown up in you, it fignifies nothing what you have chofen in the ftead of it, or why you have chofen it, you are not *That*, which alone can help you to a Place in the Divine Granary.

God wants no Services of Men to reward, he only wants to have *fuch a Life* quickened and raifed up in you, as may make it *poffible* for you to enter into, and live in Heaven.

He has created you out of his own *Eternal Nature*, and therefore you muft have either an Eternal Life, or Eternal Death according to it. If eternal Nature ftandeth *in you*, as it doth *without* you, then you are born again to the Kingdom of Heaven ; but if Nature works contrary in you to what it does in Heaven, then you are in Eternal Death : And here lies the Neceffity of our being *born* again of the *Word* and *Spirit* of God, in order to the Kingdom of Heaven. It is becaufe we are created

out

out of that eternal Nature which is the *King-dom of Heaven*; 'tis becaufe we are *fallen out* of it into a Life of temporal Nature, and therefore muft have the Life of eternal Nature *re-kindled* in us, before we can poffibly enter into the King-dom of Heaven: Therefore, look where you will, or at what you will, there is only one Thing to be done, we want Nothing elfe, but to have the *Light World*, or the Life of Eter-nal Nature kindled again in our Souls, that *Life*, and *Light*, and *Spirit* may be *That* in our Souls, which they are in Eternal Nature, out of which our Souls were created; that fo we may be heavenly Plants growing up to the Kingdom of Heaven *.

You deceive yourfelf with fancy'd Notions of the Goodnefs of God; you imagine, that fo perfeƈt a Being cannot damn you for fo *fmall* a Matter, as *chufing* a Religion according to your *own Notions*, or for not joining yourfelf with this, or that Religious Society.

But all this is great Ignorance of *God*, and *Nature*, and *Religion*. God has appointed a Religion, by which Salvation is to be had ac-cording to the *Poffibility* of Nature, where no Creature will be fav'd, or loft, but as it works with, or contrary to Nature. For as the God

of

* *Way to divine Knowledge*, Page 186——195.

of Nature cannot himſelf act *contrary* to Nature, becauſe Nature is the *Manifeſtation* of himſelf, ſo every Creature having its Life in, and from *Nature*, can have only *ſuch* a Life, or *ſuch* a Death as is according to the *Poſſibility* of Nature: And therefore, no Creature will be ſav'd, by an *arbitrary* Goodneſs of God, but becauſe of its *Conformity* to Nature, nor any Creature loſt by a Want of Compaſſion in God, but becauſe of its Salvation being *impoſ-ſible*, according to the *whole State* of Nature.

It is not for Notional, or Speculative Miſtakes, that Man will be rejected by God at the laſt Day, or for *any Crimes* that God could *over-look*, if he was ſo pleaſed; but becauſe Man has continued in his *unregenerate State*, and has refiſted and ſuppreſſed that *Birth of Life*, by which alone he could become a Member of the Kingdom of Heaven. The *Goodneſs* and *Love* of God have no *Limits* or *Bounds*, but ſuch as his Omnipotence hath: And every Thing that hath a *Poſſibility* of partaking of the Kingdom of Heaven, will *infallibly* find a Place in it.

God comes not to Judgment to diſplay any Wrath of his own, or to inflict any Puniſh-ment as from Himſelf upon Man: He only comes to declare, that all temporary Nature is

at an End, and that therefore, all Things muft
be, and ftand in their own Places in Eternal
Nature : His Sentence of *Condemnation*, is
only a leaving them that are loft, in fuch a
Mifery of their *own Nature*, as has finally rejected all that was poffible to relieve it.

You fancy that God will not reject you at the
laft Day, for having not received this, or that
Mode, or *Kind* of Religion : But here all is
Miftake again. You might as well imagine,
that no particular *kind* of Element was neceffary to extinguifh Fire, or that *Water* can fupply
the *Place* of Air in kindling it, as fuppofe that
no *particular kind* of Religion is abfolutely neceffary to raife up fuch a Divine Life in the
Soul as can only be its Salvation ; for Nature
is the *Ground* of all Creatures, it is God's Manifeftation of himfelf, it is his Inftrument in,
and by which he acts in the Production and
Government of every Life ; and therefore a
Life that is to belong to *this* World, muft be
raifed according to *temporal* Nature, and a Life
that is to live in the next World, muft be
raifed according to *Eternal* Nature.

Therefore, all the particular *Doctrines*, *Inftitutions*, *Myfteries*, and *Ordinances* of a revealed Religion that comes from the God of
Nature, muft have their *Reafon*, *Foundation*,
and

and *Neceſſity* in Nature ; and then your renouncing ſuch a revealed Religion, is renouncing
all that the God of Nature can do to ſave you.

When I ſpeak of Nature as the true Ground
and Foundation of Religion, I mean nothing
like that which you call the Religion of *Human Reaſon,* or *Nature*; for I ſpeak here of
Eternal Nature, which is the Nature of the
Kingdom of Heaven, or that Eternal State, where
all redeemed Souls muſt have their Eternal
Life, and live in Eternal Nature by a Life deriv'd from it, as Men and Animals live in temporal Nature, by a Life deriv'd from it ; for,
ſeeing Man ſtands with his Soul in Eternal Nature, as certainly as he lives outwardly in temporal Nature, and ſeeing Man can have nothing in this World, neither Happineſs, nor
Miſery from it, but what is according to temporal Nature, ſo he can with his Soul, attain
nothing, nor ſuffer nothing in the next World,
but what is according to the Eternal Nature of
that World ; and therefore, it is an infallible
Truth, that that *particular* Religion can *alone* do
us any Good, or help us to the Happineſs of
the next World, which works *with,* and *according* to Eternal Nature, and is able to *generate* that Eternal Life in us. But your Notion
of a Goodneſs of God that may be expected

at

at the laſt Day, is as groundleſs, as if you ima-
gined, that God would then ſtand over his
Creatures in a compaſſionate kind of *weighing*
or *conſidering* who ſhould be ſaved, and who
damn'd, becauſe a good-natur'd Prince might
do ſo towards Variety of Offenders.

But hear how the God of Nature himſelf
ſpeaks of this Matter: *Behold, I have ſet be-*
fore thee, Life and Death, Fire and Water, —
chuſe whether thou wilt. Here lies the *Whole*
of the Divine Mercy; 'tis all on *this ſide* the
Day of Judgment : Till the End of Time,
God is *compaſſionate* and *long-ſuffering*, and
continues to every Creature a *Power* of chuſing
Life or Death, Water or Fire ; but when the
End of Time is come, there is an End of
Choice, and the laſt Judgment is only a putting every one into the full and ſole Poſſeſſion
of *That* which he has choſen.

But your Notion of a Goodneſs of God at
the laſt Day ſuppoſes, that if a Man has erro-
neouſly choſen *Death* inſtead of *Life*, *Fire* inſtead of *Water*, that God will not ſuffer ſuch a
Creature to be deprived of Salvation through a
miſtaken Choice ; but that in ſuch a Creature,
he will make *Death* to be *Life*, and *Fire* to be
Water. But you might as well expect, that
God ſhould make a Thing to be, and not to
be

be at the fame Time; for this is as poffible as
to make Hell to be Heaven, or Death to be
Life: For Darknefs can no more be Light,
Death can no more be Life, Fire can no more
be Water in any Being through a Compaffion
of God towards it, than a *Circle* could be a
Square, a Falfhood a Truth, or *two* to be more
than *three*, by God's looking upon them.

32. Our Salvation is an *Entrance* into the
Kingdom of Heaven; now, the *Life, Light*
and *Spirit* of Heaven muft as neceffarily be in
a Creature before it can *live* in Heaven, as the
Life, Light and Spirit of this World muft be
in a Creature before it can *live* in this World:
Therefore the *one only* Religion that can fave
any one Son of fallen *Adam*, muft be that
which can *raife* or *generate* the Life, Light
and Spirit of Heaven in his Soul, that when
the Light and Spirit of this World leaves him,
he may not find himfelf in eternal Death and
Darknefs.

Now, if this Light and Spirit of Heaven is
generated in your Soul as it is generated in
Heaven, if it arifes up in your Nature *within*
you, as it does in eternal Nature *without* you,
(which is the Chriftian new Birth, or Regeneration) then you are become capable of
the Kingdom of Heaven, and nothing can
keep

keep you out of it; but if you die without this Birth of the Eternal Light and Spirit of God, then your Soul ſtands in the *ſame Diſtance* from, and *Contrariety* to the Kingdom of Heaven, as Hell does: If you die in this unregenerate State, it ſignifies nothing *how* you have liv'd, or *what* Religion you have own'd, all is left undone that was to have ſaved you: It matters not what *Form* of Life you have appeared in, what a Number of decent, engaging or glorious Exploits you have done either as a *Scholar*, a *Stateſman*, or a *Philoſopher*; if they have proceeded only from the Light and Spirit of this World, they muſt die with it, and leave your Soul in that Eternal Darkneſs, which it muſt have, ſo long as the Light and Spirit of Eternity is not generated in it.

And this is the true Ground and Reaſon, why an outward *Morality*, a *Decency* and *Beauty* of Life and Conduct with reſpect to this World, ariſing only from a *Worldly Spirit*, has nothing of Salvation in it: He that has his Virtue only from this World, is only a *Trader* of this World, and can only have a Worldly Benefit from it. For it is an undoubted Truth, that every Thing is neceſſarily bounded by, or kept within the Sphere of its *own Activity*; and therefore, to expect Heavenly Effects from

a Worldly

a Worldly Spirit, is Nonfense: As *Water* cannot rife higher in its Streams, than the Spring from whence it cometh, fo no Actions can afcend farther in their Efficacy, or rife higher in their Value, than the *Spirit* from whence they proceed. The Spirit that comes from Heaven is always in Heaven, and whatfoever it does, tends to, and reaches Heaven: The Spirit that arifes from this World, is always in it; it is as worldly when it gives *Alms*, or prays in the *Church*, as when it makes *Bargains* in the *Market*. When therefore the Gofpel faith, He that gives Alms to be feen of Men, hath his Reward; it is grounded on this general Truth, That every Thing, every Shape, or kind or degree of Virtue that *arifes* from the *Spirit* of this World, has nothing to expect but *That* which it can receive from this World: For every Action muft have its Nature, and Efficacy according to the Spirit from whence it proceeds. He that loves to fee a *Crucifix*, a worthlefs Image, folely from this Principle, becaufe from his Heart he embraces Chrift as his fuffering Lord and Pattern, does an Action poor, and needlefs in itfelf, which yet by the Spirit from whence it proceeds, *reaches* Heaven, and *helps* to kindle the heavenly Life in the Soul. On the other hand, he that from

a felfifh

a *selfish Heart*, a *Worldly Spirit*, a Love of Esteem, distinguishes himself by the most rational Virtues of an exemplary Life, has only a Piety that may be reckon'd amongst the *perishable* Things of this World.

33. You (the *Deist*) think it a *Partiality* unworthy of God, when you hear that the *Salvation* of Mankind is attributed and appropriated to *Faith* and *Prayer* in the Name of Jesus Christ. It must be answered, *First*, That there is *no Partiality* of any kind in God; every Thing is accepted by him according to its *own Nature*, and receives all the Good from him that it can possibly receive: *Secondly*, That a Morality of Life, not arising from the *Power* and *Spirit* of Jesus Christ, but brought forth by the Spirit of *this World*, is the same Thing, has the same Nature and Efficacy in a Heathen, as a Christian, does only the *same* worldly Good to the one, as it does to the other; therefore, there is not the least Partiality in God, with respect to the *Moral Works* of Mankind, considered as arising from, and directed by the Spirit of this World.

Now, were these the *only Works* that Man could do, could he only act from *the Spirit* of this World, no *Flesh* could be sav'd, that is, no earthly Creature, such as Man is, could possibly

begin

begin to be of a heavenly Nature, or have a heavenly Life *brought* forth in him; for it is only a Spirit from Heaven derived into the fallen Nature, that makes *any Beginning* of a heavenly Life in it, that can lay the *Poſſibility* of its having the leaſt Ability, Tendency, and Diſpoſition towards the Kingdom of Heaven. This Spirit derived from Heaven, is the *Birth* of the Son of God, given to the Soul as its *Saviour, Regenerator,* or *Beginner* of its Return to Heaven; it is that *Word* of Life, or *Bruiſer* of the Serpent, that was *in-ſpoken* into the firſt fallen Father of Men; 'tis this *alone* that gives to all the Race of *Adam* their *Capacity* for Salvation, their *Power* of being again Sons of God; and therefore, Faith and Prayer in the *Name* of Jeſus Chriſt, or Works done in the *Spirit* and *Power* of Jeſus Chriſt can *alone ſave* the Soul, becauſe the Soul can have *no Relation* to Heaven, *no Communion* with it, *no Beginning* or *Power* of Growth in the heavenly Life, but ſolely by the Nature and Name of Jeſus Chriſt *derived* into it. God's Redemption of Mankind is as univerſal as the Fall: It was the one Father of all Men that fell, therefore, all his Children were born into his fallen State: It was the *one Father* of all Men that was redeemed by the *in-ſpoken Word* of Life into him;

therefore,

therefore, all his Children are born into his State of Redemption, and have as certainly the same Bruiser of the Serpent in the *Birth* of their Life from him, as they have from him a *Serpentine Nature* that is to be bruised.

Hence it was, that this *Bruiser* of the Serpent, when born of a Virgin, and come to die for the World, saith of himself, I am the *Way*, the *Truth*, and the *Life* ; *no Man cometh unto the Father* but by me. Hence also the Apostle saith, *There is none other Name under Heaven given among Men, whereby we must be saved,*—because he is that *same* saving Name, or Power of Salvation which from the *Beginning* was given to *Adam*, as an in-spoken *Word* of Life, or Bruiser of the Serpent : And therefore, as sure as *Adam* had *any Power* of Salvation *derived* into him from Jesus Christ, so sure was it, that the Apostle *must tell* both Jews and Heathens, that there *was no Salvation in any other.*

Therefore, tho' Jesus Christ is the *one only* Saviour of all that can any where, or at any Time be saved, yet there is no *Partiality* in God, because, this same Jesus Christ, who came in Human Flesh to the Jews in a certain Age, was that *same Saviour* who was given to *Adam*, when all Mankind were in his Loins ; and

H   who,

who, through all Ages, and in all Countries,
from the firſt Patriarchs to the End of the
World, is the common Saviour, as he is the
common *Light that lighteth every Man* that
cometh into the World, and that *Principle* of
Life both in Jews and Heathens, by which
they had any Relation to God, or any *Power*,
or *Right*, or *Ability* to call him Father. When
therefore you look upon the Goſpel as *nar-
rowing* the Way of Salvation, or limiting it
to thoſe, who only know and believe in Jeſus
Chriſt, ſince his Appearance in the Fleſh,
you miſtake the *whole Nature* of the Chriſtian
Redemption.

And when you reject *this Saviour* that then
appeared, and *died* as a Sacrifice upon the
Croſs, you don't renounce a *particular kind* of
Religion, that was given *only* at a certain Time
to one Part of the World, but you renounce
the *one Source* and *Fountain* of all the Grace
and Mercy that God *can* beſtow upon Mankind, you renounce your Share of that firſt
Covenant which God made with *all Men* in
Adam, you go back into his *firſt fallen* State,
and ſo put yourſelf into that Condition of Eternal Death, from which there is no Poſſibility
of Deliverance, but by that one Saviour whom
you have renounced.

And

And now, my dear Friend, beware of Prejudice, or Hardnefs of Heart : One carelefs, or one relenting Thought upon all that is here laid before you, may either quite fhut out, or quite open an Entrance for true Conviction. I have fhewn you what is meant by Chriftian Redemption, and the abfolute Neceffity of a *new* and *heavenly Birth*, in order to obtain your Share of a heavenly Life in the next World : I have confirm'd the Truths of the Gofpel, by Proofs taken from what is undeniable in Nature : And I readily grant you that nothing can be true in revealed Religion, but what has its *Foundation* in Nature; becaufe a Religion coming from the God of Nature, can have no other End but to reform, and fet right the Failings, Tranfgreffions, and Violations of Nature. When the Gofpel faith, that Man fallen from the State of his Creation, and become an earthly Animal of this temporal World, muft be born again of the Son and Holy Spirit of God, in order to be a heavenly Creature ; 'tis becaufe all Nature faith, that an immortal, eternal Soul, muft have an *immortal, eternal* Light and Spirit, to make it live in Eternal Nature, as every Animal muft have a *temporal* Light and Spirit, in order to live in temporary Nature Muft you not therefore either deny the *Im-*

mortality

mortality of the Soul, or acknowledge the Neceſſity of its having an *Eternal* Light and Spirit ? When the Goſpel ſaith, that nothing can *kindle* or *generate* the heavenly Life, but the Operation of the *Light* and *Spirit* of Heaven, it ·is becauſe all Nature ſaith, that no temporal Life can be raiſed but in the *ſame manner* in temporary Nature. Muſt you not therefore be forced to confeſs, that Nature and the Goſpel both preach the *ſame Truths.*

Light and Spirit muſt be where-ever there are *living* Beings : And there muſt be the ſame Difference betwixt the Light and Spirit of different Worlds, as there is betwixt the Worlds themſelves. *Hell* muſt have its Light, or it could have no *living* Inhabitants, but its Light is not ſo *refreſhing*, not ſo *gentle*, not ſo *delightful*, not ſo *comfortable* as flaſhing Points of Fire in the thickeſt Darkneſs of Night ; and therefore their Light is called an *Eternal Darkneſs*, becauſe it can never *diſperſe*, but only horribly *diſcover* Darkneſs : Hell alſo muſt have its *Spirit* ; but it is only an inceſſant Senſibility of *wrathful Agitations*, of which the Thunder and Rage of a Tempeſt is but a low, ſhadowy Reſemblance, as being only a little outward Eruption of *That Wrath*, which is the inward, reſtleſs Eſſence of the Spirit of

Hell ;

Hell ; and therefore that Life, tho' it be a living Spirit, is juftly called an *Eternal Death*.

The Light and Spirit of God admit of no Delineation or Comparifon, they are only fo far known to any one, as they are brought into the Soul by a Birth of themfelves in it.

Now confider, I pray you : The Light and Spirit of this World can no more be the Light and Spirit of *immortal Souls*, than *Grafs* and *Hay* can be the Food of Angels ; but is as different from the Light and Spirit of Heaven, as an Angel is different from a Beaft of the Field. When therefore the Soul of a Man departs from his Body, and is *eternally* cut off from *all* temporal Light and Spirit, what is it that can keep fuch a Soul from falling into *Eternal Darknefs*, unlefs it have in itfelf, that *Light* and *Spirit*, which is of the fame Nature with the Light and Spirit of Eternity, fo that it may be in the Light of Heaven or Eternal Nature, as it was in the Light of this World in temporary Nature.

Light and Spirit there muft be in every Thing that lives, but the Death of the Body takes away the Light and Spirit of this World ; if therefore the Light and Spirit of Heaven be *not born* in the Soul when it lofes the Body, it can only have that Light and Spirit, which is the very *Death* and *Darknefs* of Hell.

When

When Man loft the Light and Spirit of his Creation, he loft it by turning the *Will* and *Defire* of his Soul into an Earthly Life ; this was his Defire of *knowing Good and Evil* in this World. His Fall therefore confifted in this, his Soul loft its firft *innate, in-breath'd* Light and Spirit of Heaven, and inftead of it, had only the Light and Spirit of Temporary Nature, to keep up for a Time fuch a Life in him from this World, as the proper Creatures of this World have : And this is the Reafon, why Man, the nobleft Creature that is in this World, has yet various Circumftances of Neceffity, Poverty, Diftrefs and Shame, that are not common to other Animals of this World. 'Tis becaufe the Creatures of this Life are here *at home,* are the proper Inhabitants of this World, and therefore that Womb out of which they are born, has provided them with all that they want ; but Man being only *fallen* into it, and as a Tranfgreffor, muft in many Refpects find himfelf in fuch Wants as other Creatures have not. *Tranfitory Time* has brought them forth, and therefore they can have no Pain, nor Concern, nor Danger in *paffing away ;* becaufe it is the *very Form* of their Nature, to begin, and to have an End : And therefore the
God

God of Nature has no outward Laws, or Directions for the Creatures of this World.

But the Soul of Man being *not born* of the Light and Spirit of this tranfitory World, but only ftanding a while as a *Stranger* upon Earth, and being under a *Neceffity* of having either the Nature of an Angel, or a Devil, when it *leaves* this World, is met by the Mercy and Goodnefs of the God of Nature, is inwardly, and outwardly called, warned, directed, and affifted *how* to regain that Light and Spirit of Heaven which it loft, when it fell under the temporary Light and Spirit of this World. And this is the whole Ground and End of re-vealed Religion, *viz.* to kindle fuch a *Begin-ning* or *Birth* of the Divine Light and Spirit in the Soul, that when Man muft take an Eter-nal Leave of the Light and Spirit of this World, he may not be in a State of Eternal Death and Darknefs.

Now, feeing the Light and Spirit of Hea-ven or Eternal Nature, is as different from the Light and Spirit of this World, as an Angel is from an Animal of the Field, if you have liv'd here only to the Spirit and Temper of this World, govern'd by its Goods and Evils, and only wife according to its Wifdom, you muft die as *deftitute* of the Light and Spirit of Hea-

H 4

ven

ven, as the Beasts that perish. You have now
an *Averfion* and *Diflike*, or at least, a *Difbelief*
of the Doctrines of Christian Regeneration,
you struggle against *this Kind* of Redemption,
you would have no Salvation from the *Light*
and *Spirit* of Eternity regenerated in your
Soul ; where then must you be, when the
Light and Spirit of this World leaves you ?

Do you think that the Light and Spirit of
God will then *feize* upon you, *fhine* up in you
by an *outward Force*, tho' they never could *be
born* in you ? Or do you think, that the Light
and Spirit of God can *now be generating* themfelves in you, and ready to appear, as foon as
you have ended a Life, that has continually
refifted them, and would have no *new Birth*
from them ? Or that God, by a compaffionate
Goodnefs, will not fuffer you to be in that
Condition, into which your *own Will* has brought
you ? No, my Friend, the *Will* that is in you,
must do *That* for you, which the Will that
was in Angels did for thofe that *flood*, and for
thofe that *fell*.

God's Goodnefs or Compaffion is always in
the *fame* infinite State, always *flowing forth*, in
and through all Nature in the fame infinite
Manner, and nothing wants it, but that which
cannot receive it : Whilft the Angels ftood,
they

they ftood incompaffed with the infinite Source
of all Goodnefs and Compaffion, God was communicated to them in as high a Degree as their
Nature could receive; and they fell, not becaufe he ceafed to be an infinite, open Fountain of all Good to them, but becaufe they
had a Will which muft direct itfelf.

For the Will, at its firft arifing in the Creature, can be fubject to no outward Power, becaufe it has no outward Maker; as it ftands in
a creaturely Form, God is its true Creator; but
as a *Will*, it has no *outward Maker*, but is a
Ray, or Spark, derived from the *Unbeginning*
Will of the Creator, and is of the fame Nature in the Creature, as it was in the Creator,
felf-exiftent, *felf-generating*, *felf-moving*, and
uncontroulable from without; and there could
not poffibly be a *free Will* in the Creature, but
by its being *directly* deriv'd, or propagated
from the fame Will in the Creator, for Nothing
can be free *now*, but that which *always* was
fo.

But if the free Will of God, which is above
and fuperior to Nature, be communicated to
the Creature, then the Creature's free Will muft
have the fame Power over its *one Nature*,
that the Will of God has over that Eternal
Nature, which is his own Manifeftation: And
therefore,

therefore, every free Creature muſt have, and
find its *own* Nature in *this*, or *that* State, as a
Birth from the free Working of its own Will.
And here appears the true Reaſon, why no
Creatures of this World can commit Sin; 'tis
becauſe they have no Will that is *ſuperior* to
Nature : Their Will in every one of them, is
only the Will of Nature ; and therefore let
them do what they will, they are always doing that which is *natural*, and conſequently,
not ſinful. But the Will of Angels and Men
being an *Offspring*, or *Ray*, derived from the
Will of God, which is *ſuperior* to Nature,
ſtands chargeable with the State and Condition
of their Nature ; and therefore it is, that the
Nature of the Devil, and the Nature of fallen
Man is imputed to both of them, as their Sin,
which could not be, but becauſe their Will
was uncontroulable, and gave Birth and Being
to that State and Condition of Nature, which
is called, and is their Sin.

Therefore, O Man ! look well to thyſelf,
and ſee what Birth thou art bringing forth,
what Nature is growing up in Thee, and be
aſſured, that ſtand thou muſt, in that State in
Nature, which the working of thy own Will
has brought forth in Thee, whether it be happy
or miſerable. Expect no Arbitrary Goodneſs
of

of God towards Thee, when thou leavest this
World; for that must grow for ever which
hath grown here. God hath created thee in
Nature, his Mercy hath shewn Thee all the
Laws and Necessities of Nature, and how
Thou may'st rise from Thy Corruption, ac-
cording to the Possibilities of Nature, and He
can only save Thee by thy conforming to the
Demands of Nature: The Greatness of the
Divine Mercy and Favour towards all Men
appears in this, that when all Nature was
fail'd, and Mankind could from Nature have
Nothing but Eternal Death, that God brought
such a Second *Adam* into the World, as being
God and Man, could make Nature begin its
Work again, where it fail'd in the first *Adam*.

The *free Grace* and Mercy by which we
are said in the Scripture to be *sav'd*, is not an
arbitrary Good Will in God, which saves
whom he pleases; as a Prince may forgive
some, and not forgive others, merely through
his own Sovereign Grace and Favour: Nothing
of this Kind hath any Place in God, or in the
Mystery of our Redemption; but the Mercy
and Grace, by which we are sav'd, is therefore
free, because God hath freely, and from his
own Goodness, put us into a *State* and Possibility of Salvation, by freely giving us Jesus
Christ,

Chriſt, (the Divine and Human Nature united in one Perſon) as the only Means of regenerating that firſt Divine and Human Life, which the whole Race of Mankind had loſt. In this Senſe alone it is, that all our Salvation is wholly owing to the free Grace of God, that is, our *State*, and *Poſſibility*, and *Means* of attaining Salvation is wholly owing to his free Grace in giving us Jeſus Chriſt; but our Salvation, canſidered as a *finiſhed Thing*, is not, cannot be found by any Act of God's free Grace towards us, but becauſe *all That* is done, alter'd, remov'd, ſuppreſſed, quickened, and recovered by us in the *State* of our Nature, which the free Grace of God had furniſhed us with the Poſſibility and Means of doing. If Nature and Creature had no Share in working out our Salvation; if it was all free Grace, effected againſt, and without the Powers of Nature, how comes it, that the fallen Angels are not to be redeemed as well as Man? Muſt we ſay that God is leſs good to them than he is to us? Or if they are not redeemed, can there be any other Reaſon for it, but becauſe it is an Impoſſibility in Nature? Muſt not an infinite Good do all the Good that is wanted, and is poſſible to be done? If free Grace can do what it pleaſes, if it wants no Concurrence of Nature and Creature, how

can

can any Being, whether Man or Angel, be eternally miserable, but through an Eternal Defect
in the Goodness of God towards it? Shall we
call that infinite Goodness, which sets Bounds
and Limits to itself, and which could do more
Good, but will not?

The Truth of the Matter is this, God is as
infinite and boundless in Love and Goodness, as
he is in *Power*, but his Omnipotence can only
do that which is possible, and nothing is possible
but that which hath its Possibility in Nature;
because Nature is God's first Power, his great,
universal Manifestation of his Deity, in and
through, and by which all his infinite Attributes break forth, and display themselves: So
that to expect, that God should do any Thing
that is above, or contrary to this Nature, is as
absurd as to expect that God should act above, or
contrary to himself: As God can only make a
Creature to be in, and through, and by Nature;
so the Reason why he cannot make a Creature
to be, and not to be at the same Time, is only
this, because it is contrary to Nature. Let no
Man therefore trust to be sav'd at the last
Day, by any *arbitrary* Goodness, or *free Grace*
of God; for Salvation is, and can be nothing
else, but the having *put off* all that is damnable
and hellish in our Nature, which Salvation can

be

be found by ho Creature but by its own full conforming to, and concurring with thofe Myfterious Means, which the free Grace of God hath afforded for the Recovery of our firft, perfect, glorious State in Nature.

C H A P.

CHAP. II.

*Of Eternal and Temporal Nature. How Na-
ture is from God, and the Scene of his Action.
How the Creatures are out of it. Temporal
Nature created out of that which is eternal.
The fallen Angels brought the first Disorders
into Nature. This World created to repair those
Disorders. Whence Good and Evil is in every
Thing of this World. How Heaven and Hell
make up the Whole of this World. How the
Fire of this World differs from eternal Fire ;
and the Matter of this World from the Ma-
teriality of Heaven. Eternal Nature is the
Kingdom of Heaven, the beatifick Manifesta-
tion of the tri-une God. God is mere Love
and Goodness. How Wrath and Anger come
to be ascrib'd to him. Of Fire in general.
Of the Unbeginning Fire. Of the Spirituality
of Fire. How Fire comes to be in material
Things. Whence the Possibility of kindling
Fire in the Things of this World. Every
Man is, and must be the Kindler of his own
Eternal Fire, &c.*

1. WAS there no *Nature*, there could
be no Creature, because the Life
of every Creature is, and can be
nothing else, but the Life of *that Nature* out
of

of which it was created, and in which it has its Being. Eternal Beings muſt have their Qualities, Nature, Form and Manner of Exiſtence out of *Eternal Nature*, and temporal Beings out of temporary Nature : Was there no Eternity, there could be no Time, was there nothing infinite, there could be nothing finite ; therefore we have here two great fundamental Truths that cannot be ſhaken ; *Firſt*, That there is, and muſt be, an *Eternal Nature* ; becauſe there is a Nature that is temporary, and that it muſt be that to Eternal Creatures, which temporal Nature is to temporal Creatures : *Secondly*, That every where, and in all Worlds, *Nature* muſt ſtand between God and the Creature, as the Foundation of all mutual Intercourſe ; God can tranſact nothing with the Creature, nor the Creature have any Communion with God, but in, and by *that Nature*, in which it ſtands.

I hope no one will here aſk me for Scripture Proofs of this, or call theſe Truths *Noſtrums*, becauſe they are not to be found in the *ſame Form* of Expreſſion in ſome particular Text of Scripture. Where do the Holy Writings tell us, that a Thing cannot be, and not be at the *ſame Time* ? Or that every *Conſequence* muſt ariſe from *Premiſes* ? And yet the Scripture

ture is continually fuppofing both thefe Truths, and there could be no Truth in the Scripture, or any where elfe, if thefe Things were not undeniable.

There is nothing faid of Man throughout all Scripture, but what fuppofes him to ftand *in Nature*, under a neceffity of chufing fome-thing that is *natural*, either Life or Death, Fire or Water. There is nothing faid of God with relation to Creatures, but what fuppofes him to be the God of *Nature*, manifefting himfelf in and through Nature, calling, affift-ing and directing every Thing to its higheft *natural* State. Nature is the Scene of his Providence, and all the Variety of his govern-ing Attributes difplay themfelves by his various Operations in and through Nature : Therefore it is equally certain, that what God does to any Creature, muft be done through the *Me-dium* of Nature, and alfo what the Creature does toward God, muft be done in and through the Powers of *that Nature* in which it ftands. No temporary Creature can turn to God, or reach after him, or have any Communion with him, but in, and according to that Relation which temporary Nature bears to God; nor can any Eternal Beings draw near to, or unite with God in any *other manner*, than that in

I   which

which Eternal Nature is united with him.
Would you know, why no Omnipotence of
God can create Temporal Animals but out
of temporary Nature, nor eternal Animals but
out of Eternal Nature; it is becaufe no Omnipotence of God can produce a vifible *Triangle*,
but out of, and by three vifible *Lines*; for, as
Lines muft be before there can be any *lineal
Figures*, fo *Nature* muft be before there can
be *natural Creatures*.

2. Every Thing that is in Being, is either
God, or Nature, or Creature; and every Thing
that is not God, is only a Manifeftation of
God; for as there is nothing, neither Nature,
nor Creature, but what muft have its Being
in, and from God, fo every Thing is, and muft
be according to its Nature, more or lefs a *Manifeftation* of God. Every thing therefore, by
its Form and Condition, fpeaks *fo much* of
God, and God in every Thing, fpeaks and
manifefts *fo much* of himfelf. Temporary
Nature is this beginning, created Syftem of
Sun, Stars, and *Elements*; 'tis temporary Nature, becaufe it begins and hath an End, and
therefore is only a temporary Manifeftation of
God, or God manifefted according to tranfitory Things.

3. Properly and ftrictly fpeaking, nothing
can begin to be: The Beginning of every
Thing

Thing is nothing more, than its beginning to be in a *new State*. Thus *Time* itself does not begin to be, but Duration, which always was, began to be meafured by the Earth's turning round, or the rifing and fetting of the Sun, and that is called the Beginning of Time, which is, properly fpeaking, only the Beginning of the Meafure of Duration : Thus it is with all temporal Nature, and all the Qualities and Powers of temporal Beings that live in it : No Quality or Power of Nature *then* began to be, but fuch Qualities and Powers as had been from all Eternity, began then to be in a *new State.* Afk what Time is, it is nothing elfe but fomething of Eternal Duration become *finite, meafurable,* and *tranfitory ?* Afk what *Fire, Light, Darknefs, Air, Water,* and *Earth* are; they are, and can be nothing elfe, but fome eternal Things become *grofs, finite, mea-furable, divifible,* and *tranfitory ?* For if there could be a temporal Fire that did not *fpring* out of Eternal Fire, then there might be Time that did not come out of Eternity.

'Tis thus with every temporary Thing, and the Qualities of it; 'tis the Beginning of Nothing, but only of a *new State* of fomething that exifted before : Therefore all temporary Nature is a Product, Offspring, or Out-birth

of

of Eternal Nature, and is nothing elſe but ſo
much of Eternal Nature chang'd from its eternal
to a temporal Condition. *Fire* did not begin
to be, Darkneſs did not begin to be, Light did
not begin to be, Water and Earth did not begin to be, when this temporary World firſt
appeared, but all theſe Things came out of
their *Eternal State*, into a lower, divided, compacted, created and tranſitory State. Hearing,
Seeing, Taſting, Smelling, Feeling, did not
then begin to be, when God firſt created the
Creatures of this World, they only came to
be Qualities and Powers of a lower, and more
imperfect Order of Beings than they had been
before.

Figures, and their Relations, did not then
begin to be, when Material *Circles* and *Squares*,
&c. were firſt made, but theſe Figures and
Relations began then to appear in a lower
State than they had done before : And ſo it
muſt be ſaid of all temporal Nature, and every
Thing in it. It is only *ſomething* of Eternal
Nature ſeparated, changed, or created into a
new, temporary State and Condition.

4. Now it may be aſk'd, why was Eternal
Nature thus degraded, debaſed, and chang'd
from its Eternal State of Perfection ? Will any
one ſay, that God of his own Will changed
Eternal

Eternal Nature, which is the *Glorious Manifestation* of his Power and Godhead, the *Seat* of his holy Refidence, his *Majeftick Kingdom* of Heaven, into this poor, miferable, Mixture of Good and Evil, into this impure State of Divifion, Groffnefs, Death, and Darknefs? No. It is the higheft of all Abfurdities, to fay fo. Now, we fufficiently know from Scripture, that a whole Hierarchy, or Hoft of Angels, renounced their Heavenly Life, and thereby raifed up a *Kingdom* that was not Heavenly. Could they not have inflam'd and difordered outward Nature in which they liv'd, they could not have deftroyed the Heavenly Nature in themfelves : For every Thing muft be according to the State of that World in which it lives ; and therefore, the State of outward Nature, and the State of inward Nature in the Angels muft ftand and fall together ; and as fure as a whole Kingdom of Angels loft their heavenly Life, fo fure is it, that their whole Kingdom loft its heavenly State and Condition : And therefore, it is an undeniable Truth, founded on Scripture Evidence, that *fome Part* of Eternal Nature was changed from its *firft State* of Glory and Perfection, *before* the Creation of Temporary Nature ; therefore, in the Creation of this poor, grofs, diforder'd,

perifhable,

perifhable, material Word, one of thefe two
Things was done, either God took the *fpoiled
Part* of Heaven or Eternal Nature, and created it into this *Temporary State* of Good and
Evil; or he degraded, and brought down fome
Part of the Kingdom of Heaven from its Glory
and Perfection, into *this Mixture* of Good
and Evil, Order and Diforder in which the
World ftands. He could not do this *latter*,
without bringing Evil into Nature, as the
Devil had done, and therefore we may be fure
he did not do it; but if he did the former,
then the Creation of this lower World, was a
glorious Act, and worthy of the infinite Goodnefs of God, it was putting an End to the Devil's
working Evil in Nature, and it was putting
the Evil that was brought into Nature, in a
way of being finally overcome, and turn'd into Good again. Will any one now call thefe
Things *whimfical Speculations?* Can any Thing
be thought of *more worthy* of God, more *conformable* to Nature, or more *confonant* to all
revealed Religion? But perhaps you will fay,
how could the Angels fpoil or deftroy that
glorious Kingdom of Eternal Nature in which
they dwelt. It may be anfwered, how could
it poffibly be otherwife? How could they live
in Eternal Nature, unlefs Nature without them,

and

and Nature within them, mutually *mix'd* and *qualified* with each other? Would you have such mighty Spirits, with their eternal Energies, have less Power in *that Nature*, or Kingdom in which they dwelt, than a kindled Piece of *Coal* hath in this World? For every Piece of *Coal* set on Fire, adds so much Heat to outward Nature, and so far alters and changes the State of it.

5. Now, let it be supposed, not only that a Piece of *Coal*, but that the Whole of every Thing in this World, that could either give or receive Fire was made to burn, what Effect would it have upon the whole Frame of Nature? Would not the whole State of Things, the Regions, Places, and Divisions of the Elements, and all the Order of temporal Nature be quite destroyed?

When therefore *every Angelical Life* kindled itself in Wrath, and became thereby divided, darkned, and separated from God, the same Kindling, Darkning, Dividing and Confusion must be brought forth in their Natural Kingdom, because they liv'd in Nature, and could have neither Love, nor Wrath, but such as they could exert in and by the Powers of Nature.

Now, all Fire, where-ever it is, is either a Fire of Wrath, or a Fire of Love: Fire not

over-

overcome or governed by *Light*, is the Fire of
Wrath, which only tears in Pieces, confumes
and devours all that it can lay hold of, and it
wills nothing elfe : But *Light* is the Fire of
Love, it is meek, amiable, full of kind Embraces, lovingly fpreading itfelf, and giving itfelf with all its Riches into every Thing that
can receive it. Thefe are the *two Fires* of
Eternal Nature, which were but one in Heaven, and can be only one where-ever Heaven
is ; and it was the *Separation* of thefe two
Fires that changed the Angels into Devils, and
made their Kingdom a Beginning of Hell.

Now, either of thefe two Fires, where-ever
it is kindled in animate or lifelefs Things,
communicates its own kind of Heat in fome
Degree to outward Nature, and fo far alters
and changes the State of it : The Wrath of a
Man, and the Wrath of a *Tempeſt* do *one* and
the *fame Thing* to outward Nature, alter its
State in the fame Manner, and only differ in
their Degree of doing it.

Fire kindled in a material Thing, can only
communicate with the Materiality of Nature ;
but the Fire of a wrathfully inflam'd Man,
being a Fire both of Body and Soul, communicates a *twofold* Heat, it ſtirs up the Fire
of

of outward Nature, as Fire does in a *Coal*, and it stirs up the Wrath of Hell as the Devils do.

The Fire of Love kindled by the Light and Spirit of God in a truly regenerated Man, communicates a twofold Blessing, it outwardly joins with the meek Light of the Sun, and helps to overcome the Wrath of outward Nature; it inwardly co-operates with the Power of Good Angels, in resisting the Wrath and Darkness of Hell: And it would be no Folly to suppose, that if all human Breath was become a *mere, unmix'd* Wrath, that all the Fire in outward Nature would immediately break forth, and bring that Dissolution upon outward Nature, which will arise from the last Fire. Therefore it is necessary, that a whole Kingdom of Angels should kindle the *same* Wrath and Disorder in outward Nature that was in themselves; for being in eternal Nature, and communicating with it, as temporal Beings do in temporal Nature, what they did in themselves, must be done in that Nature or Kingdom in which they liv'd, and mov'd, and had their Being.

What a powerful Fire there is in the Wrath of a Spirit, may be seen by the Effects of human Wrath; one sudden Thought shall in a Moment discolour, poison, inflame, swell,

distort

diftort and agitate the *whole Body* of a Man.
Whence alfo is it, that a difeafed Body infects
the Air, or that malignant Air infects a health-
ful Body? Is it not becaufe there is, and muft
be an infeparable Qualifying, Mixing and Uniting betwixt Nature and thofe Creatures that
live in it? Now, all Difeafes and Malignities,
whether in Nature or Creature, all proceed
from the finful Motions of the *Will* and *Defires*
of the Creature. This is as certain, as that
Death and all that leads to it, is the *fole Pro-*
duct of Sin; therefore it is a certain Truth,
that all the Diforder that ever was, or can be
in Nature, arifes from that Power which the
Creature hath in and upon Nature; and therefore, as fure as a whole Hoft of Heavenly Beings raifed up a fiery, wrathful, dark Nature
in themfelves, fo fure is it, that the fame
wrathful, fiery, dark Diforder was raifed up in
that Kingdom, or Nature, in which they had
their Being.

6. Now the Scriptures no where fay in exprefs Words, that the *Place* of this World was
the Place of the Angels that fell, and that
their fallen, fpoil'd and difordered Kingdom,
was by the Power of God, *chang'd* or *created*
into this temporary State of Things in which
we live; this is not exprefsly faid, becaufe it is
plainly

plainly implied and fully fignified to us by the most general Doctrines of Scripture ; for if we know, both from Nature and Scripture, that this World is a *Mixture* of Good and Evil, don't we enough know, that it could only be created out of *That* which was Good and Evil ? And if we know that Evil cannot come from God, if we know that the Devil had actually brought it forth *before* the Creation of this World ; are we not enough told, that the Evil which is in this World, is the Evil that was *brought forth* into Nature by the Devil ? And that therefore the Matter of this World, is that *very Materiality* which was fpoiled by the fallen Angels ? How can we need a particular Text of Scripture to tell us, that the *Place* of this World was the Place of the *Angels* before their *Fall*, when the whole Tenor of Scripture tells us, that it is the Place of their Habitation *now* ? For how could they have, or find Darknefs, but in that *very Place*, where they had extinguifhed the Light ? What cou'd they have to do with us, or we with them, but that we are entered into *their Poffeffions*, and have their Kingdom made over to us ? How could they go about amongft us as roaring Lions, feeking whom they may devour, but that our Creation has brought us amongft them ?

them? They cannot *possibly* be any where, but where they fell, becaufe they can live no where but in the *Evil* which they have brought forth; they can have no Wrath and Darknefs but where they broke off from Light and Love; they can communicate with no outward Nature but that which fell with them, and underwent the fame Change as they did: Therefore, tho' St. *Jude* faith with great Truth, that they *left their own Habitation*, yet, it is only as they left their own Angelical Nature, not departed from it into a diftant Place, but deform'd and chang'd it; fo that the Heaven that was within them, and without them, is *equally left*, becaufe both within them, and without them, they have no Habitation but a fiery Darknefs broken off from the Light of God.

And therefore, as Man by his Creation is brought into a Power of Commerce with thofe fallen Angels, who muft live, and could only act in that Part of Nature which they had deformed, it is plain, that this Creation placed him in *that Syftem* of Things, which was form'd and created out of their fallen Kingdom, becaufe they can act, or be acted upon no where elfe.

7. And this is the one true, and only Reafon, why there is Good and Evil throughout

all

all temporal Nature and Creature ; 'tis becaufe all this temporary Nature is a Creation out of that Strife of Evil againft Good which the fallen Angels had brought into their Kingdom. No fubtle, *evil Serpent* could have been generated, no *Tree of Knowledge* of Good and Evil could have fprung out of the Earth, but becaufe Nature in this World was *that Part* of Eternal Nature which the fallen Angels had *corrupted* ; and therefore, a Life made up of Good and Evil could be brought forth by it. Evil and Good was in the Angelical Kingdom as foon as they fet *their Wills* and *Defires* contrary to God, and the Divine Life. Had God permitted them to go on, their whole Kingdom had been like themfelves, all over *ane unmix'd* Evil, and fo had been incapable of being created into a redeemable State : But God put a Stop to the Progrefs of Evil in their Kingdom, he came upon it *whilft* it was in Strife, and *compacted* or *created* it all into a new, temporary, material State and Condition ; whence thefe two Things followed : *Firft,* That the fallen Angels loft their Power over it, and could no farther kindle their *own Fire* in it, but were as chain'd Prifoners, in an Extent of Darknefs which they could neither get out of, nor extend any farther : *Secondly,* This

new

new Creation being created out of this *begun Strife*, ftood as yet in the *Birth* of Life, and fo became capable of being affifted and bleffed by God; and finally, at the End of Time, reftored to its firft heavenly State.

Now, the Good and Evil that is in this World is *that fame* Good and Evil, and in the *fame Strife* that it was in the Kingdom of the fallen Angels, only with this happy Difference, there it was under the Devil's Power, and in a Way to be wholly evil; here it is in a new compacted, or created State under the Providence and Bleffing of God, appointed to bring forth a *new kind* of Life, and difplay the Wonders of Divine Love, till fuch Time as a new Race of Angelical Creatures born in this Mixture of Good and Evil, fhall be fit to receive the Kingdom of *Lucifer*, reftored to its firft Glory?

Is there any Part of the Chriftian Religion that does not either *fuppofe* or *fpeak* this great Truth, any Part of outward Nature that does not *confirm* it? Is there any Part of the Chriftian Religion that is not made more intelligible, more beautiful and edifying by it? Is there any Difficulty of outward Nature that is not totally removed and fatisfy'd by it?

How

How was the Philofophy' of the Antient Sages perplexed with the State of Nature? They knew God to be all Goodnefs, Love, and Perfection, and fo knew not what to do with the Mifery of Human Life, and the Diforders of outward Nature, becaufe they knew not *how* this Nature came into its *prefent State*, or from whence it was defcended. But had they known, that temporal Nature, all that we fee in this whole Frame of Things, was only the *fickly*, *defil'd* State of Eternal Things put into a temporary State of *Recovery*, that Time and all tranfitory Things were only in this War and Strife, to be finally delivered from all the Evil that was brought into Eternal Nature, their Hearts muft have praifed God for this Creation of Things as thofe *Morning Stars* did, that *fhouted for Joy* when it was firft brought forth.

8. From this true Knowledge of the *State*, and *Nature*, and *Place* of this Creation, what a Reafonablenefs, Wifdom, and Neceffity does there appear in the hardeft Sayings, Precepts and Doctrines of the Gofpel? He that thus knows what this World is, has great Reafon to be glad that he is born into it, and yet ftill greater Reafon to rejoice, in being called out of it, preferv'd from it, and fhewn how to efcape with the Prefervation of his Soul. The

Evils

Evils that are in this World, are the Evils of *Hell,*
that are tending to be nothing else but Hell ;
they are the *Remains* of the Sin and Poison
of the fallen Angels : The Good that is in
this World are the Sparks of *Life* that are to
generate *Heaven,* and gain the Restoration of
the first Kingdom of *Lucifer.* Who therefore
wou'd think of any Thing, desire any Thing,
endeavour any Thing, but to resist Evil in
every Kind, under every Shape and Colour ?
Who would have any Views, Desires and
Prayers after any Thing, but that the *Life* and
Light of Heaven may rise up in Himself, and
that God's Kingdom may come, and his Will
be done in all Nature and Creature ?

Darkness, Light, Fire and Air, Water and
Earth, stand in their temporary, created Diftinction and Strife, for no other End, with no
other View, but that they may obtain the *one
Thing needful,* their first Condition in Heaven :
And shall Man that is born into Time for no
other End, on no other Errand, but that he
may be an Angel in Eternity, think it hard
to live as if there were but one Thing needful
for him? What was the poor *Politicks,* the
earthly *Wisdom,* the *Ease, Sensuality,* and *Ad-
vancements* of this World for us, but such Fruits
as must be eaten in Hell? To be swell'd with
Pride,

Pride, to be fattened with Senfuality, to grow great through Craft, and load ourfelves with earthly Goods, is only living the Life of Beafts, that we may die the Death of Devils. On the other hand, to go ftarv'd out of this World, rich in nothing but heavenly Tempers and De-fires, is taking from *Time* all that we came for, and all that can go with us into Eternity.

9. But to return to the farther Confideration of Nature. As all temporary Nature is no-thing elfe but eternal Nature brought out of its kindled, difordered Strife, into a created or compacted Diftinction of its *feveral Parts*, fo it is plain, that the Whole of this World, in all its *working Powers*, is nothing elfe but a Mixture of Heaven and Hell. There cannot be the fmalleft Thing, or the fmalleft Quality of any Thing in this World, but what is à Quality of *Heaven* or *Hell*, difcovered under a temporal Form : Every Thing that is difa-greeable to the *Tafte*, to the *Sight*, to our *Hear-ing*, *Smelling*, or *Feeling*, has its Root and Ground, and Caufe, *in* and from *Hell*, and is as furely in its Degree the *Working* or *Mani-feftation* of Hell in this World, as the moft diabolical Malice and Wickednefs is : The *Stink* of Weeds, of Mire, of all *poifonous*, cor-rupted Things, *Shrieks*, horrible *Sounds*, *wrath-*

K   *ful*

ful Fire, *Rage of Tempefts,* and *thick Darknefs,* are all of them Things that had *no Poffibility* of Exiftence, till the fallen Angels diforder'd the *State* of their Kingdom; therefore, every Thing that is difagreeable and horrible in this Life, every Thing that can afflict and terrify our Senfes, all the Kinds of natural and moral Evil, are only *fo much* of the Nature, Effects, and Manifeftation of Hell: For Hell and Evil are only two Words for *one* and the *fame* Thing: The Extent of one is the Extent of the other, and all that can be afcribed to the one, muft be afcribed to the other. On the other hand, all that is fweet, delightful and amiable in this World, in the *Serenity* of the Air, the *Finenefs* of Seafons, the *Joy* of Light, the *Melody* of Sounds, the *Beauty* of Colours, the *Fragrancy* of Smells, the *Splendor* of precious Stones, is nothing elfe but Heaven *breaking through* the Veil of this World, *manifefting* it-felf in fuch a Degree, and darting forth in fuch Variety *fo much* of its own Nature. So that Heaven and Hell are not only as near you, as conftantly fhewing and proving them-felves to all your Senfes, as *Day* and *Night,* but Night itfelf is nothing elfe but Hell break-ing forth in *fuch a Degree,* and the Day is nothing

thing elfe but a certain *Opening* of Heaven, to fave us from the Darknefs that arifes from Hell.

O Man! confider thyfelf, here thou ftandeft in the earneft, perpetual Strife of Good and Evil, all Nature is continually at work to *bring about* the great Redemption; the whole Creation is travelling in Pain, and laborious Working, to be delivered from the *Vanity* of Time, and will thou be afleep? Every thing thou heareft, or feeft, fays nothing, fhews nothing to Thee, but what either eternal Light, or eternal Darknefs hath *brought forth*; for as Day and Night divide the whole of our Time, fo Heaven and Hell divide all our Thoughts, Words and Actions. Stir which way thou wilt, do, or defign what thou wilt, thou muft be an *Agent* with the *one* or with the *other*. Thou canft not ftand ftill, becaufe thou liveft in the *perpetual Workings* of temporal and eternal Nature; if thou workeft not with the Good, the Evil that is in Nature carries thee along with it: Thou haft the Height and Depth of Eternity in Thee, and therefore be doing what thou wilt, either in the *Clofet*, the *Field*, the *Shop*, or the *Church*, thou art fowing *That* which grows, and muft be reap'd in Eternity. Nothing of thine can vanifh away, but every Thought, Motion, and Defire of thy Heart,

K 2   has

has its *Effect* either in the Height of Heaven, or
the Depth of Hell : And as Time is upon the
Wing, to put an End to the *Strife* of Good
and Evil, and bring about the laſt great *Separation* of all Things into their Eternal State,
with ſuch Speed art Thou making Haſte either
to be wholly an Angel, or wholly a Devil : O !
therefore awake, watch and pray, and join
with all thy Force with that Goodneſs of God,
which has created Time and all Things in it,
to have a happy End in Eternity.

10. Temporal Nature opened to us by the
Spirit of God, becomes a *Volume* of holy In-
ſtruction to us, and leads us into all the Myſteries and Secrets of Eternity : For as every
Thing in temporal Nature is *deſcended* out of
that which is eternal, and ſtands as a *palpable,
viſible Out-birth* of it ; ſo when we know how
to ſeparate the *Groſſneſs, Death,* and *Darkneſs*
of Time from it, we find what it is in its eternal State. Fire, and Light, and Air in this
World are not only a true Reſemblance of the
Holy Trinity in Unity, but are the Trinity itſelf in its moſt *outward, loweſt* kind of Exiſtence or Manifeſtation ; for there could be no
Fire, Fire could not *generate* Light, Air could
not *proceed* from both, theſe three could not
be thus united, and thus divided, but becauſe
they

they have their *Root* and *Original* in the Tri-
unity of the Deity. Fire *compacted, created,
separated* from Light and Air, is the *Elemental
Fire* of this World: Fire uncreated, uncom-
pacted, unseparated from Light and Air, is
the *heavenly Fire* of Eternity: Fire kindled
in any material Thing is only Fire *breaking out
of its created, compacted* State; it is nothing
else but the awakening the *Spiritual Properties*
of that Thing, which being thus stirr'd up,
strive to get rid of that material *Creation* under
which they are imprison'd: Thus every kindled
Fire, with all its Rage and Fiercenefs, tears and
divides, scatters and confumes that *Materiality*
under which it is imprison'd; and were not
these *Spiritual Properties* imprison'd in Matter,
no material Thing could be made to burn.
And this is another Proof, that the Materiality
of this World is come out of a higher, and
spiritual State, becaufe every Matter upon
Earth can be made to *difcover* Spiritual Properties concealed in it, and is indeed a Compaction of nothing else. Fire is not, cannot
be a *material* Thing, it only makes itfelf vifible and fensible by the Destruction of Matter:
Matter is its *Death* and *Imprisonment*, and it
comes to Life but by being able to agitate,
divide, shake off, and confume that Matter

K 3   which

which held it in Death and Bondage; fo that
every Time you fee a Fire kindled, you fee
Nature ftriving in a *low Degree* to get rid of
the Groffnefs of this material Creation, and to
do that which can alone be done by the *laft
Fire*, when all the inward, fpiritual Properties
hid in every Thing, in *Rocks,* and *Stones,* and
Earth, in *Sun,* and *Stars,* and *Elements,* fhall
by the laft Trumpet be awaken'd and call'd
forth: And this is a certain Truth, that Fire
could *no where* now be kindled in any material Thing, but for *this Reafon,* becaufe all
material Nature was created to be reftored,
and ftands by Divine Appointment in a *Fitnefs*
and *Tendency* to have its Deliverance from this
created State, by *Fire*; fo that every Time you
fee a Piece of Matter *diffolved* by Fire, you
have a *full Proof,* that all the Materiality of
this World is appointed to a Diffolution by
Fire; and that then, (O glorious Day!) Sun
and Stars, and all the Elements will be delivered from Vanity, will be again that *one
eternal, harmonious, glorious* Thing which they
were, before they were compacted into *material* Diftinctions and Separations.

11. The Elements of this World ftand in
great *Strife* and *Contrariety,* and yet in great
Defire of *mixing* and *uniting* with each other;
and

and hence arifes both the *Life* and *Death* of all Temporal Things: And hereby we plainly know that the Elements of this World were once *one undivided* Thing ; for Union can *no where* be defir'd, but where there has firft been ·a *Separation* ; as fure therefore as the Elements defire each other, fo fure is it, that they have been *parted* from each other, and are only Parts of fome *one Thing* that has been divided. · When the Elements come to *fuch* a Degree of Union, a Life is produc'd ; but becaufe they have ftill a *Contrariety* to each other, they foon deftroy again that fame Life which they had built, and therefore every four-elementary Life is fhort and tranfitory.

Now, from this undeniable State of Nature, we are told thefe following great Truths : 1. That the *four* Elements are only *four Parts* of That, which before the Creation of this World, was only a *one Element*, or one *undivided Power* of Life. 2. That the Mortality of this Life is wholly and folely owing to the *divided State* of the Elements. 3. That the true, immortal Life of Nature, is only *there* to be found, where the four Elements are only *one Thing*, mere *Unity* and *Harmony* ; where Fire and Air, Water and Earth, have a much more *glorious* Union than they have in *Dia-*

K 4 *mond*

monds and precious *Stones:* For in the brighteſt Diamonds the four Elements ſtill partake of their divided State, tho' to our Eye they appear as only *one glorious* Thing ; but the Beauty of the *Diamond* is but a *Shadow,* a low Specimen of *that Glory* which will ſhine through all Nature, when Fire and Air, Water and Earth ſhall be again that *one Thing* which they were, before the Fall of Angels and the Creation of this World. 4. That the Body of *Adam* (being form'd for Immortality) could not poſſibly have the *Nature,* or be made out of the *divided State* of the Elements. The Letter of Scripture abſolutely demonſtrates this ; for if Sickneſs, Sorrow, Pain, the Trouble of Heat and Cold, all ſo many Forerunners of Death, can *only be* where the Elements are in *Diviſion* and *Contrariety* ; and if, according to Scripture, theſe Calamities did not, could not *poſſibly* touch *Adam* till he fell, then it is plain from Scripture, that before his Fall, the Diviſion and Contrariety of the Elements was not in him : And that was his Paradiſical Nature, in and by which he ſtood in a State of Superiority over all the Elements of this World. 5. That the Body of *Adam* loſt its one Elementary Glory and Immortality, and then firſt became *groſs, dark, heavy Fleſh* and *Blood,* under

der

der the Power of the four Elements, when he *lufted* to eat, and *actually* did eat of that Tree, which had its Good and Evil from the *divided State* of the Elements. 6. Hence we also know, with the greateft Certainty, the Myfte-ry of the Refurrection of the Body, that it confifts *wholely* and *folely* in the reducing the four-Elementary Body of this World, to its *firft, one Elementary* State, and then every one has that *fame Body* raifed again that dy'd, and *all* that *Adam* loft is *reftored*. For if the Body is mortal, and dies becaufe it is become a Body of the *four Elements*, it can only be raifed *im-mortal*, by having its four Elements reduced again into *one* : And here lies the *true Samenefs* of the Body that died, and that which rifes again. But to proceed :

12. As all the four Elements, by their *De-firing*, and wanting to be *united* together, prove that they are only four grofsly divided *Out-births* of That which before was *only one* heavenly, harmonious Element, fo every fingle Element fully demonftrates the fame Thing ; for every fingle Element, tho' ftanding in its *created Contrariety* to every other, has yet in its *own* divided State, all the four Elements *in itfelf* : Thus the *Air* has every Thing in it

that

that is in the Earth, and the Earth has in itſelf
every Thing that is in Fire, Water and Air,
only in a different Mixture and Compaction ;
were it not ſo, had not every Element in ſome
Degree the *whole Nature* of them all, they
could not poſſibly mix, and qualify with one
another ; and this may well paſs for a Demonſtration, that *That* out of which the four Elements are deſcended, was *one harmonious* Union
of them all, becauſe every one of the four,
has *now*, and muſt have in its divided State,
all the four in itſelf, tho' not in Equality ; for
if the four muſt be together, tho' unequally
lodg'd in every ſingle Element, it is plain, the
four muſt have been *one harmonious* Thing,
before they were brought into four *unequal Separations :* And therefore, as ſure as there are four
warring, diſagreeing Elements in *Time*, ſo ſure
is it, that *That* which is now in this fourfold
Diviſion, was and is in Eternity, *one*, in an
heavenly, harmonious Union, keeping up an
Eternal, joyful, glorious Life in *Eternal Nature,*
as its four broken Parts bring forth a poor,
miſerable, tranſitory Life in temporal Nature.

13. All *Matter* in this World is only the
Materiality of Heaven *thus* altered. The Difference between *Matter* in this World and
Matter in the other World, lies wholly and
ſolely

folely in this; in the one it is *dead*, in the other it is *living* Materiality. It is dead Materiality in this World, becaufe it is *grofs*, *dark*, *hard*, *heavy*, *divifible*, &c. It is in this State of Death, becaufe it is *feparated*, or *broken* off from the Eternal *Light*, which is the true Life, or the Power of Life in every Thing.

In eternal Nature or the Kingdom of Heaven, Materiality ftands in Life and Light; it is the Light's *glorious Body*, or that Garment wherewith Light is *cloathed*, and therefore has all the Properties of Light in it, and only differs from Light, as it is its *Brightnefs* and *Beauty*, as the *Holder* and *Difplayer* of all its Colours, Powers and Virtues. But the fame Materiality in this World, being created or compacted into a Separation from Fire united with Light, is become the Body of *Death* and *Darknefs*, and is therefore *grofs*, *thick*, *dark*, *heavy*, *divifible*, &c. for Death is nothing elfe but the fhutting up, or fhutting out the *united Power* of Fire and Light: This is the *only Death* that ever did, or can happen to any Thing, whether earthly or heavenly. Therefore, *every Degree* of Hardnefs, Darknefs, Stiffnefs, &c. is a Degree of Death; and herein confifts the Deadnefs of the Materiality of this World. When it fhall be raifed to Life,

that

that is, when the *United Power* of Fire and Light ſhall *kindle* itſelf through all temporal Nature, then *Hardneſs, Darkneſs, Diviſibility,* &c. will be all extinguiſhed together.

That the *Deadneſs* of the Earth may, and certainly will be brought to Life by the *united Power* of Fire and Light, is ſufficiently ſhewn us by the Nature and Office of the *Sun.* The *Sun* is the *united Power* of Fire and Light, and therefore the Sun is the Raiſer of Life out of the *Deadneſs* of the Earth ; but becauſe Fire and Light as united in the Sun, is only the Virtue of temporary Fire and Light, ſo it can only raiſe a ſhort and fading, tranſitory Life. But as ſure as you ſee, that Fire and Light united in the Sun, can change the *Deadneſs* of the Earth, into ſuch a beautiful Variety of a Vegetable Life, ſo ſure are you, that this dark, groſs Earth, is in its State of Death and Darkneſs, only for this Reaſon, becauſe it is *broken off* from the united Power of Fire and Light : For as ſure as the outward Operation of the Fire and Light of the Sun can change the Deadneſs of the Earth into a *Degree* of Life, ſo ſure is it, that the Earth lies in its preſent Deadneſs, becauſe it is ſeparated from its *own Eternal* Fire and Light : And as ſure as you ſee, that the Fire and Light of the Sun can

raiſe

raife a *temporal Life* out of the Earth, fo fure is it, that the united Power of *Eternal* Fire and Light can, and will turn all that is earthly, into its *firſt State* of Life and Beauty. For the Sun of this World, as it is the Union of temporal Fire and Light, has no Power, but as it is the *outward Agent*, or Temporary *Repreſentative* of Eternal Fire and Light, and therefore it can only do that in part, and imperfectly in Time, which by the Eternal Fire and Light will be *wholly* and *perfectly* done in Eternity. And therefore every Vegetable Life, every Beauty, Power, and Virtue which the Sun calls forth out of the Earth, tells us, with a *divine Certainty*, that there will come a Time, when all that is hid in the Deadneſs, Groſſneſs, and Darkneſs of the Earth, will be again call'd up to a Perfection of *Life* and *Glory of Beauty*.

14. How has the Philoſophy of the *Schools* been puzzled with the *Diviſibility* of Matter! 'Tis becauſe human Reaſon, the Miſtreſs of the Schools, partakes of the *Deadneſs* of the Earth ; and the Soul of Man muſt firſt have the Light of *Eternal Life* riſe up in him, before he can *ſee* or *find* out the Truths of Nature. Human Reaſon knew nothing of the Death of the Matter, or the Nature and Reaſon of its temporary Creation, and ſo thought

Death

Death and Divifibility to be *essential* to Matter ;
but the Light of God tells every Man this
infallible Truth, that *God made not Death* in
any Thing, that he is a God of Life, and
therefore, every Thing that comes from him,
comes into a *State* of Life. Matter is thick,
hard, heavy, divifible, and the like, only for
a *Time,* becaufe it is *compacted* or *created* into
Thicknefs, Hardnefs, and Divifibility only for
a Time : Thefe are only the Properties of its
temporal, created State, and therefore are no
more *essential* to it than the Hardnefs of *Ice* is
effential to Water. Now, that the Creation
of the Matter of this World is nothing· elfe
but a *Compaction*, that all the Elements are *fe-*
parated Compactions of That which before was
free from fuch a Compaction, is plain from
Scripture. For we are told, that all the Material Things and Elements of this World, are
to have their created State and Nature taken
from them, by being *dissolved* or *melted :* But
if this be a Scripture Truth, then it is equally
true from Scripture, that their Creation was
only a Compaction ; and a Compaction of
fomething that ftood before according to its
own Nature, abfolutely free from it. *Morta-*
lity, Corruptibility, and *Divifibility,* are not
effential Properties, but temporary Accidents,
they

they are in Things, as *Difeafes* and *Sicknefs*
are, and are as feparable from them; and that
is the true Reafon, why this *Mortal can put on
Immortality*, this *Corruptible can put on Incor-
ruptibility*, and this Divifible put on Indivifibi-
lity: For when the four Elements fhall be diffolved and loofed from their *feparate Compaction* from one another, when Fire and Air,
Water and Earth, fhall be *a one* much more
glorious and harmonious Thing than they are
now in the brighteft Diamond, then the *Divifibility* of this redeemed Materiality will be
more impoffible to be *conceived*, than the *Diftance* between Fire and Water in a *Diamond*.

15. The Reafon why all inanimate Things
of this World tend towards their utmoft Perfection in their Kind, lieth wholly and folely
in this Ground; 'tis becaufe the four Elements
of this World were once the one Element of the
Kingdom of the fallen Angels; and therefore,
Nature in this World is *always labouring* after
its *firft* Perfection of Life, or as the Scripture
fpeaks, the *whole Creation travaileth in Pain,
and groaneth to be delivered from its prefent Vanity*: And therefore it is, that all Vegetables
and Fruits naturally grafp after every Kind and
Degree of Perfection they can take in; endeavouring with all their Power, after that *firft*

Perfection

Perfection of Life which was before the Fall of
the Angels. Every *Taste* and *Colour*, and
Power and *Virtue*, wou'd be what it was before
Lucifer kindled his dark, fiery, wrathful Kingdom ; but as this cannot be, so when every
Fruit and Flower has work'd itself *as far* towards a heavenly Perfection as it can, it is
forced to wither and rot, and become a *Witness*
to this Truth, that neither Flesh nor Blood,
nor Fruit, nor Flower, can reach the Kingdom of God.

16. All the Misery and Imperfection that is
in Temporary Nature, arises from the divided
State of the Elements : Their Division is that
which brings all Kinds and Degrees of Death
and Hell into this World, and yet their being
in a certain Degree in one another, and always
endeavouring after their *first Union*, is so much
of the Nature and Perfection of Heaven still
in them. The Death that is in this World,
consists in the Grossness, Hardness and Darkness of its Materiality. The Wrath that is
in this World consists in the kindled Division
of its Qualities, whence there arises a contrary
Motion and Fermentation in all its Parts, in
which consists both the Life and Death of all
its Creatures. This Death and this Wrath is
the Nature of Hell in this World, and is the
Mani-

Manifeſtation of the *Diſorders* which the fallen
Angels have occaſioned in Nature. The Heaven in this World began when God ſaid, *Let
there be Light*, for ſo far as Light is in any
Thing, *ſo much* it has of Heaven in it, and of
the *Beginning* of a heavenly Life : This ſhews
itſelf in all Things of this World, chiefly in
the Life-giving Power of the *Sun*, in the
Sweetneſs and *Meekneſs* of Qualities and Tempers, in the *Softneſs* of Sounds, the *Beauty*
of Colours, the *Fragrancy* of Smells, and
Richneſs of Taſtes and the like ; thus far as
any Thing is tinctured with *Light*, ſo far it
ſhews its *Deſcent* from Heaven, and its partaking of ſomething heavenly and paradiſical.
Again, *Love* or Deſire of Union, is the other
Part of Heaven that is viſible in this World.
In Things without Life, it is a *ſenſeleſs Deſire*,
a friendly *mixing* and *uniting* of their Qualities,
whereby they ſtrive to be again in that firſt
State of Unity and Harmony in which they
exiſted, before they were kindled into Diviſion
by *Lucifer*. In rational Creatures, it is *Meekneſs*, *Benevolence*, *Kindneſs* and *Friendſhip*
amongſt one another : And thus far they have
Heaven and the Spirit of God in them, each
in their Sphere, being and doing that to one

another,

another, which the Divine Love is and does
to all.

Again, the Reason why Man is naturally
taken with beautiful Objects, why he admires
and rejoices at the Sight of *lucid* and *transpa-
rent* Bodies, and the *Splendor* of precious Stones,
why he is delighted with the *Beauty* of his
own Person, and is fond of his Features when
adorned with *fine Colours*, has this only true
Ground, 'tis because he was created in the
greatest Perfection of Beauty, to live amongst
all the Beauties of a *glorious Paradise*: And
therefore Man, tho' fallen, has this strong
Sensibility and reaching Desire after all the
Beauties, that can be picked up in fallen Nature. Had not this been his Case, had not
Beauty, and *Light*, and the *Glory* of Brightness
been his *first State* by Creation, he wou'd now
no more want the Beauty of Objects, than the
Ox wants to have his Pasture enclosed with
beautiful Walls, and painted Gates. Every
Vanity of fallen Man shews our first Dignity,
and the Vanity of our Desires are so many
Proofs of the *Reality* of that which we are
fallen from. Man wants to see himself in
Riches, Greatness and Power, because Human
Nature came first into the World in that State;
and therefore, what he had in *Reality* in Paradise,

radife, that is he vainly feeking for, where
he is only a poor Prifoner in the Valley and
Shadow of Death.

17. All Beings that are purely of this World,
have their Exiftence in and Dependance upon
temporal Nature. God is no Maker, Creator
or Governor of any Being or Creature of this
World, *immediately*, or by himfelf, but he creates, upholds and governs all Things of this
World, by, and through, and with temporal
Nature: As temporary Nature is nothing elfe
but Eternal Nature *feparated*, *divided*, *compacted*, made *vifible* and *changeable* for a Time;
fo Heaven is nothing elfe but the *beatifick Vifibility*, the *Majeftick Prefence* of the abyffal,
unfearchable, tri-une God: 'Tis that Light
with which the Scripture faith, God is *decked
as with a Garment*, and by which he is manifefted and made vifible to *heavenly Eyes* and
Beings; for Father, Son, and Holy Ghoft, as
they are the tri-une God, *deeper* than the Kingdom of Heaven or Eternal Nature, are invifible
to all created Eyes; but that *beatifick Vifibility*
and *outward Glory* which is called the Kingdom
of Heaven, is the *Manifeftation* of the Father,
Son, and Holy Ghoft, in, and by, and through
the glorious Union of *Eternal Fire*, and *Light*,
and *Spirit*. In the Kingdom of Heaven, thefe

are

are three and one, becaufe their Original, the
Holy Trinity, is fo, and we muft call them
by the Names of Fire, and Light, and Spirit ;
becaufe all that we have of Fire, and Light,
and Spirit in this World, has its *whole Nature*
directly from them, and is indeed nothing elfe
but the Fire, and Light, and Spirit of Eternity, brought into a *feparated, compacted*, temporal State.   So that to fpeak of a heavenly
Fire, has no more *Groffnefs* and *Offence* in it,
than when we fpeak of a heavenly *Life*, a
heavenly *Light*, or heavenly *Spirit* ; for if
there is a heavenly Light and Spirit, there
muft of all neceffity be a heavenly Fire ; and
if thefe Things were not in Heaven in a *glorious*
State of Union, they never could have been
here in this *grofs State* of a temporal Compaction and Divifion : So that as fure as there are
Fire, and Light, and Air in this World, in a
divided, compacted, imperfect State, in which
confifts the Life of temporary Nature and
Creatures, fo fure is it, that Fire, and Light,
and Spirit are in the Kingdom of Heaven,
united in *one Perfection* of Glory, in which
confifts the beatifick Vifibility of God, the
Divine Nature, as communicable to heavenly
Beings.

18. The

18. The Kingdom of Heaven ſtands in this *threefold Life*, where three are one, becauſe it is a Manifeſtation of the Deity, which is three and one; the Father has his *diſtinct* Manifeſtation in the Fire, which is always *generating* the Light; the Son has his *diſtinct* Manifeſtation of the *Light*, which is always *generated* from the Fire; the Holy Ghoſt has his *Manifeſtation* in the Spirit, that always *proceeds* from both, and is always *united* with them.

It is this Eternal Unbeginning Trinity in Unity of Fire, Light, and Spirit, that conſtitutes *Eternal Nature*, the *Kingdom of Heaven*, the *heavenly Jeruſalem*, the *Divine Life*, the *beatifick Viſibility*, the *Majeſtick Glory* and *Preſence* of God. Through this Kingdom of Heaven, or Eternal Nature, is the inviſible God, the incomprehenſible Trinity *eternally breaking* forth, and manifeſting itſelf in a boundleſs Height and Depth of blisful Wonders, opening and diſplaying itſelf to all its Creatures in an infinite Variation and endleſs Multiplicity of its Powers, Beauties, Joys and Glories. So that all the Inhabitants of Heaven are for ever Knowing, Seeing, Hearing, Feeling, and variouſly enjoying all that is great, amiable, infinite and glorious in the Divine Nature.

L 3

Nothing

Nothing afcends, or comes into this Kingdom of Heaven, but that which defcended,
or came out of it, all its Inhabitants muft be
innate Guefts, and born out of it.

19. God confidered in himfelf, as diftinct from
this Eternal Nature, or Kingdom of Heaven,
is not the *immediate* Creator of any Angels,
Spirits, or Divine Beings ; but as he creates
and governs all temporal Beings *in*, and *by*,
and *out* of temporal Nature, fo he creates and
governs all Spiritual and Heavenly Beings *in*,
and *by*, and *out* of Eternal Nature : This is as
abfolutely true, as that no Being can be *temporal*, but by partaking of temporal Nature, nor
any Being eternal, but by partaking of the eternal, divine Nature ; and therefore, whatever God
creates is not created *immediately* by *himfelf*, but
in and by, and out of *that Nature*, in which it
is to live, and move, and have its Being, temporal Beings out of temporal Nature, and eternal Beings out of the heavenly Kingdom of
Eternal Nature : And hence it is, that all Angels, and the Souls of Men are faid to be born
of God, Sons of God, and Partakers of the
Divine Nature, becaufe they are form'd out of
that Eternal Nature, which is the *unbeginning
Majefty* of God, the *Kingdom* of *Heaven*, or
Vifible Glory of the Deity. In this Eternal
Nature, which is the Majeftick Cloathing, or
Glory

Glory of the tri-une God, manifested in the
glorious Unity of divine Fire, Light, and Spi-
rit, have all the created Images of God, whe-
ther they be Angels or Men, their Exiſtence,
Union and Communion with God; becauſe
Fire, and Light, and Spirit have the *ſame Union*
and *Birth* in the Creature, as in the Creator :
And hence it is, that they are ſo many various
Mirrors of the Deity, penetrated with the
Majeſty of God, receiving and returning back
Communications of the Life of God. Now,
in this Ground, that is, in this Conſideration
of God, as manifeſting his Holy Trinity through
Nature and *Creature*, lieth the ſolid and true
Underſtanding of all that is ſo variouſly ſaid of
God, both in the Old and New Teſtament
with Relation to Mankind, both as to their
Creation, Fall, and Redemption. God is to
be conſidered throughout, as the God of Nature, only manifeſting himſelf to all his Creatures in a Variety of Attribures in and by Nature; creating, governing, bleſſing, puniſhing,
and redeeming them according to the *Powers*,
Workings, and *Poſſibilities* of Nature. Fire,
Light, and Spirit in *harmonious Union*, is the
ſubſtantial Glory, the beatifick Manifeſtation
of the tri-une God, viſible and communicable
to Creatures form'd out of it. All intelligent,

holy

holy Beings were by God form'd and created
out of, and for the Enjoyment of this Kingdom of Glory, and had Fire, and Light, and
Spirit, as the tri-une Glory of their created
Being: And herein confifted the infinite Love,
Goodnefs and Bounty of God to all his Creatures: It was their being made Creatures of
this Fire, Light, and Spirit, Partakers of that
fame Nature in which the Holy Trinity had
ftood from all Eternity *glorioufly manifefted.*
And thus they were Creatures, Subjects, and
Objects of the Divine Love; they came into
the neareft, higheft Relation to God; they
ftood in, and partook of his own *manifefted*
Nature, fo that the outward Glory and Majefty
of the tri-une God, was the very *Form,* and
Beauty, and *Brightnefs* of their own created
Nature. Every Creature which thankfully, joyfully, and abfolutely gave itfelf up to
this bleffed Union with God, became abfolutely fix'd in its firft created Glor and incapable of knowing any thing but Love, and
Joy, and Happinefs in God to Eternity:
Thus in this State, all Angels and Men came
firft out of the Hands of God. But feeing
Light proceeds from Fire by a *Birth,* and the
Spirit from both, and feeing the *Will* muft be
the *Leader* of the Birth, *Lucifer* and *Adam*
could

could both do as they did, *Lucifer* could *will*
ftrong *Might* and *Power*, to be greater than
the Light of God made him, and fo he brought
forth a Birth of *Might* and *Power*, that was
only mighty *Wrath* and *Darkneſs*, a Fire of
Nature *broken off* from its Light. *Adam* cou'd
will the *Knowledge* of *temporal Nature*, and
ſo he loſt the Light and Spirit of Heaven for
the Light and Spirit of this World: And had
Man been left in this State of temporary Nature, without a Redeemer, he muſt, when the
Light of this World had left him, have found
himſelf in the ſame abſolute Wrath and Darkneſs of Nature, which the fallen Angels are in.

20. Now, after theſe two Falls of two Orders of Creatures, the Deity itſelf came to have
new and *ſtrange* Names, new and unheard of
Tempers and Inclinations of *Wrath*, *Fury*,
and *Vengeance* aſcribed to it. I call them *new*,
becauſe they began at the *Fall* ; I call them
ſtrange, becauſe they were *foreign* to the Deity,
and could not *belong* to God in himſelf: Thus
God is in the Scriptures ſaid to be *a Conſuming*
Fire. But to whom? To the fallen Angels,
and loſt Souls. But *why*, and *how* is he ſo to
them? It is becauſe thoſe Creatures have loſt *all*
that they had from God, but *Fire* ; and therefore God can only be *found* and *manifeſted* in
them,

them, as a *Confuming Fire.* Now, is it not juftly faid, that God, who is nothing but infinite Love, is yet in *fuch Creatures* only a Confuming Fire, and that tho' God be nothing but Love, yet they are under the *Wrath* and *Vengeance* of God, becaufe they have only *that Fire* in them, which is broken off from the Light and Love of God, and fo can know, or feel nothing of God, but *his Fire* in them. As Creatures they can have no Life, but what they have *in* and *from* God; and therefore, that wrathful Life which they have, is truly faid to be a *Wrath of God* upon them. And yet it is as ftrictly true, that there is no Wrath in God himfelf, that he is not changed in *his Temper* towards the Creatures, that he does not ceafe to be one and the fame *infinite Fountain* of Goodnefs, *infinitely flowing forth* in the Riches of his Love upon all and every Life; but the Creatures have changed *their State* in *Nature,* and fo the God of Nature can only be *manifefted* in and to them, according to their *own* State in Nature: And this is the true Ground of rightly underftanding all that is faid of the *Wrath* and *Vengeance* of God in and upon the Creatures. It is only in *fuch* a Senfe as the *Curfe* or *Unhappinefs* of God may be faid to be upon them, not becaufe any Thing

curfed,

curfed, or unhappy, can be *in*, or come *from* God, but becaufe they have made *that Life* which they muft have in God, to be mere *Curfe* and *Unhappinefs* to them : For every Creature that lives, muft have its Life in and from God, and therefore God muft be in every Creature ; this is as true of Devils, as of Holy Angels : But how is God in them ? Why only as he is manifefted in *Nature.* Holy Angels have the *tri-une* Life of God in them, therefore God is in them all *Love, Goodnefs, Majefty* and *Glory,* and theirs is the Kingdom of Heaven. Devils have *nothing* of this tri-une Life left in them, but the *Fire* of Eternal Nature *broken off* from all Light and Joy ; and therefore the Life that they can have in and from God, is only a Life of *Wrath* and *Dark-nefs,* and theirs is the Kingdom of Hell : And becaufe this Life is a Strength of Life which they muft have *in* and *from* God, and which they cannot *take out* of his Hands ; therefore, is their curfed, miferable, wrathful Life truly and juftly faid to be the *Curfe,* and *Wrath,* and *Vengeance* of God in and upon them, tho' God himfelf can no more have Wrath and Vengeance, than he can have *Mifchief* and *Malice* in him : For this is a glorious, two-fold Truth, that from God confidered as in himfelf,

himſelf, nothing can come from Eternity to
Eternity, but infinite Love, Goodneſs, Happineſs, and Glory ; and alſo that infinite Love,
Goodneſs, Happineſs and Glory are, and will
be for ever and ever flowing forth from him
in the *ſame boundleſs, univerſal, infinite* manner ;
he is the ſame infinitely overflowing Fountain
of Love, Goodneſs and Glory after, as before
the *Fall* of any Creatures ; his Love, and the
infinite Workings of it can no more be *leſſened,*
than his Power can be increaſed by any outward Thing ; no Creature, or Number of
Creatures can raiſe any Anger in him, 'tis as
impoſſible as to caſt *Terror*, or *Darkneſs*, and
Pain into him, for nothing can come into
God from the Creature, nothing can be in him,
but that which the Holy Trinity in Unity is
in itſelf. All Creatures are Products of the
infinite, tri-une Love of God ; nothing *will'd,*
and *deſir'd,* and *form'd* them, but *infinite Love,*
and they have all of them all the Happineſs,
Beauty and Excellency that an infinitely powerful Love can reach out to them : The ſame
infinite Love *continues ſtill* in its *firſt creating*
Goodneſs, willing, deſiring, working, and
doing nothing with regard to all Creatures,
but what it will'd, did, and deſired in the
Creation of them : This God over Nature and
Creature,

Creature, darts *no more* Anger at Angels when
fallen, than he did in the Creation of them:
They are not in *Hell*, becaufe Father, Son,
and Holy Ghoft are *angry* at them, and fo caft
them into a Punifhment, which their Wrath
had *contrived* for them; but they are in Wrath
and Darknefs, becaufe they have done to the
Light which *infinitely* flows forth from God, as
that Man does to the Light of the Sun, who
puts out his own Eyes: He is in Darknefs,
not becaufe the Sun is *darkned* towards him,
has *lefs Light* for him, or has loft all *Inclination*
to enlighten him, but becaufe he has put out
that *Birth* of *Light* in himfelf, which alone
made him capable of feeing in the Light of the
Sun. It is thus with fallen Angels, they have
extinguifhed in themfelves that *Birth* of *Light*
and *Love*, which was their *only Capacity* for
that Happinefs, which infinitely, and every
where flows forth from God; and they no
more have their Punifhment from God himfelf
than the Man who puts out his Eyes, has his
Darknefs from the Sun itfelf.

21. God, confidered in himfelf, as the holy,
tri-une God, is not the immediate Fountain
and Original of Creatures; but God confider'd as *manifefting* himfelf in and through
Nature, is the Creator, Father and Producer
of

of all Things. The hidden Deity of Father, Son, and Holy Ghost, is from Eternity to Eternity, *manifested*, made *visible*, *perceivable*, *senpble* in the united Glory of Fire, Light and Spirit; this is the *beatifick Presence*, the *glorious Out-birth* of the Holy Trinity; this is that eternal, universal Nature, which *brings* God into all Creatures, and all Creatures into God, according to that Degree and Manner of Life which they have in Nature : For the Life of Creatures must stand in Nature, and Nature is nothing else but God made *manifest*, *visible*, and *perteptible* ; and therefore the Life of every Creature, be it what it will, a Life of Joy or Wrath, is only *so much* of God made *manifest* in it, and *perceptible* by it, and thus is God in some Creatures only a God of Wrath, and in others, only a God of Glory and Goodness:

No Creature can have Life, or live, and move, and have its Being in God, but by being form'd out of, and living in this Manifestation of Nature. Thus far Hell and Heaven, Angels and Devils are *equally* in God, that is, they equally live, move, and have their Being in that *Eternal Nature*, which is the Eternal Manifestation of God : The one have a Life of Glory, Majesty, and Love, and Bliss, the other a Life of Horror, Fire, Wrath, Misery, and Darkness.

Darkneſs. Now, all this could not poſſibly
be, there could be no Room for *this Diſtinction*
between Creatures ſtanding in Nature, the one
could not poſſibly have a Life of *Majeſtick
Bliſs* and *Glory*, the other of *fiery Horror* and
Darkneſs, but becauſe the Holy, tri-une God
is *manifeſted* in the *united* Glory and Bliſs of
Fire, Light, and Spirit. For the Creatures
could only divide *That*, which there was in
Nature to be divided, they could only divide
That, which was *united*, and diviſible; and
therefore, as ſure as Heaven is a ſplendorous
Light of bliſsful Majeſty, as ſure as Hell is a
Place of *fiery Wrath* and *Darkneſs*, ſo ſure is
it from the Scriptures, that Eternal Nature,
which is from God, or a Manifeſtation of God,
is a Nature of *united* Fire, Light, and Spirit,
otherwiſe, ſome Creatures could not have the
bliſsful Glory of Light, and others, a horrible,
fiery Darkneſs for their *ſeparate Portions*.

All therefore that has been ſaid of an Eternal
Nature, or Kingdom of Heaven, conſiſting of
united Fire, Light, and Spirit, is not only to
be look'd upon as an Opinion well grounded,
and ſufficiently diſcover'd by the Light of Nature, but as a *fundamental* Truth of reveal'd Religion, fully eſtabliſh'd by *all* that is ſaid in the
Scriptures both of Heaven and Hell. For if
God

God was not *manifested, visible, perceptible* and *communicable,* in and by this *united* Fire, and Light, and Spirit, how could there be a Heaven of *glorious Majesty?* If this Fire of Heaven could not be *separated,* or *broken off* from its heavenly Light, how could there be a Hell in Nature? Or, how could those Angels which lost the Light of Heaven, have *thereby* fallen into a State of hellish Darkness, or Fire? Is not all this the greatest of Demonstrations, that the holy Tri-unity of God is, and must be manifested in Nature, by the Union of Fire, Light, and Spirit? And is not this Demonstration wholly taken from the very Letter of the most plain Doctrines of Scripture?

Hell and Wrath could have no *Possibility* of Existence, but because the Light, and Majesty, and Glory of Heaven, must of all necessity have its Birth *in* and *from* the Fire of Nature. An Angel could not have *become* a Devil, but because the Angelick *Light* and *Glory* had, and must have *its Birth* in and from the *Fire* of Life. And thus as a Devil was *found,* where angelick Light and Glory had its Existence, so a Hell was found, where heavenly Glory was *before*; and as the Devil is nothing but a Fire-spirit *broken off* from its Angelical Light and Glory, so Hell is nothing but the Fire of Heaven *separated* from its first Light and Majesty.

And

And here we have plainly found two Worlds in Eternity; not *poſſible* to be two, nor ever *known* to be two; but by ſuch Creatures, as have in their own Natures, by their own Self-motion, ſeparated the Fire of Eternal Nature from its Eternal Light, Spirit and Majeſty. And this is alſo the Beginning, or firſt Opening of the *Wrath* of God in the Creature; which is, in other Words, only the Beginning, or firſt Opening of Pain and Miſery in the Creature, or the Origin of a helliſh, tormenting State of Life.

22. And here, in this *dark wrathful* Fire of the fallen Creature, do we truly find that *Wrath* and *Anger* and *Vengeance* of God, that cleaves to Sin, that muſt be *quench'd, atton'd,* and *ſatisfy'd* before the Sinner can be reconciled to God; that is, before it can have again that *tri-une* Life of God in it, which is its Union with the holy Trinity of God, or its regaining the Kingdom of Heaven in itſelf.

Some have objected, that by thus conſidering the *fallen* Soul, as a *dark, wrathful* Fire-Spirit, for this Reaſon, becauſe it has loſt the *Birth* of the Son and holy Spirit of God in it, that this caſts Reproach upon God the Father, as having *the Nature* of ſuch a Soul in Him. But this is a groundleſs Objection, for this State

M of

of the Soul cafts no more Reproach upon the *firft*, than upon the fecond and third Perfons of the holy Trinity. The fallen Soul, that has loft the Birth of the Son and holy Spirit of God in it, cannot be faid to have *the Nature* of the Father left in it. This would be blafphemous Nonfenfe, and is no way founded on this Doctrine. But fuch a Soul muft be faid to have *a Nature* from the Father left in it, tho' a *fpoil'd* one, and this becaufe the Father is the *Origin, Fountain* and *Creator* of all kind of Exiftence: Hell, and the Devils have their Nature from Him, becaufe every Kind of Creature muft have what it has of Life and Being from its Creator; but Hell and the Devils have not therefore *the Nature* of the Father in them. If it be afk'd what the Father is, as he is the firft Perfon in the facred Trinity, the Anfwer muft be, that as fuch, He is the *Generator* of the Son and holy Spirit: This is *the Nature* of the Father; where *this generating* is not, there is not *the Nature* of the Father. Is it not therefore highly abfurd to charge this Doctrine with afcribing *the Nature* of the Father to the *fallen* Soul, which afferts the Soul to be fallen, for *this Reafon*, becaufe it has quite *loft* and *extinguifh'd* all Power and Ability for the *Birth* of the Son and holy Spirit in it? How could it be more

roundly

roundly affirm'd, or more fully prov'd, that the fallen Soul *hath not* the Nature of the Father left in it. But to proceed:

The Reader ought not to wonder, or be offended at the frequent mention of the Word *Fire*, which is here us'd to denote the true Nature, and State of the Soul. For both Nature and Scripture speak continually the same Language. For wherever there is mention of Life, Light, or Love in the Scriptures, there Fire is *necessarily* suppofed, as being that in which all Life, and Light, and Love muft neceffarily arife ; and therefore the Scriptures fpeak as often of Fire, as they do of Life, and Light, and Love, becaufe the one neceffarily includes the other : For all Life, whether it be *vegetable*, *fenfitive*, *animal*, or *intellectual*, is only a kindled Fire of Life in fuch a Variety of States; and every dead, infenfitive Thing is only fo, becaufe its Fire is quench'd, or fhut up in a hard Compaction. If therefore we will fpeak of the *true Ground* of the fallen State of Men and Angels, we are not at Liberty to think of it under any *other Idea*, or fpeak of it in any *other manner*, than as the *darkned Fire* of their Life, or the Fire of their Life unable to kindle itfelf into Light and Love. Do not the Scriptures ftrictly confine us to this Idea of Hell ?

So

So that it is not any particular Philoſophy, or affeſted Singularity of Expreſſion, that makes me ſpeak in this manner of the Soul, but becauſe all Nature and Scripture forces us to confeſs, that the Root of all and every Life ſtands, and muſt neceſſarily ſtand in the *Properties* of Fire.

The holy Scriptures alſo ſpeak much of Fire, in the Ideas which they give us, both of the divine Nature, and of created Spirits, whether they be ſav'd, or loſt; the former as becoming Flames of heavenly Light and Love, the latter as dark Firebrands of Hell *.

No

---

* Theologia fere ſupra omnes Sacroſanſtam Ignis Figuram probaſſe reperitur. Eam enim invenies non ſolum *Retas igneas* fingere, ſed etiam ignea animalia —— quinetiam *Thronos igneos* eſſe dicit, ipſoſq; ſummos Seraphim *incenſos* eſſe ex ipſo nomine declarat, eiſq; Ignis & *Proprietatem* & *Aſtionem* tribuit : ſemperatq; ubiq; igneam figuram probat. Ac igneam quidem Formam ſignificare arbitror cœleſtium Naturarum *maximam* in Deo imitando *ſimilitudinem.* Theologi ſummam, & formâ carentem eſſentiam *ignis Specie* multis locis deſcribunt, quòd Ignis multas Divinæ, ſi diſtu fas eſt, Proprietatis, *Imagines* ac *Species* præ ſe ferat. Ignis enim, qui ſenſu percipitur, in omnibus & per omnia ſine admixtione funditur, ſecerniturq; a rebus omnibus, lucetq; totus ſimul, & abſtruſus eſt, incognituſq; manet ipſe per ſe ——Cohiberi, vinciq; non poteſt——quicquid ipſi proprius quoquo modo adhibeatur, ſui particeps facit. Renovat omnia vitali calore, illuſtrat aperto lumine ; teneri non poteſt, nec miſceri. Diſſipandi vim habet, commutari non poteſt, furſum fertur, celeritate magna præditus eſt, ſublimis eſt, nec humilitatem ullam ferre poteſt. Immobilis eſt, per ſe movetur, aliis motum affert ; comprehendendi vim habet, ipſe comprehendi non poteſt. Non eget altero : clam ſe amplificat : in materiis quæ ipſius capaces ſunt, magnitudinem ſuam declarat. Vim efficiendi habet,

No Defcription is, or can be given us either of Heaven or Hell, but where Fire is neceffarily fignified to be the *Ground* and *Foundation* both of the one and of the other. Why do all Languages, however diftant, and different from one another, all fpeak of the Coldnefs of *Death*, the Coldnefs of *Infenfibility?* Why do they all agree in fpeaking of the *Warmth* of Life, the *Heat* of Paffions, the *Burnings* of Wrath, the *Flames* of Love? It is becaufe it is the Voice or Dictate of univerfal Nature, that Fire is the *Root* or *Seat* of Life, and that every Variety of human Tempers is only the various *Workings* of the Fire of Life.—It ought to be no Reafon why we fhould think *grofsly* of Fire, becaufe it is feen in fo many *grofs Things* of this World? For how is it feen in them? Why only as a *Deftroyer*, a *Confumer*, and *Refiner* of *all Groffnefs*; as a *Kindler* of Life, and Light out of Death and Darknefs. So that in all the Appearances of Fire, even in earthly Things, we have Reafon to look upon it as fomething of a heavenly, exalting, and glorious Nature; as that which difperfes Death, Darknefs, and

M 3

Groffnefs,

---

habet, potens eft: omnibus præfto eft; nec videtur: *Attritu* autem quafi *Inquifitione* quadam connaturaliter repente apparet, rurfufq; ita avolat ut comprehendi, & detineri nequeat: in omnibus fui communionibus minui non poteft——Multas etiam alias Ignis Proprietates invenire poffumus, quæ propria funt diæ.næ actionis. S. *Dionif. Arcop. de cælefti Hierarci.* 56.

Groffnefs, and raifes up the Power and Glory
of every Life.

If you afk what Fire is in its firft, true, and
unbeginning State, not yet entred into any Creature, It is the Power and Strength, the Glory
and Majefty of eternal Nature; it is that which
generates, enriches, brightens, ftrengthens, and
difplays the Light of Heaven. It is that which
makes the eternal Light to be majeftick, the e-
ternal Love to be flaming: For the *Strength* and
Vivacity of Fire, muft be both the Majefty of
Light, and the Ardour of Love. It is the glorious *Out-birth,* the true *Reprefentative* of God
the Father *eternally generating* his only Son,
Light and Word.

If you afk what Fire is in its own fpiritual
Nature, it is merely a *Defire,* and has no other
Nature than that of a *working Defire,* which is
continually its *own Kindler.* For *every Defire*
is nothing elfe, but its *own ftriking* up, or its
own kindling itfelf into fome Kind and Degree
of Fire. And hence it is that Nature (tho'
reduc'd to great Ignorance of itfelf) has yet
forc'd all Nations and Languages to fpeak of
its Defires, as *cool, warm,* or *burning,* &c. becaufe every Defire is, fo far as it goes, a *kindled
Fire.* And it is to be obferv'd, that Fire could
have no Exiftence or Operation in material
Things, but becaufe all the Matter of this
World

World has in it more or lefs of fpiritual and heavenly Properties compacted in it, which *continually defire* to be delivered from their material Imprifonment. And the ftirring up *the Defire* of thefe fpiritual Properties, is the *kindling* of that *Heat*, and *Glance*, and *Light*, in material Things, which we call Fire, and is nothing elfe but their glorioufly breaking, and triumphantly difperfing that hard Compaction in which they were imprifon'd. And thus does every kindled Fire, as a *Flafh* or *tranfitory opening* of heavenly Glory, fhew us in little and daily, but *true* Inftances, the *Triumph* of the laft Fire, when all that is fpiritual and heavenly in this World, fhall kindle and feparate itfelf from that, which muft be the Death and Darknefs of Hell.

Now the Reafon, why there are fpiritual Properties in all the material Things of this World, is only this, it is becaufe the Matter of this World is the *Materiality* of the Kingdom of Heaven, brought down into a *created State* of Groffnefs, Death, and Imprifonment, by occafion of the Sin of thofe Angels, who firft inhabited the Place, or Extent of this material World.

Now thefe heavenly Properties, which were brought into this *created* Compaction, lye in a *continual Defire* to return to their firft State of

Glory

Glory; and this is the *groaning of the whole Creation to be delivered from Vanity*, which the Apoftle fpeaks of. And in this *continual Defire* lieth the kindling, and *all the Poffibility* of kindling any Fire in the Things of this World. Quench *this Defire*, and fuppofe there is nothing in the *Matter* of this World that defires to be reftor'd to its firft Glory, and then all the breaking forth of Fire, Light, Brightnefs, and Glance in the Things of this World, is utterly quench'd with it, and it would be the fame Impoffibility to ftrike Fire, as to ftrike Senfe and Reafon out of a Flint.

24. But you will perhaps fay, tho' this be a Truth, yet it is more *fpeculative* than *edifying*, more fitted to entertain the Curiofity, than to affift the Devotion of Chriftians. But ftay awhile, and you fhall fee it is a Truth full of the moft edifying Inftruction, and directly fpeaking to the Heart.

For if *every Defire* is in itfelf, in its own Effence, the *kindling* of Fire, then we are taught this great practical Leffon, that our *own Defire* is the Kindler of our own Fire, the Former and Raifer of *that Life* which leads us. What our Defire kindles, that becomes the Fire of our Life, and fits us either for the majeftick Glories of the Kingdom of God, or the

dark

.dark Horrors of Hell: So that our *Defire* is all, it does all, and governs all, and all that we have and are, muft arife from it, and therefore it is, that the Scripture faith, *Keep thy Heart with all Diligence, for out of it are the Iffues of Life.*

We are apt to think that our *Imaginations* and *Defires* may be play'd with, that they rife and fall away as nothing, becaufe they do not always bring forth outward and vifible Effects. But indeed they are the greateft Reality we have, and are the true *Formers* and *Raifers* of all that is real and folid in us. All outward Power that we exercife in the Things about us, is but as a *Shadow* in Comparifon of that *inward Power*, that refides in our *Will, Imagination*, and *Defires*; thefe communicate with Eternity, and kindle a Life which always reaches either Heaven or Hell. This Strength of the inward Man makes all that is the Angel, and all that is the Devil in us, and we are neither good nor bad, but according to the Working of that which is fpiritual and invifible in us. Now our Defire is not only thus powerful and productive of real Effects, but it is always alive, always working and *creating* in us, I fay creating, for it has no lefs Power, it perpetually generates either Life or Death in

us :

us: And here lies the Ground of the great
Efficacy of *Prayer*, which when it is the
Prayer of the Heart, the Prayer of Faith, has
a kindling and creating Power, and forms and
transforms the Soul into every Thing that its
Defires reach after : It has the Key to the
Kingdom of Heaven, and unlocks all its Trea-
fures, it opens, extends, and moves that in us,
which has its Being and Motion in and with
the Divine Nature, and fo brings us into a real
Union and Communion with God.

Long *Offices* of Prayer founded only from
the Mouth, or impure Hearts, may Year after
Year be repeated to no Advantage, they leave
us to grow old in our own poor, weak State:
Thefe are only the poor Prayers of Heathens,
who, as our Lord faid, *think to be heard by
their much fpeaking.* But when the Eternal
Springs of the purified Heart are ftirr'd, when
they ftretch after that God from whence they
came ; then it is, that what we afk, we receive,
and what we feek, we find. Hence it is, that
all thofe great Things are by the Scriptures attributed to Faith, that to it all Things are poffible ; that it heals the Sick, faves the Sinner,
can remove Mountains, and that all Things
are poffible to him that believeth ; 'tis becaufe
the Working of *Will* and *Defire* is the firft
Eternal

Eternal Source of all Power, *that* from which
every Thing is kindled into that Degree of Life
in which it ftandeth ; 'tis becaufe *Will* and *Defire* in us are *Creaturely Offsprings* of that firft
Will and Defire which form'd and govern'd
all Things ; and therefore, when the Creaturely Power of our Will, Imagination and
Defire leaves off its Working in Vanity, and
gives itfelf wholly unto God in a *naked* and
implicit Faith in the Divine Operation upon it,
then it is, that it does nothing in vain, it rifes
out of Time into Eternity, is in Union and
Communion with God, and fo all Things are
poffible to it. Thus is this Doctrine fo far
from being vainly fpeculative, that it opens to
us the Ground, and fhews us the Neceffity and
Excellency of the greateft Duties of the Gofpel.

25. Now, as all *Defire* throughout Nature
and Creature is but *one* and the *fame* Thing,
branching itfelf out into various Kinds and
Degrees of Exiftence and Operation, fo there
is but *one Fire* throughout all Nature and Creature, ftanding only in different States and
Conditions. The Fire that is in the *Light* of
the Sun, is the fame Fire that is in the *Darknefs* of the Flint : That Fire which is the Life
of our Bodies, is the Life of our Souls ; that
which *tears* Wood in Pieces, is the fame which
upholds

upholds the beauteous Forms of Angels: It is the fame Fire that burns *Straw*, that will at laft melt the *Sun*, the fame Fire that brightens a *Diamond*, is darkned in a *Flint*: It is the fame Fire that kindles Life in an Animal, that kindled it in Angels: In an Angel it is an Eternal Fire of an Eternal Life, in an Animal it is the fame Fire brought into a temporary Condition, and therefore can only kindle a Life that is temporary: The fame Fire that is mere Wrath in a Devil, is the Sweetnefs of flaming Love in an Angel; and the fame Fire which is the Majeftick Glory of Heaven, makes the Horror of Hell.

CHAP.

C H A P. III.

The true Ground of all the Doctrines of the Gof-
pel difcovered. Why Adam could make no
Atonement for his Sins. Why, and how Jefus
Chrift alone could make this Atonement.
Whence the Shedding of Blood for the Remiffion
of Sins. What Wrath and Anger it is, that
is quenched and aton'd by the Blood of Chrift.
Of the laft Sufferings of Chrift. Why, and
how we muft eat the Flefh and drink the Blood
of Jefus Chrift.

1. WE have now, Worthy Reader, fo
far cleared the Way, that we have
nothing to do, but to rejoice in the
moft open Illuftration, and full Proof of all
the great Doctrines of the Gofpel, and to fee
all the Objections, which *Deifts, Arians,* and
Socinians have brought againft the firft Articles
of our Faith, dafh'd to Pieces: For as foon as
we but begin to know, that the holy, tri-une
Deity from Eternity to Eternity *manifefts* itfelf
in *Nature,* by the *tri-une Birth* of Fire, Light
and Spirit, and that all Angels and Men muft
have been created out of *this Nature* ; there is
not a Doctrine in Scripture concerning the

Creation,

Creation, Fall, and Redemption of Man, but becomes the moft plainly intelligible, and all the Myfteries of our Redemption are proved and confirmed to us, by all that is vifible and perceptible in all Nature and Creature.

Here we have the plain Foundation of the whole Oeconomy of all Religion from the Beginning to the End of Time, why the *In-carnation* of the Son of God, who is the Light of the World, muft have before it the *fiery Difpenfation* of the Father delivered from *Mount Sinai*; and after it, the *pouring* out, or *proceeding* forth of the Holy Spirit upon all Flefh; it is becaufe the *tri-une Life* of the fallen Race muft be reftored according to the *tri-une Manifeftation* of the Holy Deity in Nature.

Here we know what the *Love*, and what the *Anger* of God is, what *Heaven* and *Hell*, an *Angel* and a *Devil*, a loft and a redeemed Soul are. The *Love*, and Goodnefs, and Blef-fing of God known, found, and enjoyed by any Creature, is nothing elfe but the Holy Trinity of God known, found, and enjoyed in the blifsful, glorious, *tri-une Life* of Fire, Light and Spirit, *where* Father, Son, and Holy Ghoft *perpetually* communicate their own name-lefs, numberlefs, boundlefs Powers, Riches and Glories to the created Image of their own Nature.

Nature. The *Hell* in Nature, and the hellish
Life in the Creature, the *Wrath* of God in Nature and Creature, is nothing elfe but the tri-
une, holy Life broken and deftroyed in *fome
Order* of Creatures, it is only the Fire of Heaven *feparated* from its heavenly Light and Spirit.
This is that Eternal *Anger*, and *Wrath*, and
Vengeance, that muft be *aton'd*, *fatisfy'd*, and
remov'd, that eternal Fire that muft be quench'd,
that eternal *Darknefs* that muft be changed
into Light, or there is no *Poffibility* in Nature,
that the Soul of fallen Man fhould ever fee the
Kingdom of God : And here all the Doctrines
of the *Socinians* are quite tore up by the Roots.
For in this Ground appeareth the *abfolute Neceffity* of the Incarnation, Life, Sufferings,
Death, Refurrection and Afcenfion of the Son
of God. Here lieth the *full Proof*, that through
all Nature there could no Redeemer of Man be
found, but only in the Second Perfon of the
adorable Trinity become Man. For as the
Light and Spirit of Eternal Life, is the Light
and Spirit of the Son and Holy Ghoft manifefted in Heaven, fo the Light of Eternal Life
could never come again into the *fallen Soul*,
but from him *alone*, who is the *Light* of Heaven. He muft be again in the Soul, as he was
in it, when it was firft breathed forth from
the

the Holy Trinity, he muſt be manifeſted in the Soul, as he is in Heaven, or it can never have the Life of Heaven in jt.

The *Socinians* therefore, or others, who think they pay a juſt Deference to the Wiſdom and Omnipotence of God, when they ſuppoſe there was no *abſolute Neceſſity* for the Incarnation of the Son of God; but that God, if he had ſo pleaſed, could as well have ſav'd Man ſome *other Way*, ſhew as great Ignorance both of God and Nature, as if they ſhould have ſaid, that when God makes a *blind* Man to ſee by *opening* or *giving* him Eyes, there was no Neceſſity in the *Thing* itſelf, that *Sight* ſhould be given in *that particular Way*, but that God, if he had ſo pleaſed, could have made him become a *ſeeing* Man in this World without the *Eyes*, or *Light* of this World.

For if the *Son* of God is the *Light* of Heaven, and Man only wants to be redeemed, becauſe he has *loſt* the Light of Heaven; is it not abſolutely impoſſible for Him to be redeemed any *other Way*, or by any other Thing, than by a *Birth* of this Son of God in him. Is not this Particularity the *one only* Thing that can raiſe fallen Man, as *ſeeing Eyes* are the one only Thing that can take away Blindneſs from the Man?

2. If

If *Adam* had been able to *undo* in himself all that he had *done*, if he could have *gone back* into that State from whence he was fallen, if he could have *raifed up* again in himfelf that Birth of the Holy Trinity, in which he was created, *no Saviour* had been wanted for him ; but becaufe he could not do any Thing of this, but muft be *That* which he had made himfelf to be, therefore the *Wrath* of Nature, or the Wrath of God *manifefted* in Nature, abode upon him, and *this Wrath* muft of all neceffity be *appeafed, aton'd*, and *fatisfy'd*, that is, it muft be *kindled* into Light and Love, before he could again find, and enjoy the *God of Nature*, as a God of Light and Love.

Could *Adam* himfelf have done all that which I have juft now mentioned, then his own Actions had *aton'd* and *fatisfied* the Divine Wrath, and had *reconcil'd* him to God : For nothing loft him the Love of God, but *That* which feparated him from God ; and nothing did, or ever can feparate him from God, but the Lofs of that *tri-une Life*, in which alone the Holy Trinity of Divine Love can dwell. If therefore *Adam* could have raifed again in himfelf that *tri-une Life*, then his Sin, and the Wrath of God upon him, had been *only tranfitory* ; but becaufe he did That, which

N   according

according to all the *Poſſibilities of Nature*, was
unalterable ; therefore he became a *Priſoner* of
an eternal *Wrath*, an Heir of an *everlaſting*,
painful Life, till the Love of God, who is
greater than Nature, ſhould *do That* for him
and in him, which he could by no Powers of
Nature do for himſelf, nor the higheſt of
Creatures do for him.

3. And here we ſee in the plaineſt Light,
that there was *no Anger* in God *himſelf* towards
the fallen Creature, becauſe it was *purely* and
ſolely the infinite Love of God towards him,
that did, and alone could raiſe him out of his
fallen State : All Scripture, as well as Nature,
obliges us to think thus of God. Thus it is
the whole Tenor of Scripture, that *God ſo lov'd
the World, that he ſent his only-begotten Son into
it, that the World, through him, might be ſaved :*
Is not this ſaying *more* than if it had been ſaid,
that there was *no Anger* in God himſelf towards
fallen Man ? Is he not expreſsly declared to be
infinitely flowing forth in Love towards him ?
Could God be more infinite in Love, or more
infinitely diſtant from all *Poſſibility* of Anger
towards Man, when he firſt created him, than
when he *thus* redeemed him ? God out of pure
and free Love gave his Son to be the Life of
the World, *firſt*, as an *inſpoken* and *ingrafted*
Word

Word of Life, as the *Bruiſer* of the Serpent given to *all Mankind* in their Father *Adam*. This *Word* of Life, and *Bruiſer* of the Serpent, was the *Extinguiſher* of that Wrath of God that lay upon fallen Man. Now, will the Scriptures, which tell us that the Love of God ſent his Son into the World, to redeem Man from that *belliſh Wrath* that had ſeiz'd him, allow us to ſay, that it was to extinguiſh a Wrath that was got into *God himſelf*, or that the Bruiſer of the Serpent was to *bruiſe, ſuppreſs*, or *remove* ſomething that Sin had *raiſed* in the Holy Deity *itſelf?* No ſurely, but to bruiſe, alter, and overcome an *Evil* in Nature and the Creature, that was become Man's *Separation* from the Enjoyment of the God of Love, whoſe Love ſtill exiſted in its own State, and ſtill followed him, and gave his only Son to make him capable of it. Do not the Holy Scriptures continually teach us, that the Holy Jeſus became incarnate *to deſtroy the Works of the Devil*, to overcome Death and Hell that had taken Man captive? And is not this ſufficiently telling us, *what* that Wrath was, and *where* it exiſted, which muſt be *aton'd, ſatisfy'd, and extinguiſhed*, before Man could again be alive unto God, or reconciled unto him, ſo as to have the tri-une Life of

Light

Light and Love in him? It was a Wrath of
Death, a Wrath of *Hell*, a Wrath of *Sin*,
and which only the precious, powerful Blood
of Chrift could change into a Life of Joy and
Love: And when this Wrath of Death and
Hell are *removed* from Human Nature, there
neither is, nor can be any *other Wrath* of God
abiding on it.   Are not the Devils and all loft
Souls juftly faid to be under the *eternal Wrath*
of God, and yet in *no Wrath* but that which
exifts in Hell, and in their own Hellifh Nature.

4. They therefore, who fuppofe the Wrath
and Anger of God upon fallen Man, to be a
State of Mind in God himfelf, to be a political kind of *juft Indignation*, a Point of *Honour-
able Refentment*, which the Sovereign Deity,
as Governor of the World, ought not to recede
from, but muft have a *fufficient* Satisfaction
done to his offended Authority, before he can,
confiftently with his Sovereign Honour, receive
the Sinner into his Favour, hold the Doctrine
of the *Neceffity* of Chrift's atoning Life and
Death in a miftaken Senfe.   That many good
Souls may hold this Doctrine in this Simplicity
of Belief, without any more Hurt to themfelves, than others have held the *Reality* of
Chrift's Flefh and Blood in the Sacrament under

der the Notion of the *Tranfubftantiation* of
the Bread and Wine, I make no Manner of
Doubt: But when Books are written to im-
pofe and require this Belief of others, as the
only faving Faith in the Life and Death of
Chrift, it is then an Error that ceafes to be innocent: For neither Reafon, nor Scripture
will allow us to bring Wrath into God himfelf,
as a Temper of his Mind, who is only infinite,
unalterable, overflowing Love, as unchangeable in Love, as He is in Power and Goodnefs.
The Wrath that was awakened at the Fall of
Man, that then feized upon him, as its Captive, was only a *Plague*, or *Evil*, or *Curfe*
that Sin had brought forth in Nature and
Creature; it was only the Beginning of Hell:
It was *fuch* a Wrath as God himfelf pitied
Man's lying under it; it was *fuch* a Wrath as
God himfelf furnifhed Man with a Power of
overcoming and extinguifhing, and therefore
it was not a Wrath that was according to the
Mind, *Will*, and *Liking*, or Wifdom of God;
and therefore it was not a Wrath that was in
God himfelf, or which was exercifed by his
Sovereign Wifdom over his difobedient Creatures: It was not *fuch* a Wrath, as when So-
vereign Princes are angry at Offenders, and
will not ceafe from their Refentment, 'till fome

political

political Satisfaction, or valuable Amends be made to their flighted Authority. No, no; it was such a Wrath as God himself hated, as he hates Sin and Hell, a Wrath that the God of all Nature and Creature so *willed* to be *remov'd* and *extinguished*, that seeing nothing less cou'd do it, he sent his only-begotten Son into the World, that all Mankind might be *sav'd* and *delivered* from it. For seeing the Wrath that was awakened and brought forth by the Fall, and which wanted to be appeas'd, aton'd, and quench'd, was the Wrath of *eternal Death*, and *eternal Hell*, that had taken Man captive; therefore God spared not the precious, powerful, efficacious Blood of the Holy Jesus, because that alone could extinguish this eternal Wrath of Death and Hell, and re-kindle Heaven and Eternal Life again in the Soul. And thus all that the Scriptures speak of the *Necessity* and *powerful* Atonement of the Life and Death of Christ, all that they say of the *infinite Love* of God towards fallen Man, and all that they say of the *Eternal Wrath* and *Vengeance* to which Man was become a Prey, have the most solid Foundation, and are all of them proved to be consistent, harmonious Truths of the greatest Certainty, according to the plain Letter of Scripture.

5. It

5. It is the Foundation of the Law and the Gospel, that *without shedding of Blood, there is no Remission of Sins*; and that the precious Blood of Christ could alone do this, could alone reconcile us to God, and deliver us from the Wrath to come. How, and why Blood, and only the Blood of Jesus Christ could do this, will appear as follows: *Adam* was created with a twofold Respect, to be himself a glorious, living, eternal Image of the Holy, triune God, and to be a *Father* of a new World of like Beings, all descended from himself. When *Adam* fell, he lost both these Conditions of his created State; the Holy Image of God was extinguished, his Soul lost the Light and Spirit of Heaven, and his Body became earthly, bestial, corruptible Flesh and Blood, and he could only be a *Father* of a Posterity partly *diabolical*, and partly *bestial*.

Now, if the first Purpose of God was to stand, and to take Effect; if *Adam* was still to be the Father of a Race that were to become Sons of God, then there was an absolute Necessity that all that *Adam* had *done* in and to himself, and his Posterity, by the Fall, should be *undone* again; the *Serpent* and the *Beast*, that is, the Serpentine Life, and the bestial Life in Human Nature, must both of

N 4   them

them be *overcome*, and *driven* out of it. This was the *one only*, possible Salvation for *Adam*, and every Individual of his Posterity.

Adam had kill'd that which was to have been immortal in him, he had raised that into a Life which never should have been alive in him, and therefore that which was to be *un-done* and *alter'd* both in himself and his Posterity, was this, it was to part with a *Life* that he had raised up into Being, and to get *another Life*, which he had quite extinguished.

And here appears the true, infallible Ground of *all the Sacrifice*, and all the *Blood-shedding* that is necessary to redeem and reconcile Man to God. 'Tis because the earthly, fleshly, bestial, corruptible Life under the Elements of this World, is a Life *rais'd* and *brought* into Man by the Fall, is not that Life which God created, but is an Impurity in the Sight of God, and therefore cannot enter into the Kingdom of Heaven; 'tis a Life, or Body of Sin, brought forth by Sin, and the Habitation of Sin, and therefore it is a Life that must be *given up*, its Blood must be *poured out*, before Man can be released from his Sins : This is the *one only* Ground of all the *Shedding of Blood* in Religion. Had not a Life *foreign* to the Kingdom of God, and utterly *incapable* of it, been

been *introduced* by the Fall, there had been no possible Room for the *Death* of any Creature, or the *pouring out* any Blood, as serviceable and instrumental to the raising fallen Man.

6. But now, this bestial, animal Life which is thus to be given up, and its Blood pour'd out, is but the half, and lesser half of that which is requir'd to deliver Man from all that the Fall has brought upon him. For the heavenly Life, the Birth of the Light and Holy Spirit of God which *Adam* had quite extinguished, was to be *kindled* or *regenerated* again; also his *first, glorious, immortal* Body was to be regain'd, before he could become an Inhabitant of the Kingdom of Heaven: But for all this *Adam* had no Power. See here again the true and dreadful State of the *Fall,* it was the Fall into *such* a Life, as must be *slain* and *sacrificed* before the fallen Soul cou'd come to God; and yet this Death and Sacrifice of the Body, which was thus absolutely necessary, was the most dreadful Thing that could happen to Man, because *his own* Death, come when it wou'd, would only remove him from the *Light* of this World into the Eternal Darkness, and hellish State of fallen Angels: And here we find the true Reason, why Man's own Death, tho' a Sacrifice *necessary* to be made,

made, had yet nothing of *Atonement* or *Satisfaction* in it ; it was because it left the eternal Wrath of Nature, and the Hell that was therein, unquench'd and unextinguish'd in the Soul, and therefore made no *Reconcilement* to God, no *Restoration* to the Creature of its *first State* and *Life* in God, but left the Soul in its dark, wrathful Separation from the Kingdom of Light and Love,

But here the amazing Infinity of divine Love appear'd, such a Mystery of Love as will be the universal Song of Praise to all Eternity.   Here God, the second Person in the holy Trinity, took human Nature upon him, became a suffering, dying Man, that there might be found a Man, whose Sufferings, Blood and Death had Power to *extinguish* the Wrath and Hell that Sin had brought forth, and to be a *Fountain* of the first heavenly Life to the whole Race of Mankind.

It was *human Nature* that was fallen, that had lost its first heavenly Life, and got a bestial, diabolical Life in the stead of it.   Now if *this* human Nature was to be restor'd, there was but *one possible* Way, it must go back to the State from whence it came, it must put off all that it had put on, it must regain all that it had lost : But the human Nature that fell, could do nothing
thing

thing of this, and yet all this muſt be done in and by *that* human Nature which is fallen, or it could never, to all Eternity, come out of the State of its Fall; for it could not poſſibly come out of the State of its Fall, but by *putting off* all that, which the Fall had brought upon it. And thus ſtood Man, as to all the Powers of Nature and Creature, in an *utter Impoſſibility* of Salvation, and had only a ſhort Life of this World betwixt him and Hell.

7. But let us now change the Scene, and be-hold the Wonders of a *new Creation*, where all Things are called out of the *Curſe* and *Death* of Sin, and created again to Life in Chriſt Je-ſus; where all Mankind are choſen and appoint-ed to the *Recovery* of their firſt glorious Life, by a *new Birth* from a ſecond *Adam*, who, as an *univerſal* Redeemer, takes the *Place* of the firſt fallen Father of Mankind, and ſo gives Life and Immortality, and Heaven to all that loſt them in *Adam*.

God, according to the Riches of his Love, rais'd a Man out of the Loins of *Adam*, in whoſe myſterious Perſon, the *whole* Humanity, and the *Word* of God was perſonally united; that *ſame Word* which had been *inſpoken* into *Adam* at his Fall, as a ſecret *Bruiſer of the* Ser-pent, and *real Beginning* of his Salvation; ſo

that

that in this second *Adam*, God and Man was one Perfon. And in this Union of the divine and human Nature lies the *Foundation* and *Poffibility* of our Recovery. For thus the holy Jefus became qualify'd to be the *fecond Adam*, or univerfal Regenerator of all that are born of *Adam* the firft. For being himfelf *that Deity,* which as a *Spark* or *Seed* of Life was given to *Adam*, thus all that were born of *Adam* had alfo a *Birth* from him, and fo ftood under him, as their common Father and Regenerator of a heavenly Life in them. And it was this firft infpoken *Word* of Life which was given to *Adam*, that makes all Mankind to be the *fpiritual* Children of the *fecond Adam*, tho' he was not born into the World till fo many Years after the Fall. For feeing the *fame Word* that became their perfect Redeemer in the Fulnefs of Time, was in them from the Beginning, as a Beginning of their Redemption, therefore he ftood related to all Mankind as a *Fountain* and *Deriver* of an heavenly Life into them, in the fame *univerfal manner* as *Adam* was the Fountain and Deriver of a miferable Mortality into them.

And feeing alfo this great and glorious Redeemer had in himfelf the *whole Humanity,* both as it was *before* and after the *Fall*, viz.

in

in his inward Man the *Perfection* of the firſt *Adam*, and in his outward the *Weakneſs* and *Mortality* of the fallen Nature; and ſeeing he had all this, as the *Undoer* of all that *Adam* had done, as the *Overcomer* of Death, as the *Former* and *Raiſer* of our heavenly Life, therefore it was, that all his Conqueſts over this World, Sin, Death, and Hell, were not the Conqueſts of a *ſingle Perſon* that terminated in himſelf, but had their real *Effect* and efficacious *Merit* through *all* human Nature, becauſe he was the *appointed Father* and *Regenerator* of the whole human Nature, and as ſuch, had that *ſame Relation* to it all as *Adam* had : And therefore as *Adam's* Fall, Sin and Death, did not, could not terminate in himſelf, becauſe he was our *appointed Father*, from whom we muſt have ſuch a State and Condition of Life as he had ; ſo the Righteouſneſs, Death, Reſurrection and Aſcenſion of Chriſt into the Kingdom of Heaven did not terminate in himſelf, but became ours, becauſe he is our appointed *ſecond Adam*, from whom we are to derive *ſuch* a State and Condition of Life as he had ; and therefore all that are *born again* of him, are certainly born into *his State* of Victory and Triumph over the World, Sin, Death and Hell.

8. Now

8. Now here is opened to us the true Reason of the *whole Procefs* of our Saviour's Incarnation, Paffion, Death, Refurrection and Afcenfion into Heaven : It was becaufe fallen Man was to go through *all thefe Stages* as neceffary Parts of his Return to God ; and therefore, if Man was to go out of his *fallen State*, there muft be a Son of *this fallen* Man, who, as a *Head* and *Fountain* of the whole Race, could do all this, could go back through all thefe Gates, and fo make it *poffible* for all the Individuals of human Nature, as being *born* of him, to inherit his *conquering Nature*, and follow him through all thefe Paffages to eternal Life. And thus we fee, in the ftrongeft and cleareft Light, both *why* and *how* the holy Jefus is become our great Redeemer.

Had he fail'd in any of thefe Things, had he not *been* all that he was, and *did* all that he did, he could not have made one full, perfect, fufficient Atonement and Satisfaction for the Sins of the whole World, that is, he could not have *been* and *done* that, which in the *Nature* of the Thing was *abfolutely* neceffary, and *fully* fufficient to take the whole human Race *out of* the Bondage and Captivity of their fallen State. Thus, had he not really had the divine Nature in his Perfon, he could not have *begun* to be

our

our *second Adam* from the Time of the Fall, nor could we have ftood *related* to him as Children, that had receiv'd a *new Birth* from him. Neither could he have made a *Beginning* of a divine Life in our fallen Nature, but that he was that God who could make Nature *begin again* where it had fail'd in our firft Father. Without this Divinity in his Perfon, the Perfection of his Humanity would have been as helplefs to us as the Perfection of an Angel. Again, had he not been *Man*, and in human Nature *overcome* Sin and Temptation, he could have been *no Saviour* of fallen Man, becaufe nothing that he had done had been done *in* and *to* the fallen Nature. *Adam* might as well have deriv'd Sin into the Angels by his Fall, as Chrift had deriv'd Righteoufnefs into us by his Life, if he had not *ftood* both in our Nature, and as the *common Father* and *Regenerator* of it; therefore his Incarnation was neceffary to deliver us from our Sins, and accordingly the Scripture faith, *he was manifeft in the Flefh to deftroy the Works of the Devil.* Again, if Chrift had not *renounced* this Life, as heartily and thoroughly as *Adam* chofe it, and declared abfolutely for another Kingdom in another World; if he had not *facrific'd* the Life he took up in and from this World, he could not have been

our

our Redeemer, and therefore the Scripture continually afcribes Atonement, Satisfaction, Redemption, and Remiffion of Sins to his *Sufferings* and *Death.* Again, had not our Lord entred into that State of *eternal Death* which fallen Man was eternally to inherit; had he not broke *from it* as its Conqueror, and rofe again from the Dead, he could not have deliver'd us from the Effects of our Sins, and therefore the Apoftle faith, *If Chrift be not rifen, ye are yet in your Sins.* But I muft enlarge a little upon the Nature and Merits of our Saviour's *laft Sufferings.* It is plain from Scripture that *that Death,* which our bleffed Lord dy'd on the Crofs, was *abfolutely* neceffary for our Salvation; that he, as our Saviour, *was to tafte Death for every Man* —that as the *Captain of our Salvation, he was to be made perfect through Sufferings* —— that there was no Entrance for fallen Man into Paradife till Chrift had overcome that Death and Hell, or that firft and fecond Death which ftood between us and it.

Now the abfolute Neceffity of our Saviour's doing and fuffering all this, plainly appears, as foon as we confider him as the *fecond Adam,* who, as fuch, is to *undo* all the Evil that the firft *Adam* had done in human Nature; and there-

therefore muſt enter into *every State* that belong'd to this fallen Nature, *reſtoring* in every
State that which was loſt, *quickening* that
which was extinguiſh'd, and *overcoming* in
every State that by which Man was overcome.
And therefore as *eternal Death* was as certainly brought forth in our Souls, as temporal
Death in our Bodies, as this Death was a State
that *belong'd* to fallen Man, therefore our Lord
was obliged to taſte *this dreadful Death*, to
enter into the *Realities* of it, that he might
carry our Nature *victoriouſly* through it. And
as fallen Man was to have enter'd into this e-
ternal Death at his giving up the Ghoſt in this
World, ſo the ſecond *Adam*, as *reverſing* all
that the firſt had done, was to ſtand in this *ſecond Death* upon the Croſs, and dye from it
into that Paradiſe out of which *Adam* the firſt
dy'd into this World.

Now when the Time drew near that our
bleſſed Lord was to enter upon his laſt great
Sufferings, *viz.* the *Realities* of that ſecond
Death through which he was to paſs, then it
was that all the *anguiſhing Terrors* of a loſt
Soul began to open themſelves in him; then
all that eternal Death which *Adam* had brought
into his Soul, when it loſt the Light and Spirit of Heaven, began to be *awaken'd*, and *ſtir-*

O   *ring*

-*ring* in the fecond *Adam*, who was come to ftand in the *laft State* of the fallen Soul, to be encompafs'd with that eternal Death and *Senfibility* of Hell, which muft have been the everlafting State of fallen Man.

The *Beginning* of our Lord's Entrance into the terrible Jaws of this fecond *Death*, may be juftly dated from thofe affecting Words, *My Soul is exceeding forrowful, even unto Death, tarry ye here with me and watch.* See here the Lord of Life reduc'd to fuch Diftrefs as to beg the Prayers, Watching, and Affiftance of his poor Difciples! A plain Proof that it was not the Sufferings of this World, but a State of *dreadful Dereliction* that was coming upon him. O holy Redeemer, that I knew how to defcribe the anguifhing Terrors of thy Soul, when thou waft entring into eternal Death, that no other Son of Man might fall into it.

The Progrefs of thefe Terrors are plainly fhewn us in our Lord's *Agony* in the Garden, when the *Reality* of this eternal Death fo broke in upon him, fo awaken'd and ftirr'd itfelf in him, as to force great Drops of Blood to fweat from his Body. This was that *bitter Cup* which made him withdraw himfelf, proftrate himfelf, and thrice repeat an earneft Prayer,

Prayer, that if it were poffible, it might pafs from him, but at the fame Time heartily pray'd to drink it according to the divine Will.

This was that Cup he was drinking from the fixth to the ninth Hour on the Crofs, nail'd to the Terrors of a *two-fold Death*, when he cry'd out *My God, my God, why haft thou for-faken me?*

We are not to fuppofe that our Lord's Agony was the Terrors of a Perfon that was going to be murder'd, or the Fears of that Death which Men could inflict upon him; for he had told his Difciples, not to fear them that could only kill the Body, and therefore we may be fure he had no fuch Fears himfelf. No, his Agony was his Entrance into the *laft, eternal Terrors* of the loft Soul, into the real Horrors of that dreadful, eternal Death, which Man un-redeemed muft have dyed into when he left this World. We are therefore not to confider our Lord's Death upon the Crofs, as only the Death of that mortal Body which was nail'd to it, but we are to look upon him with wound-ed Hearts, as fix'd and faften'd in the State of that *two-fold Death*, which was due to the fallen Nature, out of which he could not come till he could fay, *It is finifhed; Father, into thy Hands I commend my Spirit.*

O 2 In

In that Inftant he gave up the Ghoft of this earthly Life; and as a Proof of his having overcome all the Bars and Chains of Death and Hell, he rent the *Rocks*, open'd the *Graves*, and brought the *Dead* to Life, and triumphantly enter'd into that long fhut up Paradife, out of which *Adam* dy'd, and in which he promifed the Thief, he fhould that Day be with him.

When therefore thou beholdeft the *Crucifix*, which finely reprefents to thy Senfes the Saviour of the World hanging on the Crofs, let not thy Thoughts ftay on any Sufferings, or Death, that the Malice of Men can caufe; for he hung there in greater Diftrefs than any human Power can inflict, *forfaken* of God, *feeling*, *bearing*, and *overcoming* the Pains and Darknefs of that eternal Death which the fallen Soul of *Adam* had brought into it. For as *Adam* by his Fall, or Death in Paradife, had nothing left in his Soul, but the *Nature, Properties* and *Life* of Hell, all which muft have *awaken'd* in him in their full Strength, as foon as he had loft the Flefh, and Blood, and Light of this World, as this eternal Death was a *State* that belonged to Man by the Fall, fo there was an *abfolute* Neceffity that the Saviour of Man fhould enter into all thefe awaken'd Realities

of

of the laſt eternal Death, and come victoriouſly
out of them, or Man had never been redeemed from them. For the fallen Nature could
no way poſſibly be ſav'd, but by its *own coming* victoriouſly out of every Part of its fallen
State ; and therefore all this was to be done
by that Son of Man, from whom we had a
Power of deriving into us his victorious
Nature.

Laſtly, if our bleſſed Lord was not aſcended
into Heaven, and ſet on the Right Hand of
God, he could not deliver us from our Sins;
and therefore the Scripture aſcribes to him, as
aſcended, a perpetual Prieſthood in Heaven :
If any Man Sin, ſaith St. *John, we have an Advo-
cate with the Father, Jeſus Chriſt the Righteous,*
and *he is the Propitiation for our Sins.*

All theſe Things therefore are ſo many e-
qually eſſential Parts of our Saviour's Character,
as he is the *one Atonement,* the *full Satisfaction*
for Sin, the *Saviour* and *Deliverer* from the
Bondage, Power, and Effects of Sin. And to
aſcribe our Deliverance from Sin, or the Re-
miſſion of our Sins more to the *Life* and *Actions,* than to the *Death* of Chriſt, or to his
Death more than to his *Reſurrection* and *Aſcenſion,* is directly contrary to the plain Letter and
Tenor of the Scripture, which ſpeaks of *all*

theſe

thefe Things as *jointly* qualifying our Lord to
be the *all-fufficient* Redeemer of Mankind;
and when fpeaking feparately of any of them,
afcribes the *fame* Power, Efficacy, and redeeming Virtue to one as to the other.

And all this is very plain from the Nature
of the Thing; for fince all thefe Things are
neceffary Parts or Stages of our Return to God,
every one of them muft have the fame neceffary Share in delivering us from our finful
State; and therefore what our Saviour did; as
living, dying, rifing from the Dead, and afcending into Heaven, are Things that he did
as equally neceffary, and equally efficacious to
our full Deliverance from all the Power, Effects, and Confequences of our Sins.

And here we may fee, in the plaineft Light,
how Chrift is faid to bear *our Iniquities*, to be
made *Sin for us*, and how his Sufferings have
deliver'd us from the Guilt and Sufferings due
to our Sins, and how we are *faved* by him. It
is not by an *arbitrary*, *difcretionary* Pleafure
of God, accepting the Sufferings of an *innocent*
Perfon, as a fufficient *Amends* or *Satisfaction*
for the Sins of Criminals. This is by no means
the true Ground of this Matter. In this View
we neither think rightly of our Saviour, nor
rightly of God's receiving us to Salvation thro'
him.

him. God is reconciled to us through Jesus
Christ in *no other Sense* than as we are *new born,
new created* in Christ Jesus. This is the only
Merit we have from him. Jesus Christ was
made Sin for us, he bore our Iniquities, he saved
us, not by giving the *Merit* of his innocent
unjust Sufferings as a *full Payment* for our
Demerits, but he saved us because he made
himself *one of us*, became a Member of *our
Nature*, and *such a Member* of our Nature, as
had *Power* to heal, remove, and overcome all
the Evils that were brought into our Nature by
the Fall. He bore our Iniquities and sav'd us,
because he stood in our Nature as our *common
Father*, as one that had the same Relation to
all Mankind as *Adam* had, and from whom
we can derive all the conquering Power of *his
Nature*, and so are enabled to come out of our
Guilt and Iniquities by having his Nature *derived* into us. This is the whole of what is
meant by having our *guilty Condition transferred* upon him, and his *Merit* transferred upon
us: Our Guilt is transferred upon him in *no o-
ther* Sense than as he took upon him the State
and Condition of our fallen Nature, to bear
all its Troubles, undergo all its Sufferings, till
he had *heal'd* and *overcome* all the Effects of
Sin. His *Merit* or *Righteousness* is imputed or

deriv'd

deriv'd into us in no other Senfe, than as we receive from him a *Birth*, a *Nature*, a *Power* to become the Sons of God. Hence it appears, what vain Difputes the World has had upon this Subject, and how this edifying, glorious Part of Religion has been perplex'd and loft in the Fictions and Difficulties of fcholaftick Learning. Some People have much puzzled themfelves and others with this *Queftion*, How it is confiftent with the Goodnefs and Equity of God to *permit*, or *accept* the Sufferings of an innocent Perfon as a Satisfaction for the Guilt and Punifhment of criminal Offenders? But this Queftion can only be put by thofe, who have not yet known the moft fundamental Doctrine of the Gofpel Salvation; for according to the Gofpel, the *Queftion* fhould *proceed* thus, How it is confiftent with the Goodnefs and Equity of God, to raife *fuch an innocent, myfterious Perfon* out of the Loins of fallen Man, as was able to *remove* all the Evil and Diforder that was brought into the fallen Nature? This is the only Queftion that is according to the true Ground of our Redemption, and at once difperfes all thofe Difficulties which are the mere Products of Human Invention. The Short of the Matter is this:

Man

Man confidered as created, or fallen, or redeemed, is *That* which he is, becaufe of his State in Nature; he can have no Goodnefs in him when created, but becaufe he is brought into fuch a Participation of a *Goodnefs* that there is *in Nature*; he can have no Evil in him when *fallen*, but becaufe he is fallen from his good State *in Nature*; he can no way be redeemed, but by being brought into his firft State of Perfection *in Nature*; and therefore, this is an eternal, immutable Truth, that he can be redeemed by the God *of Nature*, only according to the *Poffibilities* of Nature: And here lies the *true Ground*, the whole Reafon of all that our Saviour *was*, and *did*, and *fuffered* on our Account: It was becaufe in and through *all Nature* there could be no other Relief found for us: It was becaufe nothing lefs than *fuch a Procefs* of fuch a *Myfterious Perfon* could have Power to undo all the Evils that were done in and to the Human Nature; and therefore it is not only confiftent with the Goodnefs and Equity of God to bring fuch a Myfterious Perfon into the World, but is the moft infinite Inftance of his moft Infinite Love to all Mankind, that can poffibly be conceived and adored by us. To proceed:

9. By

9. By the Fall of our firſt Father we have loſt our *firſt, glorious* Bodies, that *eternal, celeſtial* Fleſh and Blood which had as truly the Nature of Paradiſe and Heaven in it, as our preſent Bodies have the Nature, Mortality and Corruption of this World in them : If therefore we are to be redeemed, there is an *abſolute Neceſſity* that our Souls be *cloathed* again with this firſt paradiſical, or heavenly Fleſh and Blood, or we can never enter into the Kingdom of God. Now, this is the Reaſon, why the Scriptures ſpeak ſo particularly, ſo frequently, and ſo amphatically of the powerful Blood of Chriſt, of the great Benefit it is to us, of its *Redeeming, Quickening, Life-giving* Virtue ; it is becauſe our firſt Life, or heavenly Fleſh and Blood is *born again* in us, or *derived* again into us from this Blood of Chriſt.

Our Bleſſed Lord, who died for us, had not only that outward Fleſh and Blood, which he received from the Virgin *Mary,* and which died upon the Croſs, but he had alſo an holy Humanity of heavenly Fleſh and Blood veil'd under it, which was appointed by God to *quicken, generate,* and *bring forth* from itſelf, ſuch an body Offspring of immortal Fleſh and Blood, as *Adam* the firſt ſhould have brought forth before his Fall.

If

If our Lord Chrift had not had a *heavenly Humanity*, confifting of fuch Flefh and Blood as is not of this World, he had not been fo perfect as *Adam* was, nor could our Birth from him, raife us to *that Perfection*, which we had loft, nor could his Blood be faid to *purchafe, ranfom, redeem,* and *reftore* us; becaufe, as it is heavenly Flefh and Blood that we have loft, fo we can only have it *ranfom'd* and *reftor'd* to us, by that Blood which is of the *fame* heavenly and immortal Nature with that which we have quite loft. Our common Faith, therefore, obliges us to hold, that our Lord had the *Perfection* of the firft *Adam's* Flefh and Blood united with, and veiled under that fallen Nature, which he took upon him from the Bleffed Virgin *Mary*. Had he not taken our *fallen* Nature upon him, nothing that he had done, could have been of any Advantage to us, or brought any Ranfom or Redemption to our fallen Nature; and had he not taken *our Nature* as it was *before* the Fall, he could not have been our *fecond* Adam, or a *Reftorer* to us of *that Nature*, which we fhould have had from *Adam* if he had not fallen.

Now, what our Common Faith thus fully teaches, concerning a heavenly, as well as earthly Humanity, which our Lord had, is

alfo

also plainly fignified to us by feveral clear
Texts of Scripture; as where he faith of himfelf, *I am from above, ye are from beneath*;
again, *I am not of this World*; and further,
No one afcends into Heaven, but He that came
*down from Heaven, even the Son of Man, who
is in Heaven:* Thefe and other Texts of the
like Nature, which plainly fpeak of *fomething*
in our Bleffed Lord, which can neither be underftood of his Divinity, nor of *that* Flefh
and Blood which he received from the Virgin
Mary, has forc'd fome *Scholaftick Divines* to
hold the *Pre-exiftence* of our Saviour's Soul,
which is an Opinion utterly inconfiftent with
our Redemption; for it is as neceffary that our
Lord fhould have a Soul as well as a Body derived from *Adam,* in order to be the Redeemer
of *Adam's* Offspring: But all thefe Texts,
which a Learning, merely *literal,* has thus
miftaken, do only prove this great, neceffary,
and edifying Truth, that our Bleffed Lord had
a heavenly Humanity, which cloathed Ielf
with the Flefh and Blood of this World in the
Womb of the Virgin and from that heavenly Humanity, or Life-giving Blood it is that
our firft heavenly, immortal Flefh and Blood
is *generated* and *form'd* in us again; and therefore his Blood is truly the *Atonement*, the *Ran-*

fom

fom, the *Redemption*, the *Life* of the World ;
becaufe it brings forth, and generates from itfelf the paradifical, immortal Flefh and Blood,
as *certainly*, as *really*, as the Blood of fallen
Adam brings forth and generates from itfelf the
finful, vile, corruptible Flefh and Blood of this
Life.

Wou'd you farther know, what Blood this
is, that has this atoning, Life-giving Quality
in it ? It is that Blood which is to be receiv'd in
the Holy Sacrament. Wou'd you know, why
it quickens, raifes and reftores the inward Man
that died in Paradife ? The Anfwer is from
Chrift himfelf, *He that eateth my Flefh and
drinketh my Blood, dwelleth in me, and I in him,*
that is, *he is born of my Flefh and Blood.* Wou'd
you know, why the Apoftle faith, *That he
hath purchafed us by his Blood,* Acts xx. 28.
That we have Redemption through his Blood,
Ephef. i. 7. Why he prays *the God of Peace
——— through the Blood of the Everlafting Covenant, to make us perfect in every good Work to
do his Will* ; 'tis becaufe the Holy Jefus faith,
except *we drink his Blood, we have no Life in
us,* and therefore the drinking his Blood, is the
fame Thing as receiving *a Life* of heavenly
Flefh and Blood from him : And all this is
only faying, that our Saviour, the fecond *Adam*,

muft

must do *that* for us and in us, which the first
Adam shou'd have done ; his Blood must be
that to us by way of *Defcent*, or *Birth* from
him, which the Blood of our first Father, if
he had not fallen, wou'd have been to us; and
as this Blood of an immortal Life is loft by
the Fall, fo he from whom we receive it again
by a *fecondary Way*, is juftly and truly faid, to
purchafe, to *redeem*, and *ranfom* us by his
Blood.

Now, there is but *one redeeming, fanctifying,
Life-giving* Blood of Chrift, and it is that
which gave and fhed itfelf under the Veil of
that outward Flefh and Blood that was facri-
ficed upon the Crofs ; it is that Holy and Heavenly Flefh and Blood which is to be received
in the Holy Sacrament ; it is that holy, immortal Flefh and Blood which *Adam* had before
the Fall, of which Blood if we had *drank*,
that is, if we had been *born* of it, we had not
wanted a Saviour, but had had fuch Flefh and
Blood as could have entred into the Kingdom
of Heaven ; had we received this holy, immortal Flefh and Blood from *Adam* before his
Fall, it had been called our being *born* of his
Flefh and Blood ; but becaufe we receive that
fame Flefh and Blood from Jefus Chrift, our
fecond *Adam*, by our *Faith*, our *Hunger* and

Defire

Desire of it; therefore it is juftly call'd our
eating and drinking his Flefh and Blood.

And here we have another ftrong Scripture
Proof, that our Saviour had heavenly Flefh and
Blood veil'd under that which he receiv'd from
the Virgin *Mary*. For does not the Holy Sacrament undeniably prove to us, that he had a
heavenly Flefh entirely different from that
which was feen nail'd to the Crofs, and which
was to be a heavenly, fubftantial Food to us;
that he had a Blood entirely different from that
which was feen to run out of his mortal Body,
which Blood we are to drink of, and live for
ever?

Now, that Flefh and Blood cannot enter
into the Kingdom of God, is a Scripture Truth;
and yet it muft be affirm'd to be a Truth according to the fame Scriptures, that Flefh and
Blood can, and muft enter into the Kingdom
of God, or elfe, neither *Adam*, nor any of his
Pofterity could enter in thither; therefore, it
is a Scripture Truth, that there is a *Flefh* and
Blood that has the Nature, the Likenefs, and
Qualities of Heaven in it, that is as wholly
different from the Flefh and Blood of this
World, as Heaven is different from the Earth.
For if the Flefh and Blood that we now have,
cannot poffibly enter into the Kingdom of
Heaven,

Heaven, and yet we muſt be Fleſh and Blood,
and Chriſt our Lord muſt be Fleſh and Blood,
for ever in Heaven; then it follows, that there
is a real Fleſh and Blood that has nothing of
this World in it, that neither ariſes from it,
nor is nouriſhed by it, but will ſubſiſt eternally, when this World is diſſolved and gone.
Now, if this Fleſh and Blood is loſt by the
Fall of our firſt Father, and if the Blood
which we derive from him is the *Cauſe,* the
Seat, and *Principle* of our mortal, corruptible,
impure Life; if from the Blood of this firſt
Father, all our Unholineſs, Impurity and Miſery is derived into us, then we may clearly
underſtand what is meant by our being redeemed by the Blood of Chriſt, and why the
Scriptures ſpeak ſo much of his *atoning, quickening, Life-giving, cleanſing, ſanĉifying* Blood;
it is becauſe it is to us the Reverſe of the Blood
of *Adam,* it is the *Cauſe,* the *Seat,* the *Principle* of our Holineſs and Purity of Life; it is
that from which we derive an immortal, holy
Fleſh and Blood in the ſame Reality from this
ſecond *Adam,* as we inherit a corrupt, impure, and earthly Fleſh and Blood from our
firſt *Adam:* And therefore that which would
have been done to us by our *Birth,* if we had
been born of the holy Blood of *Adam* unfallen,

that

that we are to underſtand to be done to us, in
and by the Holy Blood of Chriſt. For the
Blood of Chriſt is that to us in the Way of
Redemption, which the Blood of our firſt Father ſhou'd have been to us in the Order of the
Creation ; for the Redemption has no other
End, but to raiſe us from our Fall, to do that
for us, which we ſhou'd have had by the Condition of our Creation, if our Father had
kept his State of Glory and Immortality ; and
this is a certain Truth, that there would have
been no eating the Fleſh, and drinking the
Blood of Chriſt in the Chriſtian Scheme of
Redemption, but that the Fleſh and Blood
which we ſhou'd have had from *Adam*, muſt
of all neceſſity be had, before we can enter
into the Kingdom of Heaven.

10. Here therefore is plainly diſcovered to
us, the true Nature, Neceſſity and Benefit of
the Holy Sacrament of the Lord's-Supper ;
both why, and how, and for what End, we
muſt of all neceſſity, eat the Fleſh, and drink
the Blood of Chriſt. No *figurative Meaning* of
the Words is here to be ſought for, we muſt
eat Chriſt's Fleſh, and drink his Blood in the
ſame Reality, as he took upon him the *real
Fleſh and Blood* of the Bleſſed Virgin : We
can have no real Relation to Chriſt, can be no

P

true

true Members of his myſtical Body, but by being real Partakers of that ſame kind of Fleſh and Blood, which was truly his, and was his, for this *very End*, that through him, the ſame might be brought forth in us : All this is ſtrictly true of the Holy Sacrament, according to the plain Letter of the Expreſſion ; which Sacrament was thus inſtituted, that the *great Service* of the Church might continually ſhew us, that the whole of our Redemption conſiſted in the receiving the *Birth*, *Spirit*, *Life* and *Nature* of Jeſus Chriſt into us, in being born of him, and *cloathed* with a heavenly Fleſh and Blood from him, juſt as the whole of our Fall conſiſts in our being born of *Adam's* ſinful Nature and Spirit, and in having a vile, corrupt and impure Fleſh and Blood from him.

But what Fleſh and Blood are we to eat and drink ? Not ſuch as we have already, not ſuch as any Offspring of *Adam* hath, not ſuch as can have its Life and Death by, and from the Elements of this World ; and therefore, not that outward, viſible, mortal Fleſh and Blood of Chriſt, which he took from the Virgin *Mary*, and was ſeen in the Croſs, but a *heavenly*, *immortal* Fleſh and Blood, which came down from Heaven, which hath the *Nature*, *Qualities*, and *Life* of Heaven in it,

according

according to which our Lord said of himself,
that he was a *Son of Man came down from
Heaven*, that *he was not of this World*, that
he was from Above, &c. that *very* Flesh and
Blood which we should have received from
Adam, if we had kept his first glorious and
immortal Nature. For as the Flesh and Blood
which we lost by his Fall, was the Flesh and
Blood of *Eternal Life*, so it is the same Flesh
and Blood of Eternal Life which is offered to
us in the Holy Sacrament, that we may eat,
and live for ever : This is the adorable Height
and Depth of this Divine Mystery, which
brings Heaven and Immortality again into us,
and gives us *Power to become Sons of God*. Woe
be to those who come to it with the Mouths of
Beasts, and the Minds of *Serpents* ! who, with
impenitent Hearts, devoted to the Lusts of the
Flesh, the Lusts of the Eyes, and the Pride of
Life, for worldly Ends, outward Appearances,
and secular Conformity, boldly meddle with
those Mysteries that are only to be approached
by those that are of a *pure Heart*, and who
worship God in *Spirit and in Truth*. Justly
may it be said of such, that they *eat and drink
Damnation to themselves, not discerning*, that is,
not regarding, not reverencing, not humbly
adoring the Mysteries of the *Lord's* Body.

P 2

If

If you afk how the eating and drinking the
Body and Blood of Chrift, is the receiving that
Flefh and Blood of Eternal Life, which we
fhould have had from *Adam* himfelf, it is for
this plain Reafon, becaufe the *fame kind* of
Flefh and Blood is in Chrift, that was in *Adam*,
and is in Chrift as it was in *Adam*, for this
very End, that it might *be derived* into all his
Offspring: So that we come to the Sacrament
of the Bleffed Body and Blood of Chrift, becaufe he is *our Second Adam*, from whom we
muft now receive that eternal, celeftial Flefh
and Blood which we fhould have had from our
firft Father; and therefore it is, that the A-
poftle faith, the *firft Adam was made a living
Soul*, that is, had a *Life in himfelf* which could
have brought forth an eternal, ever-living Off-
fpring; but having brought forth a dead Race,
the laft Adam, as the Reftorer of the Life that
was loft, *was made a quickening Spirit*, becaufe quickening again *that Life* which *Adam*
as a *living Soul*, fhould have brought forth.

And thus we have the *plain* and *full Truth* of
the moft myfterious Part of this Holy Sacrament, delivered from the tedious Strife of
Words, and that Thicknefs of Darknefs which
learned Contenders on all Sides have brought
into it. The Letter and Spirit of Scripture are

here

here both preferved, and the Myftery appears fo
amiable, fo intelligible, and fo beneficial, as
muft needs raife a true and earneft Devotion
in every one that is capable of hungering and
thirfting after Eternal Life. And this true and
found Knowledge of the Holy Sacrament cou'd
never have been loft, if this Scripture Truth
had not been over-look'd ; namely, that Chrift
is *our fecond Adam*, that he is to do *that* for us,
which *Adam* fhould have done ; that we are
to have *that Life* from him, as a *Quickening
Spirit*, which we fhould have had from *Adam*
as a *living Soul*; and that our Redemption is
only doing a *fecond Time*, or in a fecond *Way*,
that which fhou'd have been done by the firft
Order of our Creation : This plain Doctrine
attended do, would fufficiently fhew us, that
the Flefh and Blood of *Eternal Life*, which
we are to receive from Chrift, muft be *that
Flefh and Blood* of Eternal Life which we loft
in *Adam*. Now, if we had received this immortal Flefh and Blood by our *Defcent* from
Adam, we muft in the Strictnefs of the Expreffion have been faid to partake of the Flefh
and Blood of *Adam* ; fo feeing we *now* receive
it from Chrift, we muft in the fame Strictnefs
of the Expreffion, be faid to be *real Partakers*
of the Flefh and Blood of Chrift, becaufe he

P 3

hath

hath the fame heavenly Flefh and Blood which *Adam* had, and for the *fame End* that *Adam* had it; namely, that it may come *by* and *through* him into us. And thus is this great Sacrament, which is a continual Part of our Chriftian Worfhip, a continual Communication to us of all the Benefits of our Second *Adam*; for in and by the Body and Blood of Chrift, to which the Divine Nature is united, we receive all that Life, Immortality, and Redemption, which Chrift, as living, fuffering, dying, rifing from the Dead, and afcending into Heaven, brought to Human Nature; fo that this great Myftery is that, in which all the Bleffings of our Redemption and new Life in Chrift are center'd. And they that hold a Sacrament fhort of *this Reality* of the true Body and Blood of Jefus Chrift, cannot be faid to hold that Sacrament of *Eternal Life,* which was inftituted by our Bleffed Lord and Saviour.

F I N I S.

SOME

ANIMADVERSIONS

UPON

Dr. *Trap*'s late REPLY.

HAD I the Spirit of an *Adverfary*,
or were inclined to find Entertain-
ment fot the *Satirical Reader*, it
wou'd not be eafy for me to over-
look the Opportunity which Dr. *Trap's* Reply
has put into my Hands; but as I don't want
to leffen any Appearance of Ability which the
Doctor has fhewn on this Occafion, or have
any Wifh that his *Pen* had not all its Advan-
tages; fo whatever *perfonally* concerns him,
either as a *Writer*, a *Scholar*, a *Difputant*, a
Divine, or a *Chriftian*, fhall have no Reflection
from me; and tho' by this means, fome fort
of Readers may be lefs pleafed, yet, the more
Chriftian Reader will be glad to find, that

thus

thus I muſt leave *two Thirds* of his Reply un-
touch'd ; and as I neither have, nor (by the
Grace of God) ever will have any *perſonal Con-*
tention with any Man whatever, ſo all the
Triumph which the Doctor has gained over me
by that Flow of Wrath and Contempt which
he has let looſe upon me, I ſhall leave him
quietly to enjoy.

It would be no Pleaſure to me, nor Benefit
to the World, to diſcover that *Malignity* of
Spirit, that *undiſtinguiſhing Head,* that *diaboli-*
cal Calumny, that *ſhameful Ignorance,* that *un-*
thinking Temper, that *blundering* Mind, that
perverſe Diſpoſition, that *indecent Sufficiency,*
that *unbecoming Preſumption,* that *nauſeous*
Dulneſs, that *Ignorance* of *Logic,* that *Inſenſi-*
bility of Argument, that Want of *Grammar,*
which he has ſo heartily laid to my Charge ;
and if he has any Readers that thank him for
this, I ſhall make no Attempt to leſſen their
Number.

As I deſire nothing for myſelf, or the Reader, but good *Eyes,* and a good *Heart,* ſeri-
ouſly attentive to Things uſeful and edifying,
and always open to the Light and Influence of
the Holy Spirit of God, ſo I ſhall endeavour to
ſay nothing but what is *ſuitable* to ſuch a State
of Mind, both in myſelf and the Reader.

The

The Doctor, by way of Plea for a certain Freedom in Drinking, had appeal'd to our Saviour's Miracle at the Marriage Feast, where he turn'd Water into Wine, *at a Time* when the Guests had already drank enough, and *had indulg'd something to Pleasure and Chearfulness.* Therefore more Wine, or a Continuance of Drinking, when Man have *already indulged something to Pleasure and Chearfulness,* has Authority from our Saviour's Conduct at the Feast.

One would imagine no one need be help'd to look with a just Indignation at this Abuse and Prophanation of our Lord's Miracle. Did the Saviour, of the World *mean,* or *intend* to teach any Thing like this in what he did ? Was this the *Spirit* of his Mind when he *thus tim'd* this Miracle, did he intend to convey *this Instruction* to them ? Now, if our Lord had not this Spirit, did not mean *thus* to instruct the Feasters by thus *timing* his Miracle, Is it not a great Profanation of it to appeal to it for that Instruction, which was not meant or intended by it ? Had any one of those *Guests* then present, come up to our Lord and said, Sir, we have heard indeed a Report that you require a Man to deny himself, to hate even his own Life in this World, and to forsake all that he hath in

order

order to be your Difciple, but now we per-
ceive, not by Words, but by your *miraculous
Actions*, that you are *no Enemy* to thefe kind of
Pleafures and Indulgences, fince you have
work'd a Miracle to help us to *more Wine,*
when we had already drank enough, and had
indulged fomething to Pleafure and Chearfulnefs.
What would our Lord have faid to fo fagacious
an Obferver ? Would he have told him, that
Flefh and Blood had not revealed fo great a
Truth unto him ? Would he have acquiefced in
the *Propriety* and *Juftnefs* of his Obfervation,
and pronounced him rightly *difpofed* to by one
of his Difciples ? But if fuch an Obfervation
could not have been approv'd by our Lord as a
Sign of a good Mind, how is the Doctor to be
excufed, who not only looks *thus* at it himfelf,
but propofes it to the World to be confidered
in *that View ?* In order to vindicate our Saviour's Conduct in this Matter, I ventur'd, without any Help from *Commentators* or *Schoolmen,*
to tell the Doctor, " That the Wine here fpo-
" ken of, was not *common Wine,* and there-
" fore had no Relation to our common Drink-
" ing——that it was not Wine from the Juice
" of the Grape——that it had nothing in it
" but what came from a heavenly Hand——
" that it muft have in it the *Purity* and *Vir-*

" tue

" *tue* of him that made it——that it had as
" good Qualities in it, and was fitted to have
" the fame Effect upon fome that drank it as
" the Clay which he moiften'd with his Spit-
" tle had upon the Eyes of the Blind——that
" it was Water only *fo alter'd,* and endued
" with fuch Qualities, as he pleafed to put in-
" to it ; and therefore we may be fure it was
" Water as *highly bleffed* for their Ufe as they
" were capable of ; we may be fure it was fit-
" ter to allay the Heat and Diforder of their
" Drinking, than if it had been Water *unal-*
" *ter'd* by our Saviour. How fuitable was this
" Miracle to a Feaft ? How worthy of fo di-
" vine a Perfon ! to make them cooler by giv-
" ing them Water made fitter for that Purpofe,
" and to raife their Faith by its miraculoufly
" feeming to be the beft of Wine.* "

Now how can it be prov'd that this Interpretation is not a true one, not a fafe one, not
a good one ? That our Saviour could do all this
which is here mention'd, that he could convert Water into a Wine of this Nature, is undeniable ; therefore if it had not this Nature
and Qualities in it, it could only be becaufe he
chofe to make it as bad as that Wine, which

has

* Serious Anfwer, &c. p. 48.

has the *Curse* of the Earth in it. But who will undertake to prove that Wine thus brought forth by a divine Power, muft have the *Nature* of Wine that is fqueez'd from the Grape under the *Curfe* of Sin?

The Doctor confutes my Interpretation, by calling it a *fenfelefs, impious, profane, ridiculous Noftrum, a Whimfy* of my own Brain, diluting *the glorious Miracle into nothing.* He has alfo accepted the Help of a learned *Affiftant*, one *Philoclericus,* who backs this Confutation by faying, that *it has evaporated the Miracle into nothing.* They both agree that I have brought it to nothing, and only differ in my manner of doing it. The one holds it to be by *Dilution*, and the other by *Evaporation.*

To fet this Matter therefore in a *clear Light*, let it be fuppos'd, that the *Ruler of the Feaft* fhould have come to our Saviour, and faid, Sir, having been furpriz'd at the extraordinary Difference between the laft Cup of Wine that was brought to me, and that which had been ufed in the Feaft before, I call'd the *Bridegroom* to tell him my Wonder at that extraordinary Wine which he had kept to the laft; but being fince inform'd by them that drew it, that this Wine was by thy *Word of Power* drawn from Veffels brim full of Water, I now come to fall

down

down before thee, and confefs that thou art
come from God, and haft given me a Wine
that has *not the Nature* of the earthly Grape in
it : But as God gave our Fathers *Manna* to eat,
which was juftly call'd *Angels Food*, and *Bread
from Heaven*, fo this Wine, which thou by a
divine Power has given us, muft be look'd upon, not as the *poor Juice* of the Grape, but as
Wine given us *from Heaven.*

Now had the Doctor and his *learned Affiftant* been there, and had been fuch Chriftians
as they are now, they muft both have fallen
upon the Ruler of the Feaft, as a *fenfelefs, impious, profane, ridiculous* Wretch, that had *dilu-
ted* and *evaporated* our Lord's glorious Miracle
into nothing : Though it was impoffible in the
Nature of the Thing, for all the Difciples of our
Lord, though ever fo full of Faith in him, to
make higher Profeffion of the *Reality* of this
glorious Miracle than the Ruler here has done;
and yet he has faid nothing but what is faid in
the Account which I have given of the Wine.
And indeed it muft be ftrangely abfurd for any
one to fuggeft, that the *Reality* of the Miracle
is hurt by this Account of the Wine. For is
not as great a divine Power requir'd to change
Water into a Wine, that has a *better Nature* and
Qualities than common Wine, as to make it
have

have no more Goodnefs and Virtue in it than
is in the *ordinary Juice* from the Grape ? Or is
it not rightly called Wine by thofe that drew
it, or by him that drank it, becaufe it was
Wine in Perfection, in fuch Perfection, as the
Grape could never give fince *Adam* brought
the Curfe into the World.

The Doctor fays, he *believes* it was juft the
fame fort of Wine as if it had been from the
Juice of the Grape, and his Reafon is, *becaufe
it is a Part of his Faith that our Saviour had
the Power of creating,* p. 56. Now this is the
very worft Reafon the Doctor could poffibly have
thought of. For the Doctor, I will venture
to fay, is fo orthodox a Schoolman as to hold
the common Notion of Creating, *viz.* that it
is a *Power of making fomething to be out of nothing.* But Wine thus created is the laft Thing
the Doctor fhould have had Recourfe to ; *firft,*
becaufe it is directly contrary to the Letter of
the Text, which exprefsly faith, the Water was
made Wine, therefore not a *created Wine.* Se-
condly, becaufe Wine fo created, could not
poffibly be *juft the fame Sort of Wine, as if it
had been from the Juice of the Grape,* becaufe
as the Grape and every earthly Thing ftands in
a State of Evil, Corruption, and Curfe through
the Sin of the fallen Creatures, it is abfolutely

impoffible

impoffible that any Thing *immediately* created by God *out of Nothing*, fhould have any Thing of that Evil, Corruption, or Curfe in it which Sin alone has brought into the Creatures.

The Truth of the Matter is, here was no more a *Creation* of Wine in this Miracle, than Wine is created *every Time* the Vine has ripe Grapes upon it. Water, together with Earth, is every Year turn'd into the Juice of the Grape by the Power of the Sun, from God's *eternal Word*, firft faying, *Let the Earth bring forth, the Fruit-tree yielding Fruit,* &c.

This fame *eternal*, ever *fpeaking*, ever *operating Word* of God, being become Man, could as well turn Water into Wine in a quicker Way by his own Power, as by the Help of the Vine once in a Year. Seeing therefore this Wine was not raifed from Water and Earth, according to the common Courfe of Vegetation in fallen Nature, but by the immediate Agency of the God of Nature upon Water alone, it is reafonable and abfolutely neceffary to fuppofe, that it was Wine very much freed from all that Evil, Wrath, and Curfe, which is infeparable from the *ordinary Workings* of the prefent State of Nature. Hence it appears, that the Interpretation here given, is fo far from being a profane,

fane, impious, fenfeleſs *Noſtrum*, is ſo far
from having any Thing of Force, or Fiction
in it, that it is the *firſt*, moſt *eaſy*, *natural*,
and *direct* Senſe, in which the Miracle can be
juſtly underſtood. And therefore every ſober
Chriſtian ought to reject the Doctor's Uſe of
this Miracle as inconſiſtent with Piety. Great
Intemperance, we all know, is carry'd on by
ſuch as pretend not to exceed the lawful Bounds
of Pleaſure and Indulgence. And is it conſiſt-
ent with Chriſtian Piety, or Prudence, to fur-
niſh ſuch People with a Pretext for what they
do, from our Saviour's Example and Conduct?
Or is he to be blam'd, who by a juſt, innocent, and ſafe Interpretation of the Miracle,
leaves ſuch People no Claim to its Authority?
Surely it is a ſad Miſtake to draw Arguments
for ſenſual Indulgence from him, who came to
teach and ſave the World by every Kind and
Degree of poſſible Self-denial.

But I ſhall add but one Argument more,
which is ſufficient of itſelf to ſhew how unjuſt-
ly the Doctor draws an Argument from our
Saviour's turning Water into Wine, when more
than was neceſſary had been already drank,
and *ſomething*, as he ſays, *had been indulged to
Pleaſure and Chearfulneſs*; and my Argument is
this : It is undeniably plain from the whole
Story

Story of this Matter, that there was no more
Water turn'd into Wine than that *one Cup*,
which was carry'd to the Ruler of the Feaſt,
and therefore neither Foundation nor Excuſe
for the Doctor's Argument from it.

. When the Veſſels were empty, our Lord ordered them to be filled, and to be filled up to
the Brim *with Water*. Such an Order as this
muſt, at leaſt in the Execution of it, draw the
Eyes and Attention of many that were preſent.
Not a Syllable is ever mention'd of any Wine
in the Veſſels ; they are only repreſented to us
as ſtanding brim-full of Water. Our Lord
only bids a Servant to draw from theſe Pots
thus full of Water, and what he drew and carry'd to the Ruler from Veſſels full of Water,
was ſuch Wine as ſtrangely ſurpriz'd him with
its peculiar Excellency. The Wine was only
found in that Cup into which our Saviour ordered the Servant to draw, and bear to the Ruler; and as he gave this Command but once,
ſo it is certain there was but this one Cup of
miraculous Wine. A haſty Reader, that has
his Eye upon the Increaſe of the Liquor, and
wants to have an Argument for his Purpoſe
from it, may hurry himſelf into a Fancy, that
our Saviour made all the Water Pots ſtand
brim-full of Wine. But the Story itſelf plainly repreſents quite another Matter, and is only

Q

a Rea Relation of *one Cup* of miraculous Wine, The Care that our Lord took, that all the Veffels fhould be fill'd with Water up to the Top, was not, that the Guefts might have all the Wine thefe Veffels could hold, but that all the Veffels being filled up to the Top, and made vifible to all Beholders, might be fo many plain Proofs that the Wine which he ordered to be drawn, could only be drawn from one of thofe Veffels which fo many Beholders faw to be brim-full of Water, both before and after the Drawing of the Cup of Wine. And herein lay the Strength, and Certainty, and Glory of the Miracle ; that fo many Witneffes were forced to fee and own, that by the Word of our Lord, Wine was drawn from Pots juft fill'd, and ftill remaining full to the Top with Water. And when this Miracle had thus inconteftably manifefted itfelf, the whole Affair was over, and the Guefts were left, not to rejoice over full Pots of Water turn'd into Wine, but to make fober Reflections upon the Divinity of that Perfon, who had put fuch an aftonifhing End to their Drinking. Great and holy Jefus ! How like thyfelf, the Saviour of the World, haft thou acted at this Feaft ! How couldft thou more fink the Value, extinguifh the Defire, fuppreff all Thoughts of Pleafure and Indulgence in earthly Wine, than by fhew-

ing

ing the Feasters, that from the pooreſt of the Elements thou couldſt call forth ſuch Wine as no Grape could give? How couldſt thou more effectually take from them their ſenſual Joy, or more powerfully call them to deny themſelves and come after thee, than by thus miraculouſly ſhewing them, that the richeſt Delights of ſenſual Gratifications were far ſhort of what thou couldſt give to thoſe, that would leave all earthly Delights for thee.

The next Thing of Importance which I ſhall ſpeak to, ſhall be with Regard to what I have ſaid to the Clergy. The miſerable State of Religion, and the great Corruption of Manners, ſo inconteſtably apparent in this Iſland, gave me a juſt Occaſion to deſire all the Clergy, from the higheſt to the loweſt in the Order, to conſider their Conduct, and ſee how free they were from the common Corruption, and how juſtly every one could clear himſelf from having any Share in this general Depravity of Manners. I was not inſenſible that this was a dangerous Attempt, that would expoſe me to the Reſentment of not a few of my Brethren: But as I wrote for no other End but to do as much Good as I could to thoſe who were capable of it, ſo I had no Care but how to ſpeak diſagreeable Truths, in as Chriſtian and inoffenſive a manner as I could; how I have ſucceed-

ed

ed in this, is left to the World to judge. And
as it is but too apparent, that the *Root* of all
the Evil, which but too much fpreads itfelf
through the whole Body of the Clergy, is
owing to a *worldly*, *trading* Spirit, too vifible
from the Top to the Bottom of the Order, fo
I pointed at it in the fofteft and moft affecting
manner that I could, in the following Words,
grounded on a plain Apoftolical Doctrine and
Practice.

St. *Paul*, I had obferv'd, had faid, it was
lawful for thofe that preach the Gofpel to live
by the Gofpel, and yet makes it Matter of the
greateft Joy and Comfort to himfelf that he
had wholly abftain'd from this *lawful Thing*;
and declares, it were better for him to dye
than that *this* Rejoicing fhould be taken from
him. He appeals to his daily and nightly
working with his own Hands, that fo he might
preach the Gofpel *freely*, and not be chargeable
to thofe that heard him. And this he faid he
did, not for want of Authority to do otherwife,
but that he might make himfelf an Enfample
unto them to follow him. Here, I fay,
" What fine and awakening Inftructions are
" here given to us of the *Clergy*, in a practi-
" cal Matter of the greateft Moment? How
" ought every one to be frighted at the
" Thoughts

" Thoughts of defiring or feeking a *fecond Liv-*
" *ing,* or of rejoicing at *great Pay* where there
" is but *little Duty,* when the Apoftle's *rejoi-*
" *cing* confifted in *this,* that he had paffed
" through all the Fatigues and Perils of preach-
" ing the Gofpel without any Pay at all ?
" How cautious, nay, how fearful ought we
" to be, of going fo far as the fecular Laws
" permit us, when the Apoftle thought it
" more defirable to lofe his Life, than to go fo
" far as the very Law of the Gofpel would
" have fuffer'd him ?

" It is looked upon as lawful to get feveral
" Preferments, and to make a Gain of the
" Gofpel, by hiring others to do Duty for us
" at a lower Rate. ——— It is look'd upon as
" lawful to quit a *Cure* of Souls of a fmall In-
" come, for *no other* Reafon, but becaufe we
" can get another of a greater.———It is look'd
" upon as lawful for a Clergyman to take the
" Revenues of the Church, which he ferves, to
" his *own Ufe,* though he has more than a fuf-
" ficient Competency of his own, and much
" more than the Apoftle could get by his La-
" bour. ——— It is look'd upon as lawful for
" the Clergy to live in State and Equipage, to
" buy Purple and fine Linnen out of the Re-
" venues of the Church.———It is look'd upon

" as

" as lawful for Clergymen to enrich their Fa-
" milies, to bring up their Children in the fa-
" shionable Vanities, and corrupting Methods
" of a worldly and expensive Life, by Money
" got by preaching the Gospel of Jesus Christ.
" But now, supposing all this to be *lawful*,
" what Comfort and Joy might we treasure
" up to ourselves, what Glory and Honour
" might we bring to Religion, what Force
" and Power might we give to the Gospel,
" what Benefit and Edification should we do
" to our Neighbour, if we *wholly* abstain'd
" from all these lawful Things ? Not by work-
" ing Day and Night with our own Hands,
" as the great Apostle did, but by limiting our
" Wants and Desires according to the plain
" Demands of Nature, and a religious Self-
" Denial."

Now, there are but two possible ways of
justly replying to this ; *first*, either by shewing
that these Observations are falsely drawn from
the Apostle's Doctrine and Practice, that I have
mistaken the Spirit of St. *Paul*, and the Genius of the Gospel, that I am here doing what
the Apostle would not do, was he here in Person; and representing such Things as Corruptions, which the Apostle would be glad to see
flourishing in the Church of Christ: Or, *se-*
condly

condly, that tho' thefe Things are plainly con-
demnable from the Apoftle's Doctrine and
Practice, yet they are not chargeable upon the
Spirit, Temper and Practice of the Clergy of
this Land. Now, tho' not a Word to the
Purpofe could poffibly be faid, but by one
of thefe two Ways, yet the Doctor fhuts his
Eyes to both of them, and then pronounc'd
the following Sentence upon Me, *That a Qua-
ker, or Infidel, could not well have reflected with
more Virulency upon the Clergy of our Church,
then I have done in thefe Expreffions.*

Muft I then fuppofe, that the Doctor in his
Sermons, never mentions any Failings that concerns his Auditors, or lays before them any of
their unchriftian Ways of Life? If he does, I
defire to know how he clears himfelf from *vi-
rulently* reflecting upon them and their Chriftianity? The *Quakers,* and *Infidels,* are ready
enough, and able enough to fhew, that moft
Congregations of Chriftians are fadly fallen
away from the Religion of the Gofpel; and
does the Doctor forbear this Charge, is he
afham'd to call his Flock to a more Chriftian
Life, or afraid to remind them of their Departure from the Gofpel, left he fhould feem to
join with Quakers and Infidels, who make
great Complaints of the Corruptions of Chri-

Q 4   ftians?

ftians ? Or, how can the Doctor defire to be
thought to have any *true Love*, or *juſt Eſteem*
for thofe Chriſtians, whom he is fo often re-
minding of the Corruption and Depravity of
their Manners, fo contrary to the Religion of
Jefus Chriſt ? Now, if the Doctor knows
how to untye this *Knot*, and to extricate himfelf from the Charge of *virulent reflecting* upon his Pariſhioners, as *Quakers* and *Infidels* do,
then he has diſſolved his Charge againſt me
into a mere nothing.

If it was a Thing required of me, I know
no more how to raife in myfelf the leaft Spark
of Rancour, or Ill-will towards the Clergy, as
fuch, than I know how to work myfelf up
into a Hatred of the Light of the Sun. It is
as natural to me, to wiſh them all their Perfection, as to wiſh Peace and Happineſs to
myfelf both here and hereafter ; and when I
point at any Failings in their Conduct, it is
only with fuch a Spirit as I would pluck a
Brother out of the Fire.

In that Part of my *Anfwer*, which is ad-
drefs'd to the younger Clergy, I faid, " Lay
" this down for an infallible Principle ; that
" an entire, abfolute Renunciation of all
" worldly *Intereſt*, is the only poſſible Foun-
" dation of that exalted Virtue, which your
" Station

" Station requires; without this, all Attempts
" after an exemplary Piety are in vain :
" *(and then, by way of Limitation and*
" *Explication of this, it thus immediately fol-*
" *lows :)* If you want any Thing from the
" World by way of *Figure* and *Exaltation,*
" you fhut the Power of your Redeemer out
" of your own Souls, and inftead of convert-
" ing, you corrupt the Hearts of thofe that
" are about you. Deteft therefore, with the
" *utmoft Abhorrence,* all Defires of making
" your Fortunes, either by *Perferments,* or
" *rich Marriages,* and let it be your only Am-
" bition, to ftand at the *Top* of every Virtue,
" as vifible Guides and Paterns to all that af-
" pire after the Perfection of Holinefs," *p.* 61.

Now, one would imagine there was no Part
of the Chriftian World, however corrupted by
Divifion, where this Doctrine would not be
admitted at leaft in Theory ; or, that the Gofpel of Chrift fhould be thought to be reproached, where fuch Advice as this was given
to young Divines : And yet it is of this very
Advice, that Dr. *Trap* fays, he *hopes they* will
have more *Grace* and Senfe *than to follow it :*
That it is *falfe Doctrine, tending to the Reproach and Scandal of the Chriftian Religion,*
p. 87.

Is

Is it then come to this, that unless young Divines chuse to serve *Mammon* as well as God, their Profeffion is a renouncing of *Grace* and *Senfe*, and a *Reproach to Religion*? And muft they that pretend to act in Chrift's Name, as Succeffors in his Office, take Care that they renounce not the Politicks of the Kingdom of this World? For my part, I thought it as fafe, as Chriftian, as confiftent with the Honour of the Gospel, to give this Advice: thus to fupprefs all worldly Views, as to refift all the Temptations of the Devil.

Had *Martin Luther*, when he gave his Reafons and Motives for withdrawing from Communion with the *Pope*, been able to have added this; that the *Advice* here given, had been formally condemn'd by the *Pope* in a great Council, the Defenders of that Church would have found it as hard to have made fuch a *Decree* confiftent with the Gospel, as the felling of Indulgencies: And it may well be fuppofed, that no Proteftant Writer, when fetting forth the *Marks* of Antichrift, and the *Beaft* in that Church, would have forgot to have made this *Condemnation* to be one of them.

For who can fhew it to be fo contrary to the whole Spirit of the Gospel, to call in the

Affiftance

Affiftance of the Saints, or to deny the *Cup* to the Laity in the Manner the Church of *Rome* does, who can fhew this to put fo entire a Stop to the Salvation by the Gofpel, as to condemn the *Advice* here given to young Divines as a Scandal and Reproach to Chriftianity ? For all the Ends and Defigns of the Gofpel may be purfued, and Men may arife out of the Corruption of their Nature, notwithftanding thefe two Miftakes : But to condemn it as an Error inconfiftent with *Grace* and *Senfe*, a Scandal and Reproach to Chriftianity, for young Divines to renounce worldly Views, and devote themfelves wholly to God, is ftriking at the whole Root of all Holinefs of Life, and no lefs than a Denial of the whole Spirit of the Gofpel.

Our Church requires all its Candidates for Holy Orders, to make Profeffion of their being mov'd and called by the Holy Ghoft to enter into the Service of the Church : This, I fhould think, is Proof enough, that the Spirit of this World ought not to be alive in them, when they make this Profeffion ; and yet, if any young Perfons fhould come to be ordain'd, thus dead to all wordly Views, thus wholly devoted to God, as I have here recommended, they ought, according to the Doctor, to be rejected

jected by the Bishop, as being led by a Spirit that has lost all *Grace* and *Sense*, and is a *Scandal* and *Reproach* to the Christian Religion.

It is needless to quote particular Texts of Scripture, teaching the same that I have here taught; as, that our Saviour assures us, that we *cannot serve God and Mammon :* That St. *Paul* requires us, *having Food and Raiment, to be therewith content*, for this Reason, *because they that will be rich, fall into divers Temptations of the Devil :* That St. *John* forbids us to *love the World, or the Things of the World,* for this Reason, because all that is in the World, the *Lust of the Flesh, the Lust of the Eyes, and the Pride of Life, is not of the Father, but is of the World.* It is needless to have Recourse to particular Texts of this kind, because the whole Nature and Reason of our Redemption is a standing, plain Proof of the same Thing; for we want to be redeemed for no other Reason, but because we are born Children of this World, and have by Nature only the Life, Spirit and Temper of this World in us : This is our Fall, our Curse, our Separation from God ; and therefore we can have no Redemption, but by a Renunciation of all the Workings of the Life of this World in us, by a total dying to, and denying ourselves ; because all that we are,

as

as to our State, Spirit and Life in this World, is a Life that carries us from God, a Life that should not have been raised up in us; 'tis a Life begun by the Fall, a Life of Sin and Corruption, which cannot enter into Heaven. The Life that we have in this World, from the Fall of *Adam*, is not to be *naturally* destroyed or murder'd, nor are the Necessaries and Conveniencies of Life to be rejected, nor is any one to renounce his Share in the Employments that are necessary and useful to Social Life. The Renunciation of this World reaches no farther than the renouncing the Spirit, Temper, and Inclinations of this worldly Life : We may stand in our Stations, when we stand in them as the Servants of God, as Citizens of the new *Jerusalem*, who have amongst earthly Things, our Conversation in Heaven : We may keep our Possessions, when we possess them as the Things of God, and use them not as Nature, but as the Spirit directs us; when we do thus, we have the Poverty of Spirit, which the Gospel requires, and come up to the very Letter of that Command given to the young Man, *to sell all that he had, and give to the Poor.*

But now, if our natural Life in this World, is a corrupt, impure, disorderly, bestial, diabolical

bolical Life brought forth by the *Fall*, if we
want to be redeemed becaufe we have this State
of Life in and from this World, if we want
to be born again of the Son of God, born
again of the Holy Spirit, becaufe our natural
Birth is according to the Spirit of this World;
if nothing of the Beaft, or the Devil, no kind
or degree of Selfifhnefs, Envy, Pride and Vanity can enter into the Kingdom of God, then
it is plain from the Nature of the Thing, that
all Religion which leaves this Nature alive and
unrenounced, which lets Selfifhnefs, Pride,
Wrath, and Vanity fubfift in us, which bring
us to our Graves in the fame Nature in which
we were born, is not the Religion that can fave
us. If this Nature in all its moft fecret Workings
is not renounc'd and deny'd, it matters not
what we are, or what we have been doing,
it fignifies little in what Chair we have fat,
whether in *Italy*, or *England*, how long we
have been Preachers, how many Hereticks and
Schifmaticks we have oppofed, or how many
Books we have written in Defence of Orthodoxy; it is as vain to appeal to this, as to
our having preached and *prophefy'd* in the
Name of Chrift, in the Streets and Fields:
For if this Nature is allowed to live in us, all
our good Works have been govern'd by it,
they

they have sprung from *Selfishness*, are animated
with Pride, and only serve to gratify our own
natural Passions. When therefore the Doctor
calls upon young Divines to have *more Grace
and Sense* than to be driven from Thoughts of
advancing themselves by *Preferments and rich
Marriages*, he would do well to confider, how
little short this is of calling them to break their
very Baptifmal Vow, of *renouncing the Pomps
and Vanities of the World*. And if young Candidates for Holy Orders, looking only at their
Baptifmal Vow, fhould be led into this Degree
of Self-denial and Detachment from the World,
does the Doctor think, that the Apoftles, from
whom this Baptifmal Vow is defcended, will
rife up in the Day of Judgment, and condemn fuch grofs Ignorance and Abufe of it?
Does he think, that there are any departed
Saints that will join with him in faying, that
fuch a Spirit is a *Scandal* and *Reproach* to the
Gofpel? What more favourable Difpofition
could the Adverfary of Mankind wifh to fee,
either in young or old Divines, than a wanting
and defiring to have Figure in the World,
either by Preferments or rich Marriages?
Would he find it difficult to enter into thofe
Hearts, where the Luft of the Flefh, the Luft
of the Eyes, and the Pride of Life had thus
entered?

enter'd ? Or would he look upon fuch as but half fitted for him, in Comparifon of thofe who enter'd into holy Orders in a Spirit of Self-denial, and Renunciation of the Pomps and Vanities of the World ? Does the Doctor think that thefe grofs Inftances of worldly Ambition have no Affinity with thofe Pomps and Vanities, which muft be renounced' in Baptifm ?

John the *Baptift* was but the Preparer of the Way for evangelical Purity of Life ; but does the Doctor think that if the *Baptift* was now to come amongft us, as fome have thought he will come again before the End of the Church, that he would look at Things as the Doctor does, that he would fee fuch Perfections and fuch Corruptions, fuch Orthodoxy and fuch Enthufiafm as the Doctor fees ; that this *burning and fhining Light* would fee no *Generation of Vipers* but where the Doctor fees them ; that he would preach no where but in Churches ; that he would fpare no Clergy, nor any Church, but that which is eftablifh'd in this Ifland ; that he would complain of the Hardfhips of our Clergy, and the fuffering Spirit which they are forced to practife, as the Doctor does ; that he would plead for a prieftly Liberty of coveting Preferments and rich Marriages, as the Doctor doth ;

doth, that he would condemn the *Treatife upon Chriftian Perfection* amongft the *moft pernicious Books* of the Age, that he would recommend *Wharton's Defenfe of Pluralities,* and the
Doctor's Difcourfe of the *Folly, Sin, and Danger of being righteous over-much,* as the true
Fruits of that Spirit which firft preach'd the
Gofpel? He that can believe this, muft believe
that the Baptift was come to confefs the Errors and Miftakes of his firft Appearance in
the World.

I fhall therefore proceed to tell young Divines, that a total Renunciation of the Spirit,
Temper, and Inclinations of this Life, is the
one Thing neceffary to confecrate them to their
holy Office; that, as fure as the Church of
Chrift is not a Kingdom of this World, as fure
as Jefus Chrift came to deliver us from this evil
World, as fure as he requires us to be born a-
gain from above, to hate even our own Life
in this World, and to forfake all and follow
him, fo fure is it that no one has the *Call* of
the Holy Spirit to the Miniftry of the Gofpel,
nor the leaft Ground of hoping to be led and
govern'd by it in his Miniftry, till he at leaft
prays, defires, and heartily endeavours to have
all that Difregard of worldly Profperity, Figure, and Diftinction, which the Spirit of Je-

R.   fus

fus Chrift, the Maxims of the Gofpel, and the
Practice of the Apoftles fet before him. Till
this Renunciation of the World is made, we cannot enter into the Miniftry at its *own Door*,
but, like Thieves and Robbers, climb over its
Walls; and then it will be no Wonder if we
do no more Good to the Church than Thieves
do the Houfe they break open and plunder. If
a young Minifter wants to act the Part, and
have the Appearance of a fine Gentleman, to
go on in the common Spirit of the World, to
cover a fecular Spirit with an ecclefiaftick Garb,
and make his Fortunes in the Church, he muft
be told, that it is much fafer to be a *Publican*
and a *Sinner*, than to be a *Trader* in fpiritual
Things; that he who with unfanctify'd Hands
attends at the Altar, is farther from the Kingdom of God, than he who has not yet made
one Step towards it.

Covetoufnefs is *Idolatry*; it is a heathenifh,
Antichriftian Vice, tho' only trafficking in
worldly Matters; but when it takes Poffeffion
of the Altar, and makes a Trade of the Myfteries of Salvation, and turns Godlinefs into
Gain, it has a Blacknefs of Vice and Depravity
which much exceeds that of the worldly Mi-
fer. The Spirit of an Ecclefiaftick fhould be
the Spirit of Heaven, knowing nothing of this
World,

World, but how to efcape its Snares and
Temptations, burning in the Love of God,
and holding out Light and Direction to all
that afpire after every Perfection of the Chriftian Life.

'Tis too commonly thought, that when a
young Student has taken his Degree, and fhewn
fome Signs of a Genius for Learning, that he
is well prepared to enter into the Service of the
Church. But alas ! all the Accomplifhments
of human Learning are but the Ornaments of
the *Old Man*, which leave the Soul in its Slavery to Sin, full of all the Diforders and Corruptions of the fallen Nature, and under the
Blindnefs and Perverfenefs of fome of Paffions. If it were not thus, how could the Errors of all Churches have the *greateft* Scholars
for their *Champions ?* All the learned Catholick
World is amazed at the Prejudice, the Blindnefs, the Perverfenefs, the Partiality, the
Weaknefs, the Sophiftry, the Unfairnefs of
Proteftant Critics. All the Proteftant World is
in the fame Degree of Wonder at the fame
Diforders in *Catholick Difputants.* Is not this
a Demonftration of the *Nature, Power,* and
Place of human Learning ? Of its great Ufefulnefs and Benefit to Religion ? Does not this
enough fhew, that it is the Effect and Offspring

of

of the old Man, has his Nature and Qualities, dwells in him, and is govern'd by him? Is not this a Demonſtration, that the *greateſt Degrees* of hiſtorical, verbal, critical Knowledge are no real Hindrance of ſpiritual Blindneſs? Is not this a Demonſtration, that human Learning is as different from divine Light as Heaven is from Earth, the new from the old Man; and that conſidered in itſelf, it leaves us in our firſt State of Slavery to blind and corrupt Paſſions? Now nothing can deliver a Man from this State, but a Spirit born into him from a-bove, a Light from the Spirit of God derived into his Soul, which alone can bring forth a *new Man* created in Chriſt Jeſus. Nothing can make way for this new Birth from above, but a total Renunciation and Dying to all that we are by our natural Birth in this World. 'Tis only *this Separation* from Things below, that can make us Partakers of the Truth and Light that comes from above. Take away *all Selfiſhneſs* from the Papiſt and the Proteſtant, or let them both be dead to the Workings of this Spirit, and then they will be as fully a-greed about Goſpel Truths, as they are in the Form of a *Square* and a *Circle*. For nothing ſtands in the way of divine Truth, or hinders its plain and full Entrance into us, but this *Par-tiality*

tiality or *Selfishness*, which adheres to every one who does not make it his first Maxim, Prayer, and Endeavour to dye to, and deny himself in all the Tempers and Inclinations of our fallen Nature. This Self-denial is the continual Doctrine of our Lord; it is by him made the Beginning of all Conversion to God, and he that cannot, or will not begin there, can make no Beginning of that Life, Light, and Salvation to which he is called in Christ Jesus: Therefore he that offers himself for holy Orders, without this Spirit of Self-denial, is a miserable Intruder into the Mysteries of Salvation; he only hardens and fixes himself in the Corruptions of his own Nature, and instead of becoming an Instrument of saving others, his very Office makes his own Salvation more dangerous.

I doubt not but some will here charge me with pleading for Poverty in the Ministry, and with Enmity to that Maintenance which they have both from the Law and the Gospel. But this is so far from being true, that I wish every good Minister, whom the Spirit of God has called to his Office, and governs in it, had much more of this World's Goods than are needful for his own reasonable Subsistence; because it is certain, that such a one's Money would all be put into the *Poor's Bag*, and he would as gladly and liberally administer to their temporal as to their spiritual Necessities. I write against nothing but *Avarice*, *Selfishness*, *Pride*, and *Ambition*, and the making the Provisions of the Church *subservient* to these Tempers. A Provision arising from the Gospel, is *consecrated* by the Gospel, and is profaned by being touch'd and used by a worldly Spirit. And he who turns this Provision of the Gospel into a Support and Gratification of worldly Passions, sins against the Nature and Law of the Gospel more than he that pays his Tithes with Reluctance.

I can easily believe there are Clergy in this Land, who labour in the Gospel, without having a sufficient Subsistence from it; but if much of this Evil was to be charged upon *Pluralities*, *Commendams*, and such like spiritual Trading, there would be no Injustice in it. And if the inferior Clergy had their Labours only undervalued by the Laity, they would be in much better Condition than they are.

When it is complain'd by what shameful *Qualifications*, empty *Titles*, and unworthy Pretences, Numbers of Persons get *loaded* and *dignified* with Variety of Preferments; it is answered, in Excuse of this great Evil, That if

Pre-

Preferments might not be thus crowded together, great *Learning*, diftinguifh'd *Abilities*,
and eminent *Labours* for the Service of Religion, muft go unrewarded.

As this Anfwer is not fetch'd from the Gofpel, or the Primitive Church, fo I fhall fhew,
that it is as little fupported by Reafon. For if
this great Learning is truly Gofpel Learning, if
this eminent Labour is truly pious Labour,
what State of Life can fo little want to be rewarded ? How can Imagination itfelf place a
Man more *above* the Thoughts and Defires of
worldly Advancement ? If fuch a one is full of
the Light and Spirit of the Gofpel, if his Labours have been like thofe of an Apoftle, muft
he not like an Apoftle be *dead* to the World ?
Can fuch a one look upon his Labour as a
Hardfhip, becaufe it has left him as *low*, and as
far from the *Pomp* of the World as it found
him ? Can he repine becaufe the Gofpel has not
prov'd a good *worldly Bargain* to him ? If the
Spirit of God has begun, and directed all his
Labours, animated all his Studies and Defigns,
can fuch a one think it hard, that he has not
by fuch Labours purchafed to himfelf a Share
in the State and Pride of Human Life ?

If by a *great Divine*, is only meant a Perfon well fkill'd in *Critical Contention*, who can

artfully

artfully, plaufibly, fcholaftically defend a Set
of Notions, amongft which he happened to be
born, and bred, fuch a Divine, I own, may
be very *impatient*, and *much cool'd* in his Zeal,
unlefs he finds himfelf well rewarded; but if
an eminent Divine is to be underftood in a
Senfe fuitable to the Gofpel, he is that *particular Perfon* that muft needs have the
greateft *Contempt* and *Diflike* of every Thing,
that has but the *Appearance* of the Pomp and
Vanity of this World in it. If therefore it
was urged, that this Conjunction of Preferments and dignifying Rewards was neceffary
to bring *ambitious Scholars* into the Church, or
to keep them in it, there would be fome Senfe,
tho' no Gofpel in the Pretence; but to talk of
them as neceffary to be the Rewards of eminent Piety and Apoftolick Labour, is as abfurd, as to fay, that thofe who have truly put
on Chrift, who ftand in the higheft Degree of
a renewed Nature, who beft know and feel the
Bleffing of a mortify'd, heavenly Spirit, have lefs
Reafon to be *content with Food and Raiment*, than
thofe who ftand in a lower Degree of the Chriftian Life; 'tis faying, that a *Bifhop*, becaufe
having moft of the *Spirit* and *Office* of an
Apoftle in him, may well defire more of the
Pride and *Figure* of this World, than the
lower

lower Clergy, who have lefs of the Apoftolical Spirit and Perfection in them.

To want to ftand in fome Degree of worldly Figure, is the State of a *Babe* in the Chriftian Life, that hath hardly tafted the Milk of
Evangelical Nourifhment, and therefore can
no way become thofe, who are to lead and
compel others to the Perfection and Fulnefs
of the Stature in Chrift Jefus.

A *great Divine* is but a *cant* Expreffion, unlefs it fignifies a Man *greatly advanced* in the
Divine Life, whofe own Experience and Example is a Demonftration of the *Reality* of all
the Graces and Virtues of the Gofpel. No
Divine has any more of the Gofpel in him,
than that which proves itfelf by the Spirit,
Actions, and Form of his Life, the reft is but
Hypocrify, not Theology : If therefore Poverty of Spirit, a Difregard of worldly Figure, a
total Self-denial is any Part of the Gofpel, an
eminent Divine, or one advanced in the Spirit
and Life of Jefus, can have no Wifh with regard to the Figure, Pride and Pomp of this
Life, but to be placed out of every Appearance
of it : And if the firft and higheft in Divine
Knowledge are not the foremoft in Poverty of
Spirit, and the outward Humility of Chrift
and his Apoftles ; if eminent Divines want and
desire

defire to have a Dignity of worldly Figure, to have Refpect by any other Means than by the Divine Virtues and Graces of an Evangelical Spirit and Converfation, and are not content with all the Contempt that fuch a Life can expofe them to, they may be *great Scholars*, but they are *little Divines*, and muft be thought to be much wanting in that which is the chief Part of the Minifters of Jefus Chrift. But to proceed:

The next Thing I faid to the young Clergy, was this; " Confider yourfelves *menely* as the " Meffengers of God, that are fent into the " World *folely* on his Errand; and think it " Happinefs enough that you are called to the " fame Bufinefs for which the Son of God " was born into the World," *p.* 81.

Now, I thought what I *here* faid, was as unexceptionable, as pious, as unfit to be condemn'd by a Profeffor of Chriftian Theology, as if I had only recommended the loving of God with all our Heart and Soul, and Mind and Strength; and that if any Clergyman diflik'd it, he would be forced to keep his Diflike to himfelf: But the Doctor is very open in his Indignation at it; the fame Anfwer, he fays, is to be given here, as before, *viz. that it is*

falfe

falſe Doctrine, tending to the Scandal and Re-
proach of the Chriſtian Religion.

Our Bleſſed Lord, when he ſent the firſt
Preachers of the Goſpel into the World, ſaid
unto them, *As my Father hath ſent me, ſo ſend*
I you———*go ye and teach all Nations*———*and lo*
I am with you to the End of the World. Now
let it be ſuppoſed, that theſe firſt Preachers of
the Goſpel fully believed, that from the Time
of their Appointment to this high Office, they
were to conſider themſelves merely as the Meſſengers
of God, ſent into the World ſolely on his Errand,
and that *it was Happineſs enough for them to be*
called to that Buſineſs, for which *the Son* of God
was born into the World ; if they had this Belief,
what follows ? Why, according to the Doctor,
it follows, that they ſet out from the very firſt
in one of the greateſt Errors, had miſtaken
the Nature and Intent of their Miſſion, and
had gone into the World upon a Principle that
was falſe in itſelf, and *ſcandalous* and *reproachful*
to the Chriſtian Religion.

But if this Belief is not to be condemn'd
in the firſt Clergy, as a falſe Opinion of their
Office, ſcandalous and reproachful to the Chriſtian Religion, I deſire to know why thoſe
Clergy, who claim their Succeſſion from the
firſt, and expect the Preſence of Chriſt in and
with

with their Miniſtry, are not to be called upon
to be of the ſame Spirit and Belief with the
firſt of their Order; or how it can be a Scandal
to the Goſpel, for the modern Clergy to be as
wholly devoted to the Service of God, as the
Apoſtles were: Surely there is ſomething ſo ex-
travagant in the Doctor's Condemnation of the
Advice here given to young Divines, as muſt
ſhock even the common Reader; and if it
could be ſuppoſed, that there are others amongſt
the learned Clergy, who are in this like mind-
ed with the Doctor, and glad to ſee this Advice condemn'd in this manner, if it could be
ſuppoſed, that there are not Numbers amongſt
them of Rank and Eminence that want and
deſire to bear their Teſtimony againſt it, have
we not too much Reaſon to fear that, which
God threatened to the Angel of the Church at
Ephesus, namely, *the Removal of our Candleſtick
out of its Place.*

The Doctor ſets it out as an extraordinary
Preſumption in *ſuch a Man* as I am, to pretend
to give Advice to young Divines, when it is ſo
ſufficiently done already by the *Offices of our
Church, the Charges, Inſtructions and Exhorta-
tions of our Biſhops at their Viſitation, and ſo
many excellent Ordination and Viſitation Sermons*, p. 87. Now, granting the Plenty and
Excellency

Excellency of all thefe, yet I have fome hope, that my Prefumption may be found to be only like that of the *poor Widow*, who after fo many rich Oblations of great People, *prefum'd* to put her little *Mite* into the Treafury. And if it be true, that the Things here fuggefted by me, are only fuch as have been already fully fet forth by fo many great Bifhops and excellent Preachers, how will the Doctor come off for condemning it, as falfe Doctrine, fcandalous, and *reproachful* to the Chriftian Religion ?

Dr. *Trap* gives a Reafon for his condemning this Advice, which is thus expreffed : *It is,* fays he, *falfe to fay, that Clergymen ought to mind nothing, in any Degree, but their Profeffion and Duty, as Clergymen ; they are Hufbands, Parents, Men, as well as Clergymen, and muft in fome meafure be concerned in the Affairs of the World,* p. 88.

Part of this I own to be very true, *viz.* that they are Men, and have the Wants of Human Nature which muft be fupplied ; and for a full Proof of this, the Doctor might have juftly appeal'd to St. *Paul*, who, tho' miraculoufly called to be an Apoftle, and feparated from the World to be *merely* a Meffenger and Apoftle of Jefus Chrift ; yet, after this high Apoftlefhip, work'd at his *Trade*, and often

fpent

ſpent ſome Part of the Day and the Night in making Tents : Therefore, if all thoſe whom I have exhorted to conſider themſelves as ſo highly ſet apart for the ſole Service of God, ſhould ſhew ſuch a Degree of worldly Care as St. *Paul* did, when he work'd at his Trade, they might yet juſtly be ſaid to act ſuitably to their Station, as the Miniſters of God, that are wholly devoted to his Service ; for if they ſhould refuſe to live, how could it be their Deſire to live wholly to the Service of God ; or, who can ſay that St. *Paul* departed from his Character, as a Miniſter of God, when he laboured with his own Hands, that he might glorioully and freely preach the Goſpel ? For it was for the Sake of the Goſpel, to promote and recommend the Goſpel, to make his Preaching the more ſucceſsful ; it was to ſhew that he had fully renounc'd the World, deſir'd nothing from it, but for the Glory and Love of God, would preach Salvation *freely* to the World : And thus have all the Miniſters of the Goſpel an Example in St. *Paul,* how they may make their *Care* of a Livelihood a *Part* of their Service to God.

But, when the Doctor ſays, that Clergymen are *Huſbands* and *Parents*, I muſt object a little ; becauſe no Scripture, or Antiquity ſhews

me,

me, that thefe Characters muſt belong to a
Preacher of the Goſpel; and therefore, when
a Clergyman excuſes himſelf from any Heights
of the Miniſterial Service, by ſaying, *he has
marry'd a Wife*, and *therefore cannot come* up
to them; it ſeems to be no better an Excuſe,
than if he had ſaid, *he had hir'd a Farm*, or
bought five Yoke of Oxen.

I know very well, that the *Reformation* has
allowed Prieſts and Biſhops not only to look out
for Wives, but to have as many as they pleaſe, one
after another: But this is only to be conſider'd
as a *bare Allowance*, and perhaps granted upon
ſuch a Motive, as *Moſes* of old made one to the
Jews, for *the Hardneſs of their Hearts*, tho'
from the Beginning it was not ſo; and therefore
when *Elogiums* are ſometimes made from the
Pulpit on this Matter, I think they had better
been ſpar'd; an Allowance granted to Weakneſs, is but an indifferent Subject to be made
a Matter of Glory.

The Doctor ſhould alſo have obſerv'd, that
my Addreſs was made to the young Clergy,
and ſuch as are only upon entring into holy
Orders, *nine in ten* of which, may be ſuppoſed
to be neither *Huſbands* nor *Fathers*. He ſhould
alſo have remember'd that our *Univerſities* are
full of Clergy, who are obliged to live *un-
marry'd*,

marry'd, that they may have proper *Leifure*
and *Freedom* to attend their Studies without
Impediment from worldly Cares. And therefore if I pointed at fuch a Dedication of the
Clergy to the Service of God, as *Hufbands* and
Fathers cannot enter into, yet the Matter is
not blameable, becaufe there are fo many that
have not yet entred into this State of Subjection to the World; but are at Liberty to devote
themfelves wholly to the Service of the Gofpel.
And therefore if to fuch as thefe, I can fo reprefent the Weight, the Duties, the heavenly Nature of the Priefthood, as to prevent or extinguifh in them all Thoughts and Defires of being thus marry'd to the World, what hurt have
I done them, or the marry'd Clergy, or the
Gofpel of Jefus Chrift ?

Virginity or *Celibacy*, when entred into from
a Principle of *divine* Love, from a Heart burning with the Defire of living *wholly* and *folely*
to God, is a State that gives Wings to all our
Endeavours, and truly fits the Soul for the higheft Growth of every heavenly Virtue : And if
he that is confecrated to the Service of the Altar, defires not to keep his Heart from carnal
Love ; if he feels not fuch an Afcent of his
Soul towards Heaven, as to have no Wifh,
but that his *whole Body, Soul,* and *Spirit,* may

be

be prefented to God in its utmoft Degree of
Purity, he muft be faid to have his Lamp
much lefs kindled, than many of the Laity,
both *Men* and *Women* have had, in all Ages of
the Church. Cuftom and common Practice
has too great a Power over our Judgments, and
reconciles us to any Thing ; but if a Chriftian,
who liv'd when Chriftianity was is its Glory,
when the firft *Apologifts* for it, appeal'd to the
Numbers of *both Sexes*, devoted to the Chafti-
ty of the fingle Life, as an *invincible Proof* of
the Power, and Divinity of the Gofpel ; if a
Chriftian of thofe Days was now to come into
the World, he muft needs be much more fhock-
ed at Reverend Doctors in Sacerdotal Robes,
making Love to Women, than at feeing a *Monk*
in his *Cell, kiffing* a wooden Crucifix.

The Knowledge and Love of the Virgin
State began with Chriftianity, when the Na-
ture of our Corruption, and the Nature of our
Redemption were fo fully difcovered by the
Light of the Gofpel. Then it was, that a new
Degree of heavenly Love was kindled in the hu-
man Nature, and brought forth a State of Life
that had not been defir'd, till the Son of the
Virgin came into the World. *John* the *Bap-
tift* may be look'd upon as the Beginner of the
Gofpel Difpenfation ; this *burning and fhining*

S   *Light*

Light was in his Perſon, the Figure of *Judaiſm*
ending in Chriſtianity. In his outward Birth
and State he was a *Jew*, in his inward Spirit
and Character he belong'd to the Goſpel. He
came out of the Wilderneſs burning and ſhining, to preach the Kingdom of Heaven *at
Hand.* This may ſhew us that Heat and Light
from above, kindled in a State of great Self-denial, are neceſſary to make us able Miniſters of
the Goſpel ; and that if we pretend to the Miniſtry without theſe Qualifications, and come
only burning and ſhining with the Spirit of this
World, we are only as well fitted to hinder, as
the Baptiſt was to prepare the Way to the
Kingdom of Heaven. Look at this great Saint,
all ye that deſire to preach the Goſpel. He
came forth in the higheſt Degrees of *Mortification* and *Chaſtity* of Life. But why did he ſo
come ? It was to ſhew the World that theſe
two great Virtues muſt form the Spirit of every
Preacher of the Goſpel. His Character does
not call you to a Wilderneſs beyond *Jordan,*
or to be cloathed with Camels Hair, *&c.* Such
Circumſtances are particular to himſelf ; but it
calls you to his inward Spirit of Self-denial, to
ſtand in his State of Death to the World, and
all carnal Love, if you would not only preach,
but prove the Perfection of the Goſpel : For if
the

the *Baptiſt* was to be thus dead to the Fleſh and
the World, that he might only preach thus
much, that the Kingdom of Heaven *was at
Hand*; can a leſs Self-denial be required of
thoſe, who are to preach that which is much
more, namely, that the Kingdom of Heaven
is come?

Now if this holy *Baptiſt*, when he came to
Jeruſalem, and had preach'd a-while upon Pe-
nitence, and the Kingdom of Heaven *at hand*,
had made an Offering of his Heart to ſome fine
young Lady of great Accompliſhments, had not
this put an End to all that was burning and
ſhining in his Character? And if thoſe Clergy
who date their Miſſion from Jeſus Chriſt himſelf, who claim being ſent by him as he was by
his Father, to ſtand as his *Repreſentatives*, ap-
plying the *Means* and *Myſteries* of Salvation to
all that deſire to be *born again* from above, if they,
whether they be *Vicars*, *Rectors*, *Arch-Deacons*,
Deans, or *Biſhops*, ſhould look upon their Office
to be as *ſacred*, and their Station as *high* in the
Kingdom of God, as the *Baptiſt's* was; if they
ſhould look upon *Love-Addreſſes* to the Sex, as
unbecoming, as *foreign*, as *oppoſite* to their Character, as to the *Baptiſt's*; could any one ſay,
that they took too much upon them, or paid
too great a Reverence to the Holineſs and Purity

rity of that Priesthood, which they deriv'd from the very Person and Office of Jesus Christ.

Our blessed Lord improv'd upon these two Articles of Mortification and Chastity, and sets them before every Preacher of the Gospel in a yet fuller Light. It is needless to shew how much he speaks of the Nature and Necessity of a total Self-denial; but what he says of the Virgin-Life, as to be chosen by those who are able to chuse it, for the Kingdom of Heaven's sake, *Matth.* xix. 12. is more than a Volume of human Eloquence in Praise of it. What Wonder is it, if after this, great Numbers both of Men and Women were found in the first Ages of the Church, that chose to know no Love, but that of God in a single Life?

St. *Paul* has done every thing to hinder a Minister of Jesus Christ from entring into Marriage, except calling it a sinful State, when he says, *He that is married, careth for the Things of the World, how he may please his Wife*; and how could he more powerfully press the Virgin Life upon the Clergy, than when he says, *He that is unmarried, careth for the Things that belong to the Lord, how he may please the Lord.* Now, who would imagine, that after this Determination of the Matter, by

so

fo great an Apoftle, there fhould be any need of Church Authority to reftrain any one in Holy Orders, from feeking after a Wife? Yet it muft be fuppofed, that even in the primitive Church there was fome Fear at leaft, that fuch a Reftraint would foon be needful; becaufe the twenty-feventh *Apoftolical Cannon* orders, that none amongft the Clergy be permitted to *enter* into Wedlock, except thofe, who have no higher an Office in the Church, than that of mere *Singers* and *Readers*.

When our Bleffed Lord fent the firft Preachers of the Gofpel into the World, he took them from amongft *marry'd Men, Fifhermen, Publicans,* and *Tentmakers*; and there was no more Reafon to look upon a Perfon as unfit to be an Apoftle, becaufe he had a Wife, than becaufe he had a Trade: And therefore, St. *Paul* does not tell *Timothy* and *Titus* to ordain no marry'd Perfon, for then no Elders could have been ordained in the Church, but he only enjoins them to lay Hands only on fuch as were in the moft perfect Condition of the marry'd Life, who had been the Hufbands but of one Wife, and whofe whole Family was a *Proof* of their Wifdom and Piety.

Hence it was, that the primitive Church made fo great a Difference between a marry'd

Clergyman

Clergyman, and a Clergyman that marry'd ;
the former was allowed for the Reasons above-
mention'd, but the latter always censured as a
thing *highly reproachful*, as a departing from
that Self-denial, Devotion and Confecration to
God, in which every one in Holy Orders ought
to live : But when Christianity had breathed a
while in the World, there soon became less
Occasion to ordain Persons that were marry'd ;
for the *Apologists* appeal to the Numbers of
both Sexes confecrated to God in a Virgin
Life, as one great Proof of the Divinity of
the Christian Religion. But when such Arguments as these were used, to set forth the Glory
of the Gospel, need any one be told, that it
must have been *highly shameful* in those Days,
for a Priest of such a Religion, to be *looking out*
for a Wife ? There is scarce a *Saint,* or *eminent* Father of the first Ages, who did not write
set Discourses, and preach entire Homilies in
Praise of this Virgin Perfection of Life ; but
surely this was enough telling the World, that
that Order of Men who officiated in the Mysteries of this Divine Religion, and were
Teachers of its Perfection, were Persons devoted to God in a Holy Virginity of Life : And
if it be ask'd, why amongst all our modern
fine Sermons, we have none upon the *Per-*
fection

fection and Advantage of a holy Virginity; the Reafon can be only this, becaufe our Priefts and Bifhops marry as often, as the Common People of the World. In the Primitive Church, if a *Subdeacon* married a *Widow*, he was degraded from his Office; and the Reafon was, becaufe he who tempted a Woman to marry a *fecond Time*, was looked upon to be a Corrupter of Human Nature: Thefe were the Sentiments of the Church, when it might be truly called the Spoufe of Jefus Chrift.

I fhall conclude this Matter with a Paffage taken from the *Serious Call to a devout and Holy Life*; it is a Quotation from the great and learned *Eufebius*, who liv'd at the time of the firft *general Council*, when the Faith of our *Nicene Creed* was eftablifhed: His Words are thefe, " There hath been, *faith he*, inftituted
" in the Church of Chrift, *two Ways* or
" *Manners* of Living; the *one* raifed above the
" ordinary State of Nature, and *common Ways*
" of Living, rejects *Wedlock, Poffeffions*, and
" *Worldy Goods*, and being wholly feparated
" and removed from the ordinary Converfation
" of Common Life, is appropriated and de-
" voted folely to the Worfhip and Service of
" God, through an *exceeding Degree of hea-*
" *venly Love :* They who are of this Order
" of

" of People, feem dead to the Life of this
" World, and having their *Bodies* only upon
" Earth, are in their *Minds* and *Contemplations*
" dwelling in Heaven ; from whence, like fo
" many heavenly Inhabitants, they look down
" upon Human Life, making *Interceffions* and
" *Oblations* for the whole Race of Mankind ;
" and this, not with the Blood of Beafts, or
" the Fat, or Smoak and burning of Bodies,
" but with the *higheft Exercifes* of true Piety,
" with cleanfed and purified Hearts, and with
" a *whole Form* of Life ftrictly devoted to
" Virtue : Thefe are their Sacrifices, which
" they are continually offering unto God, and
" implore his Mercy and Favour for themfelves
" and their fellow Creatures. Chriftianity
" receives *this* as the perfect Manner of Life.

" The *other* is of a *lower Form*, and fuiting
" itfelf more to the Condition of Human Na-
" ture, admits of *chafte Wedlock*, the Care of
" Children and Families, of Trade and Bufi-
" nefs, and goes through all the Employments
" of Life, under a Senfe of Piety and Fear of
" God : Now, they who have chofen this
" Manner of Life, have their fet Times for
" *Retirement* and *Spiritual Exercifes*, and par-
" ticular Days are fet apart for their hearing
" and learning the Word of God : And *this*

" Order

" *Order* of People are confidered as in the *fe-*
" *cond State* of Piety" *. Here you fee the Perfection of the Chriftian Life plainly fet out, and
how it was, that Numbers of private Perfons,
Men and Women, who had no Share in the
Ecclefiaftical Office, yet, by this Perfection of
Life, made themfelves *holy and heavenly Inter-*
ceffors for the whole Race of Mankind. Now,
are we not here obliged to fuppofe, that in this
Father's Days, the Clergy were in *this Number*
of People, that were thus heavenly in the *whole*
Form of their Life, thus *devoted* to God and
the *Edification* of the Church, by embracing
the perfect Life of Chriftianity? If they were
not, do they not ftand plainly condemned by
the Religion of the Gofpel, fince this Father
affures us, that *Chriftianity held this to be the*
perfect Manner of Life? I fhall only add thus
much here, that till fuch *a Degree* of heavenly Love, fuch a *Senfe* of the Purity, Holinefs
and heavenly Nature of the facred Calling,
till fuch a *Defire* of Perfection is awakened in
the Clergy, as fhuts out all *carnal* Love and
worldly Tempers from their Hearts, they cannot be fuch *Priefts* and *Interceffors* with God,
fuch *Patterns* of Purity and Holinefs, fuch
Kindlers of divine Love and heavenly Defires
amongft Men, as the Nature of their Office
both intends and requires of them.

* Serious Call, &c. p. 134.

If

If a *Candidate* for Holy Orders dares not make this *total Donation* of himself to God, to be an Inftrument of his good Pleafure only in the Service of the Gofpel, if it is not the real State of his Heart, to wifh nothing for himfelf in this World, but the moft *perfect* Purification of his Nature, the *higheft* Advancement in all Divine Virtues; if he defires any thing in and by his Office, but a *Concurrence* with Jefus Chrift in the Salvation of Souls; if he has *any Referves* of Self-feeking, or Self-advancement in the World, any flefhly Paffions which he hopes to make confiftent with the Duties of his Profeffion; if he is not feparated in *Will* and *Defire* from all that is not God, and the Service of God, he muft be faid to want the beft Proofs of his being called by the Holy Ghoft.

Dr. *Trap*'s violent Condemnation of what I faid to the young Clergy, and Candidates for Holy Orders, made it neceffary for me to enter thus far into this Subject. If any thing that I have faid to thefe Perfons, concerning the Excellency, the Advantage, the Purity, the Neceffity of a Virgin Life, in order to their own Perfection, and the full Edification of the Church, gives Offence to any of the marry'd Clergy, it can only be to thofe, who don't wifh to fee

the

the Church in a better State, than that, in which they found it; and to ſuch there need no Apology be made.

But to turn to another Matter; I had ſaid, that "Salvation wholly conſiſts in the Incar-"nation of the Son of God in the Soul or "Life of Man; that that which was *done* and "*born* in the Virgin *Mary*, muſt be done, "and born in us: As our Sin and Death is "*Adam in us*, ſo our Life and Salvation is "*Chriſt in us*——As we are earthly, corrupt "Men, by having the Nature and Life of "*Adam* the firſt propagated in us, ſo we muſt "become new and heavenly Men, by having "the Life and Nature of *Adam* the ſecond "regenerated in us: But if we are to be like "him in *Nature*, as we are like to *Adam* in "Nature, then there is an *abſolute Neceſſity*, "that *that* which was *done* and *born* in the "Virgin *Mary*, be alſo by the ſame Power of "the Holy Ghoſt, *done* and *born* in us. The "Myſtery of Chriſt's Birth muſt be the My-"ſtery of our Birth, we cannot be his Sons "but by having the Birth of his Life derived "into us: The new Paradiſical Man muſt be "brought forth in the ſame Manner in every "*individual* Perſon. That which brought "forth this *Holy Birth* in the firſt *Adam* at his

"Creation

" Creation, and in the fecond *Adam* in the
" Virgin *Mary*, *that alone* can bring it forth
" in any one of their Offspring"*. Now,
there feems to be nothing in all this, but what
is eafily to be apprehended, and fully believ'd by
every one, that knows any thing of the Chriftian Life; but the Doctor makes *two Replies* to
this Doctrine: The firft is this, *Was fuch
Words*, fays he, *ever heard amongft Chriftians
before?* + Yes, good Sir, they have often been
heard before, by fuch as *have Ears to hear*; for
they are the very Words which Chrift, and his
Apoftles have as plainly fpoken, as they have
fpoke any one Article of the Apoftles Creed:
They are only as different from the Words of
Chrift and his Apoftles, as the *Englifh* Words
of the Bible, are different from thofe *Greek*
Words, in which the Gofpels were written.
When the Scripture faith, that Chrift muft be
form'd in us, does it not fay, that Chrift muft
be born, or become incarnate to us? When
it faith, Chrift was born of the Virgin *Mary*,
doth it not fay, that Chrift was incarnate of
the Virgin *Mary?* Or is there any thing
to fright a learned Divine, who has for forty
Years been told, that Chrift muft be *formed in*
us,

* Serious Anfwer, *p.* 41.　　　+ Reply, *p.* 47.

us, revealed in us, that he muſt *put on* Chriſt, to be told, that Chriſt muſt *become incarnate* in us, that he muſt bring forth himſelf in us, and have *ſuch a Birth* in our Soul and Life, as he had in the Virgin *Mary?* For where-ever he is born, muſt he not be born in the *ſame Manner?* Was it not the *Word* of God, that by the Power of the Holy Ghoſt became Man in the Virgin *Mary?* And is there any Thing in this Birth on this wiſe that is inconſiſtent with the Birth of our new Man in Chriſt Jeſus? Muſt not the *ſame Word* of God, by the *ſame Operation* of the Holy Spirit, bring forth that in us, which is the new Man in Chriſt Jeſus, or Chriſt formed in us? When our Lord ſaith, that we muſt be born again from Above, of the Word of God, is it more or leſs than ſay-ing, that *that* Word which was born in the Virgin *Mary,* and was incarnate in her, muſt be *born* and *incarnate* in us? When the Apo-ſtle ſaith, that we muſt be born again of the *incorruptible Seed of the Word,* is not this expreſsly ſaying, that *that muſt be done and born in us,* which was done and born in the Virgin *Mary?* If he ſays, that Chriſt muſt be formed in us, does he not ſay, that he muſt have ſuch a Birth and Form in us, as he had

in

in the Virgin *Mary*; only with this Difference, that in the Birth of Chrift, the *Fulnefs* of the Deity, or eternal Word became Man, and dwelt perfonally in him; but in us, only a *Spark*, or *Seed of* the *Word* is form'd and rais'd up into a new, heavenly Man. Is there now any Thing in all this, but the moft comfortable, fubftantial Part of our Redemption fet out in the plaineft Words of Scripture? Reject this Doctrine, fay that you cannot, you will not, you defire not to have Chrift *thus born and formed* in you, and then you reject all that Salvation, which the *Word* of God, born of a Virgin hath brought into the World. For the Scripture is abfolutely plain in telling us, that loft Man cannot be made alive again unto God, but folely by this way, by being born again of the *Word* and holy *Spirit* of God; if therefore we defire not, but reject *fuch a Birth*, as was brought forth by the *Word* and holy *Spirit* of God in the Virgin *Mary*; do we not plainly reject *that Birth* in which all our Salvation confifts? And therefore to fay that *that* muft be *done* and *born* in us, which was done and born in the Virgin *Mary*, is as plain, as fcriptural, as to fay, that we muft be born again of the *Word* and holy *Spirit* of God. And on this Ground

it

it is, that *Chrift in us*, is said to be our *Hope
of Glory.*——*And that the Kingdom of Heaven
is within us*——that we muft be in Chrift new
Creatures——that we muft put on Chrift——
that he muft be formed in us, reveal'd, manifefted in us——that he is our Life——that he
brings us forth out of himfelf, as the Vine
does its Branches —— that unlefs we eat his
Flefh and drink his Blood we have no Life in
us. These, and many other the like Sayings
of Scripture, which are the ftrongeft, deepeft
Expreffions of the Nature and Manner of our
Salvation, are all grounded on this Truth, *viz.*
That the Myftery of Chrift's Birth is the Myftery of our New Birth; that *that* muft be done
and born in us, which was done and born in
the Virgin *Mary*, namely a New Man brought
forth in the Likenefs of Chrift, by a Birth from
the Word, and holy Spirit of God.

But the Doctor has a *fecond Reply* to this
Matter, which ftands thus expreffed. *Whether,* fays he, *you confider the* Divinity, *or the*
Senfe *of this, could* George Fox *himfelf have
out-done it?* p. 48. This Reply, confider'd in
itfelf, might have its Place amongft thofe *alge-
braic Quantities,* that are fome Degrees lefs
than nothing; but with Regard to the Doctor's
Purpofe it has *fomething* in it, for it is an Appeal

peal to *that* which is very powerful, which has
suppress'd many a good Truth; it is an Appeal
to *vulgar Prejudice*, and shews that the
Doctor is not without his Expectations from
that Quarter. And thus it is, that the *Catholick Artist* in his Country, plays a *Martin Luther*, when he wants to reproach *that*, which
he knows not how to confute. What Degree
of Sense, or Divinity *George Fox* was posses-
sed of, I cannot pretend to say, having never
read any of his Writings; but if he has said any
good and divine Truths, I should be as well
pleased in seeing them in his Books, as in any
of the *Fathers* of the primitive Church. For as
the Gospel requires me to be as glad to see *Piety*, *Equity*, strict *Sobriety*, and extensive *Charity* in a *Jew*, or a *Gentile*, as in a Christian;
as it obliges me to look with Pleasure upon
their Virtues, and be thankful to God, that
such Persons have *so much* of true and sound
Christianity in them; so it cannot be an unchri-
stian Spirit, to be as glad to see Truths in one
Party of Christians, as in another; and to look
with Pleasure upon any good Doctrines, that are
held by any Sect of Christian People, and be
thankful to God, that they have so much of
the genuine, saving Truths of the Gospel a-
mongst them. For if we have no Anger or

Com-

Complaint againſt thoſe that are divided from
us, but what proceeds from a Chriſtian Fear,
that what they *hold* and *practiſe* will not be ſo
beneficial to them, as our Religion will be to us,
muſt we not have the utmoſt *Readineſs* and
Willingneſs to find, own, and rejoice in thoſe
good Doctrines and Practices which they ſtill
retain and profeſs? If a poor *Pilgrim*, under a
Neceſſity of travelling a dangerous and difficult
Road by himſelf, had, through his *own Perverſeneſs* loſt the Uſe of a *Leg*, and the Sight of
one Eye, could we be ſaid to have any *charitable Concern* for his Perverſeneſs and Misfortune,
unleſs we were glad to ſee, that he had one good
Leg, and one good Eye ſtill left, and unleſs
we hop'd and deſir'd they might bring him at
laſt to his Journey's End. Now let every Part
of the Church which takes itſelf to be *found* and
good, and is only angry at every other Part,
becauſe they have *leſſen'd the Means* of their own
Salvation; let her but have thus much Charity
in her Anger, and then ſhe will be glad to ſee,
in every perverſe Diviſion, ſomething like the
one *good Leg*, and the one *good Eye* of the
Pilgrim, and which ſhe will hope and wiſh
may do them the ſame Good.

Selfiſhneſs and *Partiality* are very inhuman
and baſe Qualities, even in the Things of this

T   World,

World, but in the Doctrines of Religion they
are of a baser Nature. Now this is the *greatest*
Evil that the Division of the Church has
brought forth; it raises in every Communion
a *selfish*, *partial* Orthodoxy, which consists in
courageously defending all that it has, and condemning all that it has not. And thus every
Champion is train'd up in Defence of their *own*
Truth, their *own Learning*, and their *own*
Church, and he has the most Merit, the most
Honour, who likes every Thing, defends every
Thing amongst themselves, and leaves nothing
uncensured in those that are of a different Communion. Now how can Truth, and Goodness,
and Union, and Religion be more *struck at*,
than by such Defenders of it? If you ask why
the great Bishop of *Meaux* wrote so many
learned Books against all Parts of the *Reforma-*
tion, it is because he was born in *France*, and
bred up in the Bosom of *Mother Church*. Had
he been born in *England*, had *Oxford*, or *Cam-*
bridge been his *Alma Mater*, he might have
rival'd our great Bishop *Stillingfleet*, and would
have wrote as many learned *Folio*'s against the
Church of *Rome* as he has done. And yet I
will venture to say, that if each Church could
produce but one Man a-piece that had the *Pie-*
ty of an Apostle, and the *impartial Love* of the
first

firſt Chriſtians, in the firſt Church at *Jeruſa-*
lem, that a Proteſtant and a *Papiſt* of this
Stamp, would not want *half a Sheet* of Paper
to hold their Articles of Union, nor be half an
Hour before they were of one Religion. If
therefore it ſhould be ſaid, that Churches are
divided, eſtrang'd, and made unfriendly to
one another, by a *Learning*, a *Logic*, a *Hiſto-*
ry, a *Criticiſm* in the Hands of *Partiality*, it
would be ſaying that, which every particular
Church too much proves to be true. Aſk why
even the beſt amongſt the Catholicks are very
ſhy of owning the *Validity* of the Orders of our
Church, it is becauſe they are afraid of remo-
ving any *Odium* from the Reformation? Aſk
why no Proteſtants any where touch upon the
Benefit or Neceſſity of Celibacy in thoſe, who
are ſeparated from worldly Buſineſs to preach
the Goſpel, 'tis becauſe that would be ſeeming
to *leſſen* the Romiſh Error of not ſuffering
Marriage in her Clergy? Aſk why even the
moſt worthy and pious amongſt the Clergy of
the eſtabliſhed Church, are afraid to aſſert the
Sufficiency of the Divine Light, the Neceſſity
of ſeeking only to the Guidance and Inſpiration
of the holy Spirit, 'tis becauſe the *Quakers*, who
have broken off from the Church, have made
this Doctrine their Corner Stone.

If we lov'd Truth as fuch ; if we fought it
for its own Sake ; if we lov'd our Neighbour as
ourfelves ; if we defir'd nothing by our Religion but to be acceptable to God ; if we equally
defir'd the Salvation of all Men ; if we were a-
fraid of Error only becaufe of its hurtful Nature to us, and our Fellow-Churches, then
nothing of this Spirit could have any Place in
us.

There is therefore a *Catholick* Spirit, a *Communion of Saints* in the Love of God and all
Goodnefs, which no one can learn from that
which is called *Orthodoxy* in particular Churches,
but is only to be had by a *total Dying* to all
worldly Views, by a *pure Love* of God, and
by fuch an *Unction* from above, as delivers the
Mind from all *Selfifhnefs*, and makes it love
Truth and Goodnefs with an Equality of Affection in every Man, whether he be *Chriftian, Jew,*
or *Gentile.* He that would obtain this Divine
and Catholick Spirit in this difordered, divided
State of Things, and live in a divided Part of
the Church without partaking of its Divifion,
muft have thefe *three Truths* deeply fixed in his
Mind : *Firft*, that univerfal Love, which gives
the whole Strength of the Heart to God, and
make us love every Man as we love ourfelves,
the Nobleft, the moft Divine, the God-like

State of the Soul, and is the utmoſt Perfection
to which the moſt perfect Religion can raiſe us;
and that no Religion does any Man any Good,
but ſo far as it brings this Perfection of Love
into him. This Truth will ſhew us, that *true
Orthodoxy* can no where be found, but in a
pure diſintereſted Love of God, and our Neighbour. *Secondly,* That in the *preſent divided*
State of the Church, Truth itſelf is torn and
divided aſunder ; and that therefore he can be
the only *true Catholick,* who has more of Truth,
and leſs of Error, than is hedged in by any divided Part. This Truth will enable us to live
in a divided Part, *unhurt* by its Diviſion, and
keep us in a true Liberty and Fitneſs to be edify'd and aſſiſted by all the Good that we hear
or ſee in any other Part of the Church. And
thus uniting in Heart and Spirit with all that
is *holy* and *good* in all Churches, we enter into
the true *Communion of Saints,* and become real
Members of the holy Catholick Church, tho'
we are confin'd to the outward Worſhip of
only one particular Part of it. It is thus, that
the Angels, as miniſtring Spirits, aſſiſt, join,
unite, and co-operate with every Thing that
is holy and good, in every Diviſion of Mankind. *Thirdly,* he muſt always have in Mind
this great Truth, that it is the Glory of the di-

T 3 vine

vine Juſtice to have no Reſpect of *Parties* or *Perſons*, but to ſtand equally diſpoſed to that which is right and wrong, as well in the *Jew* as in the *Gentile*. He therefore that would like as God likes, and condemn as God condemns, muſt have neither the *Eyes* of the *Papiſt* nor the *Proteſtant*; he muſt like no Truth the leſs becauſe *Ignatius Lyola*, or *John Bunyan*, were very zealous for it; nor have the leſs Averſion to any Error, becauſe Dr. *Trap* or *George Fox* had brought it forth. Now if this univerſal Love, and impartial Juſtice, is the Spirit which will judge the World at the laſt Day, how can this Spirit be *too ſoon*, or *too much* in us; Or what can do us more Hurt than that which is an *Hindrance* of it? When I was a young Scholar of the *Univerſity*, I heard a great *Religioniſt* ſay in my *Father's* Houſe, that if he could believe the late *King of France* to be in Heaven, he could not tell how to wiſh to go thither himſelf. This was exceeding ſhocking to all that heard it: Yet *ſomething* of this kind of Temper muſt be ſuppoſed to be more or leſs in thoſe, who have, as a Point of *Orthodoxy*, work'd themſelves up into a hearty *Contempt* and *Hatred* of thoſe that are divided from them. He that has been all his Life long uſed ɔ look with great Abhorrence upon thoſe

whom

whom he has called *superstitious Bigots, dreaming Visionaries, false Saints, canting Enthusiasts,* &c. must naturally expect they will be treated by God as they have been by him ; and if he had the *Keys* of the Kingdom of Heaven, such People would find it hard to get a Place in it. But it stands us greatly in Hand to get rid of this Temper *before* we dye ; for if nothing but *universal Love* can enter into the Kingdom of God, what can be more necessary for us, than to be full of this Love before we dye ?

We often hear of People of great *Zeal* and *Orthodoxy,* declaring on their *Death-beds* their strict Attachment to the Church of *England,* and making *solemn Protestations* against all other Churches ; but how much better would it be, if such a Person was to say, " In this " *divided State* of Christendom, I must con- " form to some outwardly divided Part of it, " and therefore I have chosen to live and dye " in outward Communion with the Church " of *England* ; fully believing, that if I wor- " ship God in *Spirit and in Truth* in this di- " vided Part of the Church, I shall be as ac- " ceptable to him, as if I had been a faithful " Member of the *one whole* Church, before it " was broken into separate Parts. But as I am " now going out of this disordered Division,

T 4 " into

" into a more *univerſal State* of Things, as I
" am now falling into the Hands of the great
" Creator and Lover of *all Souls* ; as I am go-
" ing to the God of *all Churches*, to a King-
" dom of *univerſal Love*, which muſt have
" its Inhabitants from *all People, Nations, and*
" *Languages* of the Earth ; ſo in this Spirit of
" univerſal Love, I deſire to perform my laſt
" Act of Communion in this divided Church,
" uniting and joining in Heart and Spirit with
" all that is *Chriſtian, Holy, Good,* and *Ac-*
" *ceptable* to God in all other Churches ; pray-
" ing, from the Bottom of my Soul, that
" every Church may have *its Saints* ; that
" God's Kingdom may come, his Will be
" done in every Diviſion of Chriſtians and
" Men, and that *every Thing that hath Breath*
" *may praiſe the Lord.*"

Need any one now be told the ſuperior Excellency of this Spirit, or its Fitneſs to be admitted into the Kingdom of univerſal Love ?
Need we any Proof that nothing but this *Catholick* Spirit will carry us *unhurt* by Schiſm,
through all thoſe Diviſions which the Devil,
the World, and fleſhly Wiſdom have brought
into the Church ? *Again,* We have often ſeen
learned Proteſtants very zealous in pulling to
Pieces the Lives of the Saints of the *Romiſh*
Church

Church, and casting all the Reproach and Ridicule they can, upon their wondrous Spirit; tho' the Lives of the Saints of the primitive Church, written by the Fathers of the greatest Name and Authority, are as fit for to be exposed in the same Manner. Now, whence does this proceed? Why, from a *secret Touch* of that Spirit which could not bear to have the late King of *France* in Heaven; it proceeds from a *partial, selfish* Orthodoxy, which cannot bear to hear, or own, that the Spirit and Blessing of God are so visible in a Church from which it is divided, and against which it has so much preach'd: But if a Person be of this Spirit, what does it signify *where* he has his outward Church? If a *Romish Priest* in the North of *England* could not bear the Splendor of a Life *so devoted* to God, so fruitful in all the Works of Piety and Goodness, as was that of the late Lady *Elizabeth Hastings*, if he should want to sully the Brightness of her Christian Graces, and prove her to have been no *Saint*, lest it should appear, that the Spirit of God was not *confin'd* to the *Romish* Church, would not such a Zeal shew a worse Spirit, than that of *Superstition*, a greater Depravity of Heart, than the saying now and then an *Ave Mary*.

The

The more we believe, or know of the Cor-
ruptions and Hindrances of true Piety in the
Church of *Rome*, the more we fhou'd rejoice
to hear, that in every Age fo many eminent
Spirits, great Saints, have appeared in it, whom
we fhould thankfully behold as fo many *great
Lights* hung out by God, to fhew the true
Way to Heaven, as fo many joyful Proofs that
Chrift is ftill prefent in that Church, as well as
in other Churches; and that the Gates of Hell
have not prevailed, or quite overcome it ?
Who that has the leaft Spark of Heaven in his
Soul, can help thinking and rejoicing in this
manner at the Appearance of a St. *Bernard*, a
Terefa, a *Francis* de *Sales*, &c. in that
Church ? Who can help praifing God, that
her *invented Devotions*, *fuperftitious* Ufe of
Images, *Invocation* of Saints, *&c.* have not fo
fuppreffed any of the Graces and Virtues of an
Evangelical Perfection of Life, but that amongft
Cardinals, *Jefuits*, *Priefts*, *Friars*, *Monks* and
Nuns, Numbers have been found, who feem'd
to live for no other End, but to give Glory to
God and Edification to Men, and whofe Writings have every Thing in them, that can guide
the Soul out of the Corruption of this Life into
the higheft Union with God. And he who
through a *partial Orthodoxy* is diverted from
feeding in thefe green Paftures of Life, whofe

juft

just Abhorrence of Jesuitical *Craft* and *worldly
Policy* keeps him from knowing and reading
the Works of an *Alvares du Pas*, a *Rodrigues,*
a *Du Pont*, a *Guilloree*, a *Pere Surin*, and
such like Jesuits, has a greater Loss than he
can easily imagine : And if any Clergyman
can read the Life of *Bartholomeus a Martyri-
bis*, a *Spanish* Archbishop, who sat with great
Influence at the very Council of *Trent*, without being edify'd by it, and desiring to read
it again and again, I know not why he should
like the Lives of the best of the Apostolical
Fathers ; And if any Protestant Bishop should
read the *Stimulus Pastorum* wrote by this Po-
pish Prelate, he must be forced to confess it to
be a Book, that would have done Honour to
the best Archbishop, that the Reformation has
to boast of. O my God, how shall I unlock
this Mystery of Things ; in the Land of *Darkness*, over-run with *Superstition*, where Divine
Worship seems to be all *Shew* and *Ceremony*,
there both amongst Priests and People, thou
hast those, who are fired with the pure Love
of thee, who renounce every thing for thee,
who are devoted wholly and solely to thee,
who think of nothing, write of nothing, desire nothing but the Honour, and Praise, and
Adoration that is due to thee, and who call all
the

the World to the *Maxims* of the Gofpel, the
Holinefs and Perfection of the Life of Chrift.
But in the Regions where *Light* is fprung up,
whence Superftition is *fled,* where all that is
outward in Religion feems to be *prun'd, drefs'd,*
and put in its *true Order ;* there a cleanfed
Shell, a *whited Sepulchre,* feems too generally
to cover a *dead* Chriftianity.

. The Error of all Errors, and that which
makes the blackeft Charge againft the *Romifh*
Church, is *Perfecution,* a religious Sword drawn
againft the Liberty and Freedom of ferving
God according to our beft Light, that is,
againft our *worfhipping the Father in Spirit and
in Truth :* This is the great *Whore,* the *Beaft,*
the *Dragon,* the *Antichrift.* Now, tho' this
is the frightful Monfter of that Church, yet,
even here, who, except it be the Church of
England, can throw the firft Stone at her ?
Where muft we look for a Church that has fo
renounc'd this *perfecuting Beaft,* as they have
renounc'd the Ufe of *Incenfe,* the *Sprinklings*
of Holy Water, or the *extreme Unction* of dying Perfons ? What Part of the Reformation
abroad has not practifed and defended Perfecution ? What Sect of Diffenters at home have
not, in their Day of Power, dreadfully condemn'd *Toleration ?*

When

When it fhall pleafe God to difpofe the
Hearts of all Princes in the Chriftian World
entirely to deftroy this *Antichriftian Beaft*, and
leave all their Subjects in that religious Freedom
which they have from God; then the *Light* of
the Gofpel, the *Benefit* of its Faith, the *Power*
of its Minifters, the *Ufefulnefs* of its Rites, the
Benediction of its Sacraments will have proper
Time and *Place* to fhew themfelves; and that
Religion which has the moft of a *Divine
Power* in it, whofe *Offices* and *Services* do
moft good to the Heart, whofe Minifters are
moft of all *devoted* to God, and have the *moft
Proof* of the Power and Prefence of Chrift
with them, will become, as it ought to be,
the moft univerfal; and by this Deftruction of
the *Beaft*, nothing but the Errors, Delufions,
Corruptions and Fictions of every Religion,
will be left in a helplefs State. All that I have
faid on this Matter, has been occafioned by
the Doctor's Appeal to *vulgar Prejudice*; and
all that I have faid is only to intimate thus
much, that the *greateft Evil* which the Divifion of the Church brings forth, is a *Sectari-
an, felfifh* Spirit, that with the Orthodoxy of
the *Old Jews*, would have God to be *only their*
God, and themfelves only, *his chofen* People. If
therefore we would be true Chriftians of the
Catholick

Catholick Church, we must put off this *Selfish-ness* and *Partiality* of the carnal *Jew*, we must enter into a Catholick Affection for all Men, love the Spirit of the Gospel wherever we see it; not work ourselves up into an Abhorrence of a *George Fox*, or an *Ignatius Lyola*; but be equally glad of the Light of the Gospel where-ever it shines, or from what Quarter it comes; and give the same Thanks and Praise to God for an *eminent* Example of Piety, where-ever it appears, either in *Papist* or *Protestant*.

To return. Dr. *Trap* supposing the World running into a Charity that would ruin Wife and Family, asks his charitable *Half-thinker* thus; " Did you never hear that *Charity begins* " at home? Did you never read that of St. " *Paul*, If any provide not for his own, and " especially those of his own House, he hath " denied the Faith, and is worse than an In- " fidel." The Doctor's Proverb I meddled not with, but the Text of St. *Paul* I rescued from his gross Misapplication of it. That Text has no more Relation to an *excessive Charity*, the Sin the Doctor was opposing, than to an *ex-cessive Fasting*. The Apostle neither thought of this Sin in this Place, nor in any other Part of his Writings; nor does he ever give the smallest *Hint* of the Danger of falling into it.

The

The one Thing in Queſtion was this, whether poor Widows, who had near Relations, that could ſupply their Wants, ſhould be maintain'd by the Charity of the Church : The Apoſtle determines the Matter thus ; that if ſuch Perſons, who were thus able, did not *thus provide* for, that is, *ſupply* the Wants of their poor Kindred, they were ſo far from having the *Faith* of Chriſtians, that they wanted a *Goodneſs* that was to be found amongſt Infidels : This is the whole of the Apoſtle's Doctrine in this Text. He ſpeaks of *providing* for thoſe of our own Houſe or Family, in *no other* Senſe, than as it ſignifies our *Charity* to them, when they fall into Diſtreſs : But the Doctor, either led away with, or *truſting* to the *Sound* of the *Engliſh* Word, *provide*, grafts all theſe following Errors upon this plain Text. When it is ſaid, a Perſon has *provided* well for his Family, every one ſuppoſes that he has *laid up well in Store*, or got an *Eſtate* to be divided amongſt them for their future Subſiſtence, from *this Uſe* of the *Engliſh* Word, *provide*, in the Text ; the Doctor would have it believ'd, that the Apoſtle teaches every Head of a Family to be carefully and continually laying up in Store, and making ſome fix'd Proviſion for the future Maintenance of his Kindred. But the Apoſtle

is

is as *infinitely diftant* from this Thought or Direction, as from teaching them to get their
Cellars well fill'd with ftrong Liquors: When
he here fays, *provide*, he fays only this, Shut
not your Eyes to the Wants of your poor Kindred, but provide them *with what* they have
need of, and don't let them fall to the Charge
of the Church. The Doctor's *fecond Error* is
this; that, according to this Text, a Chriftian
ought not to *hinder* himfelf from thus laying
up in Store for his Family, or leave them to
live by their Labour and Induftry, through an
Extent of Charity to his poor Neighbours.
Tho' the Apoftle has not one fingle Syllable
about this Matter; and is as far from faying
any Thing like it, as from faying, that a Chriftian, when he *makes a Feaft*, fhould only in-
vite his rich Kindred and Acquaintance. The
one has as much of the Apoftle and the Gofpel
for it, as the other. The Doctor's *third* Error
is this; that, according to this Text, he, who
by a *daily, continual* Charity, has incapacitated
himfelf to lay up in Store, a fixed Provifion
for the future Maintenance of his Family, is
condemn'd by the Apoftle, as *denying the Faith,*
and *worfe than an Infidel*: Tho' the Apoftle
fpeaks no more here of *fuch a Perfon*, or any
more condemns him, than he fpeaks in the
Praife

Praife of *Ananias* and *Saphira*, who kept
back Part of the Price of the Land they had
fold.

The Perfon here condemn'd, is not he, who
through a *continual* Charity, or loving his
Neighbour as himfelf, is *hindred* from laying
up in Store; not he, who, through a Chriftian
Love of relieving the diftreffed Members of
Chrift, is content with helping his own Family to Food and Raiment, fuch a Perfon is not
thought of, much lefs condemn'd by the Apoftle; but it is that Chriftian, who being *able*,
is yet unwilling to *fupport* his near Relations,
that are fallen into Poverty, but through a for-
did Selfifhnefs, leaves them to be maintained
by the Church; this is the only Chriftian the
Apoftle here condémns, as having put off the
Piety of the Gofpel, and wanting even the
Virtue of good-natur'd Infidels.

I faid further, Had the Apoftle known a
Parent in his Days, who, through his *great*
Charity for others, had reduced his own Family to a want of Relief, he would have been
fo far from rebuking him as an *half-thinking*
Fool, or expofing him to others, as guilty of
Madnefs, that he would have told them, that
fuch a one had confecrated himfelf and Family to the Church, as the proper Objects of their

U   Care.

Care. To which the Doctor gives this Anſwer *This he affirms, and this I deny; and as he produces no other Proof, ſo I give no other Anſwer,* p. 69. Had the Doctor ſaid, as his Affirmation has no Senſe in it, ſo there need be no Senſe in my Denial of it, he had anſwered as well as he has here done. What I affirm'd, did not conſiſt as the Doctor's *Denial* doth, only of *two Words*; but was, a large Propoſition that carry'd its *own Proof* along with it, becauſe I ſaid nothing of the Apoſtle, but what the Nature of the Thing oblig'd me to ſay of every ſober Chriſtian. For if any Chriſtian could be ſuppoſed to want Compaſſion and Affection for ſuch a Sufferer, from his *own Charity* to others, he muſt be ſuch a one as the Apoſtle affirms to *have denied the Faith, and to be worſe than an Infidel.* But to ſhew the Doctor what I ſaid, has its Proof from the common Voice of Chriſtianity in the Apoſtles Days, may ſufficiently appear from the following Paſſage of St. *Clement,* who was a Companion and Fellow-labourer of the Apoſtle, and Biſhop of no leſs a Church than that of *Rome.* " We have known *many* amongſt us, " (ſays St. *Clement*) who have delivered them-" ſelves into Bonds and Slavery, that they " might reſtore others to their Liberty ; *many* " who have hired out themſelves Servants unto " others,

" others, that by their Wages they might feed
" and fuſtain them that wanted " *.

Will the Doctor now ſay, that this is no
Proof of that which I affirmed of the Apoſtle,
that he would have had a Love for thoſe who
were become Sufferers by their own Charity to
others ? Does not this Apoſtolical Biſhop make
it his Boaſt, and the Glory of Chriſtianity ;
not that they had ſome, but *many* ſuch amongſt
them ?

It was not only in the firſt Church at *Jeruſalem*, that the Chriſtians had all things common. For St. *Barnabas* writing to ſome con-
verted *Jews*, teaches them to have all Things
common, to call nothing their own in this
World, becauſe they were called to the common
Enjoyment of the Things of Eternity. *Com-
municabis in omnibus rebus proximo tuo ; nihil
dices quicquam tibi proprium, ſi enim Communi-
catis in Vicem, in bonis, incorruptibilibus, quan-
to magis in corruptibilibus* †.

An Age after this, *Juſtin Martyr* thus
glories of the Power of the Goſpel-Faith ; *We*,
ſays he, *who before* were became Chriſtians,
loved our Wealth and Poſſeſſions above all Things,
*now give up all Propriety in them, that they
may be in common for all that want them.* Qui

U 2   *Pecuniarum*

*Pecuniarum & Poſſeſſionum Fructus ac Proven-
tus præ rebus omnibus adamabamus, nunc etiam
quæ habemus in Commune conferimus, & cum
indigentibus quibuſcunque communicamus* *.
What a *lean, beatheniſh* Figure muſt the
Doctor's Proverb of *Charity beginning at home,*
have made in the Days of St. *Barnabas, Clement,* or *Juſtin Martyr?* Or who durſt then
have made ſuch an Uſe of the Text of St. *Paul,*
as the Doctor has done, or coupled it with
ſuch a Proverb? Were any of theſe firſt Saints
to judge of this Matter, the Doctor might, for
ought I know, have a *worſe Reprimand* from
them for ſo doing, than if he had only coupled *Cardinals with Pluraliſts.*

In order to ſhew the Doctor that he was
very unſeaſonably preaching againſt the *Sin*
and *Folly* of an exceſſive Charity, when yet
every Part of the Church wanted to be ſhewn
how they were fallen from the Goſpel-degree
of it, I ſet before him an *imaginary* Biſhop of
Wincheſter, yet drawn according to the Model
of the Holy Biſhops of the firſt Ages. I ſuppoſed this Biſhop ſo born again from Above,
ſo fill'd with the Spirit of Jeſus Chriſt, that he
look'd upon all the *Revenues* of his *See,* with
no other Eyes, than as our Saviour look'd at
that

* 2 Apol.

that *Bag* that was carried along with him by his Difciples, as *fo much* for his own Neceffities, and the Neceffities of others. I fuppofed that in this Spirit, he fo expended his yearly Income, that he chofe to bring up his Children as much *Strangers* to all worldly Figure, and in as *low a State* of Labour as that to which our Lord and his Apoftles had been us'd. I fuppos'd, that by a Piety of Life and Converfation, equal to this exalted Charity, he had *inftill'd* fuch an heavenly Spirit into his Wife and Children, as made them *highly thankful* for their Condition, and full of Praife to God for the Bleffing of fuch a *Relation*. Dr. *Trap,* tho' an antient Divine, feems to ftart back with Fright, at the *Sight* of this Apoftolical Bifhop, and fuppofes, that if fuch a Monfter of a Man was now to get into a Bifhoprick, he muft needs make his Children extraordinary wicked, fill them with Abhorrence of his Memory, and fpread Infidelity in the World, by making Chriftianity a Jeft to Infidels, *p.* 71.

I fay, fays the Doctor, *very clearly and plainly,* that *fuch a Bifhop muft be a Mad-man,* p. 70. Now, if the Doctor will prove from the Scriptures this Bifhop to be a *Mad-man,* it muft be for the following Reafons ; *Firft,* becaufe he had fo *mean a Spirit,* as to fuffer

U 3   the

the Son of a *Bishop* to work under a *Carpenter*, as the Redeemer of Mankind had done. *Secondly*, becaufe he taught himfelf and his Family to believe *that* which St. *Paul* believed, that *having Food and Raiment, we ought to be therewith content.* *Thirdly*, becaufe he came up to the very Letter of the great Commandment, of *loving our Neighbour as ourfelves.* *Fourthly*, becaufe he feem'd to imitate the Spirit of the firft Chriftians at *Jerufalem*, who accounted *nothing to be their own that they poffefs'd.* *Fifthly*, becaufe he had turned himfelf and Family from all the Vanity of this World, the *Luft* of the *Flefh*, the *Luft* of the *Eyes*, and the *Pride of Life.* *Sixthly*, becaufe he feem'd to have *this* of the Apoftle *fixed* in his Mind, *He that faith, he abideth in Chrift, ought fo to walk, as he walked.* *Seventhly*, becaufe his Life was fafhioned according to this Doctrine of the Holy Jefus, *Learn of me, for I am meek, and lowly of Heart : I am among you, as he that ferveth : Whofoever will be great among you, let him be your Minifter ; even as the Son of Man came not to be miniftred unto, but to minifter.* For it may be faid with the greateft Certainty, that if the Doctor will have *any Proof* from the Scripture of the Madnefs of this Bi-

fhop,

fhop, it muft be as abfurd as the Reafons here
alledg'd.

Come we now to confider this Bifhop according to the Spirit, Practice and Laws of
the Church in all Ages. Any one vers'd ever
fo little in the Hiftory of the Church, muft
fee at the firft Sight, that this *fuppofed* Bifhop
is a *true Copy* of the firft Apoftolical Fathers.
And if this Bifhop was to be accounted a
Madman, becaufe of the *Manner* of his Life,
we muft come down feveral Ages after *Conftan-
tine*, to the *Mitre* and *Triple Crown*, before
we could find a Bifhop in *his Senfes*. The
Clements, the *Polycarps*, the *Ignatius's*, the
Irenæus's, the *Cyprians*, the *Gregory's*, the
Bafils, the *Ambrofe's*, the *Chryfoftoms*, the *Hil-
lary's*, the *Auguftin's*, and a Number that have
long graced our *Calendars*, as Saints, muft take
their Place among *Bedlamites*; for they were
all of them to a *Tittle*, the very Man I have
fuppofed at *Winchefter*. They confidered every
Penny that was brought in by the Gofpel, as a
Provifion for the Poor, and themfelves as only
entitled to their common Share out of it.
They durft no more raife any of their Relations into a *Splendor* of Life, or give them
any *Figure* from the Revenues of the Church,
than commit *Sacrilege*. They gloried as much

U 4   in

in their own *ſtriƈt* Poverty and Want of worldly Figure, as in their having *totally* renounced
Idols.

But we have much more than primitive
Example for our Biſhop of *Wincheſter*; the
Doƈtrine and Laws of the Church have una-
nimouſly from Age to Age, to the very Council of *Trent*, required every Biſhop to be of the
ſame Spirit of which we have ſuppoſed him.
The Church, both by the Doƈtrine of Fathers, and the Canons of Councils conſtantly
maintains; *Firſt*, that the Clergy are not *Pro-
prietors*, but barely *Stewards* of the Benefices
they enjoy; having them for no other End,
but for their own neceſſary, frugal Subſiſtence,
and the Relief of the Poor. *Secondly*, that a
Clergyman uſing his Benefice for his *own Indulgence*, or the enriching his *own Family*, is
guilty of Sacrilege, and is a Robber and Mur-
derer of the Poor. *Thirdly*, that if a Clergyman has a reaſonable Subſiſtence of his own,
and is not in the *State* of the Poor, that then,
let his Benefice be what it will, he has no
Right to uſe any Part of it for himſelf, nor for
his Kindred, unleſs they be fit to be conſidered
amongſt thoſe Poor that are to be relieved by
the Church. *Fourthly*, that every Biſhop and
Clergyman is to live in an humble, lowly, fru-

gal,

gal, outward State of Life, feeking for no Honour or Dignity in the World, but that which arifes from the Diftinction and Luftre of his Virtues. *Fifthly*, that a *Benefic'd* Clergyman ufing the Goods of the Church for his own Indulgence, or raifing Fortunes for his Children, or their expenfive Education, is facrilegious, and a Robber of the Poor. *Sixthly*, that every Clergyman is to die out of the Church as *poor* as he entred into it. *Seventhly*, that a Clergyman *dying*, cannot *leave* or *bequeath* any Thing to his Children or Friends, but *barely that* which he had *independently* of the Church.

May

(*a*) Nihil ecclefia nifi Fidem poffidet——Poffeffio ecclefia eft Egenorum fumptus, *Amb. Ep.* 31. (*b*) Si Pauperum Compauperes fumus, & *noftra* funt, & *illorum.* Si autem privatim quæ nobis fufficiunt, poffidemus, non funt illa *noftrum*, fed Pauperum *Procurationem* gerimus, non Proprietatem nobis Ufurpatione damnabili vindicamus, *Auguf. Ep.* 50. *ad Bonif.* (*c*) Quoniam quicquid habent Clerici, Pauperum eft——Qui bonis Parentum & opibus fuftentari poffent, fi quod Pauperum eft, accipiunt *Sacrilegium profectò* committunt, & per Abufionem Talium, Judicium fibi manducant, & bibunt, *Hieron. Ep. ad Damaf.* (*d*) Epifcopus vilem *Suppellectilem*, & *Menfam*, ac *Victum Pauperem* habeat, & Dignitatis fua Authoritatem Fide & Vitæ meritis quærat, *Concil. Carthag.* 4. (*e*) Memento quod *Pauperem Vitam* Sacerdos gerere debet, & ideo fi fuperbiam habet, fi magno gaudet Beneficio, præter Victum & Veftitum *quod fupereft*, Pauperibus dare non differat, quia omnia *Pauperum* funt. *Aug. Serm.* 37. *ad Fratres.* (*f*) Hujus tu e vicino fectare Veftigia, & cæterorum, qui Virtutis illius fimiles funt, quos Sacerdotium & *humiliores* facit, & *pauperes. Hieron. Ep.* 4. *ad Ruftic.* (*g*) Præcipimus ut in poteftate fua Epifcopus Ecclefiæ Res habeat——ex iis autem quibus indiget, (fi tamen indiget) ad fuas neceffitates percipiat. *Canon. Apoft.* 40.—eas veluti

Deo

May it not therefore well be wonder'd what
could provoke Dr. *Trap* to cenſure our Biſhop
as a Madman, whoſe *whole Form* of Life, and
Uſe of his Biſhoprick, is not only after the Model of the firſt and greateſt Saints that ever were
Biſhops, but alſo ſuch as the whole Church
from the Beginning, both in Council and out
of Council, from Age to Age, hath *abſolutely*
requir'd

Deo contemplante diſpenſet ; nec ei liceat ex iis aliquid contin-
gere, aut Parentibus propriis (quæ Dei ſunt) condonare. Quod
ſi Pauperes ſunt, tanquam Pauperibus ſubminiſtret, ne eorum
occaſione Eccleſiæ Res deprædantur, *Can. Apoſt.* 39. (*b*) Ma-
nifeſta ſint quæ pertinere videntur ad Eccleſiam cum Notitia
Preſbiterorum & Diaconorum, ut ſi contigerit Epiſcopo mi-
grare de Seculo, nec *Res Eccleſiæ* depereant, nec quæ *propria*
probantur Epiſcopi, ſub Occaſione Rerum Eccleſiæ pervadan-
tur : juſtum enim eſt ut ſua Epiſcopus quibus voluerit, derelin-
quat, & quæ Eccleſiæ ſunt, eidem conſervantur Eccleſia. *Concil. Antiocb*, chap. 24. (*i*) Quicunque Clerici, qui nihil ha-
bentes ordinantur, & *tempore Epiſcopatus*, vel *Clericatus ſui*,
agros, vel quæcunque predia nomine ſuo comparant, tanquam
Rerum dominicarum *Invaſionis Crimine* teneantur obnoxii, niſi
admoniti, Eccleſiæ eadem ipſa contulerint. (*N. B.*) Si autem
ipſis proprie aliquid *liberalitate* alicujus, vel *Succeſſione* Cogna-
tionis obvenerit, faciant inde quod ipſorum Propoſito congruit.
(*k*) Sacerdotes ipſis quoque Filiis ſuis, quibus paterna debetur
Hæreditas, nihil debent derelinquere, niſi quod ſibi a Parentibus derelictum eſt : *Ergo qui ditior eſt* Sacerdos, quam venit ad
Sacerdotium, quicquid plus habuerit, *non filiis debet dare*, ſed
Pauperibus, & Sanctis fratribus, ut reddat ea quæ Domini ſunt,
Domino ſuo. *Hieron. in Ezecb.* chap. 46. (*l*) Timeant Clerici,
timeant Miniſtri Eccleſiâ, qui *in terris Sanctorum* quas poſſident,
tam iniqua gerunt, ut Stipendiis quæ ſufficere debeant, minime
contenti, Superſtua quibus egeni ſuſtendandi forent, impiè, ſa-
crilege, ſibi retineant, & in uſus ſuæ Superbiæ atque Luxuriæ
victum Pauperum conſumere non vereantur, duplici profecto
Iniquitate peccantes, quod & *aliena* diripiunt, & *Sacris* in ſuis
vinitatibus abutuntur. St. *Bernard, Serm.* 23. *in Cantic.* Vide,
lege, & relege. S. *Proſperum* de Vitâ centemplativâ.

requir'd of every benefic'd Clergyman, who
would not be condemn'd by her, as facrilegious, and a Robber of the Poor. They who
would fee the whole of this Matter fet in a clear
Light, may read an excellent Treatife of the
learned *Dupin*, wrote near the End of his Life,
where this Truth is by him afferted and inconteftably prov'd, *viz.* That whatever Changes
have been made in the *Nature* and *Tenure* of
the Goods and Revenues of the Church, or
however they have been varioufly divided a-
mongft Ecclefiafticks, yet this has remained
always unchangeable and undeniable, That a
Clergyman was no Proprietor of his Benefice;
that he could only take fo much of it to his
own Ufe, as was *neceffary* to his Subfiftence,
and then the Remainder, be it what it would,
belong'd to the Poor. This, fays he, is ftrictly maintained by the Canons of Councils, both
before and after the Divifion of ecclefiaftical
Revenues. *C'eft ce que portent precifement les
Canons, & avant, & apres la Partition des
Biens ecclefiaftiques* *.

But now if this be the Cafe, if this be an in-
contestable Doctrine, fupported by every Authority that can be brought for any one Doctrine of the Gofpel, have we not here an *utter*

* Traite Philof. & Theolog. fur l'amour de Dieu, *p.* 415.

ter Condemnation of Pluralities? Is it not an
Affront to the Gofpel, to the plaineft Maxims
of Right and Wrong, the whole Authority of
the Church, to offer one fingle Word in Defence of them? Logical, fcholaftic Diftinctions and Definitions of the Nature of *Parifhes*
and *Refidence,* can fignify no more here, where
the *whole Nature* of the Thing is to be avoid-
ed, than the *fame Art* of Words, when ufed
by *Jefuitical Cafuifts,* can juftify the Violation
of moral Duties. And if Dr. *Trap* was only
to look at this one Doctrine, he would have no
reafon to think it fo fad a Thing, to fee *Pluralifts*
coupled with *Cardinals. See,* fays the learned
*Dupin, Rules which will appear hard to many
of the benefic'd Clergy, but yet,* fays he, *they are
true, conformable to natural Equity, the Laws,
Cuftom, and Tradition of the Church, and the
Practice of the moft holy Bifhops; and wo be to
thofe that obferve them not.* Malheur a Ceux
qui ne les fuivent pas*. And therefore he con-
cludes thus, *There may be many amongft the benefic'd Clergy who err in this Matter, through
an Ignorance of that which is required of them;
therefore what I have faid ought to be taken in
good Part, as proceeding from Charity, and a
fincere Love of Truth.*

I come

* Ibid. *p.* 442.

I come now to that which the Doctor says
of Enthufiafm and Enthufiafts. Speaking to
the younger Clergy of the Means of attaining
divine Knowledge, I had thefe Words, " The
" Book of all Books is your own Heart, in
" which are written the deepeft Leffons of di-
" vine Inftruction ; learn therefore to be deep-
" ly attentive to the *Prefence* of God in your
" Hearts, who is always fpeaking, always in-
" ftructing, always illuminating that Heart
" that is attentive to him." Now can any
Thing be conceived more fcriptural, or more
inoffenfive than all this ?. Is there any thing
to fupprefs or hurt the Piety and Devotion of
that Heart, which would place its all in God ?
Which defires to be moved and guided in
all Things by his holy Spirit. How can we
worfhip God in Spirit and in Truth, how can
we pray unto him, turn to him, how can we
raife any Act of Faith or Hope in him, Refignation unto him, or Dependance upon him,
but by thus thinking of him ? Take any
Thing from God that I have here afcrib'd to
him, fuppofe him not to be thus inwardly
fpeaking, inftructing, illuminating, and then
tell me why my Heart fhould feek him, or,
how it can find him ? A Page or two after this,
to fhew the deep and intimate Union the Soul

has

has with its Creator, I said, " God is an *all-*
" *speaking, all-working, all-illuminating* Ef-
" fence, poffeffing the Depth, and bringing
" forth the Life of every Creature according to
" its Nature. Our Life is *out of* this divine
" Effence, and is itfelf a *creaturely Similitude* of
" it; and when we turn from *all Impediments,*
" this divine Effence becomes as certainly the
" true Light of our Minds *here,* as it will be
" *hereafter.*" Now is there any Thing here
to fhock, or fright, or delude the Piety of any
Chriftian? Is it a monftrous Thing to be told,
that the Light of Heaven reaches us in this
World, that we have this Communion with
God; that when we turn rightly to him, he
dwells in us and we in him; that we receive his
Operation and Light upon us in this Life, as
we fhall do in the next, only with this Difference, that now what is done *in Faith* will
then be in *open Vifion?* How can we believe
any thing that is faid of the Light and holy
Spirit of God in the Scripture, without believing this? If this be not true, how can we believe that Jefus Chrift is the Light which lighteth every Man that cometh into the World?
Or is there any Thing here more faid of God,
than when the Apoftle faith, that *in him we
move, and have our Being?* If the *Word*
of

of God was not an *ever-speaking* Word, how could Nature and Creature *speak forth* any Thing? If God was *ever* silent could any Thing else speak? Again, if Nature is *constantly* at Work; if there could be no Nature but because there is a *continual stirring* and *working* which cannot cease; is not this a sufficient Proof that there is an *all-working Deity?* And if we are told, that, in the Kingdom of Heaven, there shall be no Sun, nor Moon, but the *Lamb shall be the Light thereof,* is not this telling us, that God himself is the uncreated Light, always in the same State of Infinity, and therefore an *all-illuminating* Being? And if there is *always* Light *in Nature,* a Light that cannot be extinguished, must it not come from the *all-illuminating* Being? Yet Dr. *Trap* says, all this *is Enthusiasm, if ever there was any in the World;* that they are the *Words of Falshood and Phrenzy* *. If the Doctor had been clear in this Matter, it had been very easy for him to have shewn his Reader wherein this Enthusiasm and Frenzy lay; and it was also very necessary for him to have here said something very plain and clear concerning the Nature and Ground of Enthusiasm: For if his Reader, without any clear and distinct Notion
of

* Pag. 86.

of Enthufiafm, is taught to cry out againft a Doctrine, which only teaches, that God is always fpeaking, inftructing, and illuminating that Heart that is in great *Purity* turn'd to him; if he is taught boldly and blindly to condemn *this* as Enthufiafm and Frenzy, how fhall fuch a one be able to defend himfelf, when he is told by others, that two Thirds of the New Teftament is Enthufiafm ? As where it is faid, *I am the Light* and Life of the World ——The Kingdom of Heaven is within you —— Except ye eat my Flefh and drink my Blood, ye have no Life in you——If any Man love me, my Father will love him, and we will come unto him, and *make our Abode with him*——No Man can come unto me, except the Father draweth him——The natural Man cannot receive and know the Things of the Spirit of God——He breathed on them, and faid, Receive ye the Holy Ghoft——The Spirit of Truth, he dwelleth in you, and fhall be with you——No Man can fay, *Abba* Father, or that Jefus is the Lord, but by the Holy Ghoft ——As many as are led by the Spirit of God, they are the Sons of God. *In our Liturgy* we pray that God would prevent us in *all our* Doings, and further us with his *continual Help* ——That we may obey the godly Motions of

the

the Spirit in Righteoufnefs and true Holinefs
——— That by his holy Infpiration we may
think thofe Things that be good, and by his
merciful Guiding may perform the fame ———
That his holy Spirit may in all Things direct
and rule our Hearts, &c. Now what muft the
unlearned Reader, or the learned Doctor himfelf do with thefe and the like Places of Scripture, and Prayers of the Church, if it be *Enthufiafm*, *Falfehood*, and *Frenzy* to fay, that
God is intimately prefent in the Depth of our
Souls, always fpeaking, inftructing, enlighten-
ing that Heart, which is truly turned to him?
Or how can thefe Scriptures and Prayers have
the *leaft Truth* or *Reafonablenefs* in them, but
upon this Suppofition, that God is an all-fpeak-
ing, all-knowing, all-illuminating Being, out
of whom we are born, and in whom we live,
and move, and have our Being. But I fhall
here fpeak a Word or two of the true Ground,
and Nature of Enthufiafm.

In *Will*, *Imagination*, and *Defire*, confifts
the Life, or fiery Driving of every intelligent
Creature. And as every intelligent Creature is its
own *Self-mover*, fo every intelligent Creature has
Power of *kindling* and *inflaming* its Will, Imagination and Defire as it pleafes, with Shadows,
Fictions, or Realities; with Things carnal or

fpiritual,

spiritual, temporal or eternal. And *this kind-ling* of the Will, Imagination, and Desire, when raised into a *ruling Degree* of Life, is properly that which is to be understood by Enthusiasm: And therefore Enthusiasm is, and must be of as *many Kinds* as those Objects are, which can kindle and enflame the Wills, Imaginations, and Desires of Men. And to appropriate Enthusiasm to Religion, is the same Ignorance of Nature, as to appropriate *Love* to Religion; for Enthusiasm, a kindled, inflamed Spirit of Life, is as *common*, as *universal*, as *essential* to human Nature, as *Love* is; it goes into *every Kind* of Life as Love does, and has only such a Variety of Degrees in Mankind as Love hath. And here we may see the Reason, why no People are so angry at Religious Enthusiasts, as those that are the *deepest* in some Enthusiasm of *another Kind*.

He whose Fire is kindled from the Divinity of *Tully's* Rhetorick, who travels over high Mountains to salute the dear Ground that *Marcus Tullius Cicero* walk'd upon; whose *noble Soul* would be ready to break out of his Body, if he could see a *Desk*, a *Rostrum* from whence *Cicero* had pour'd forth his Thunder of Words, may well be unable to bear the *Dulness* of those, who go on *Pilgrimages* only to visit the
Sepulchre,

Sepulchre, whence the *Redeemer of the World*
rofe from the dead, or who grow devout at the
Sight of a *Crucifix*, becaufe the Son of God
hung as a Sacrifice thereon.

He whofe heated Brain is all over painted
with the *antient Hieroglyphicks*; who knows
how and *why* they were *this* and *that*, better
than he can find out the Cuftoms and Ufages
of his *own Parifh*; who can clear up every
Thing that is *doubtful* in Antiquity, and yet
be forc'd to live in Doubt about that which paffes in his own Neighbourhood; who has found
out the Sentiments of the *firft Philofophers* with
fuch Certainty, as he cannot find out the *real
Opinion* of any of his Contemporaries; he that
has gone thus high into the *Clouds*, and dug
thus deep into the *Dark* for thefe *glorious Dif-
coveries*, may well defpife thofe Chriftians, as
brain-fick Vifionaries, who are fometimes finding a *moral*, and *fpiritual* Senfe in the bare
Letter and Hiftory of Scripture-Facts.

It matters not what our Wills and Imaginations are employed about; wherever they *fall*
and love to *dwell*, there they *kindle* a Fire, and
that becomes the *Flame of Life*, to which every Thing elfe appears as *dead*, and *infipid*, and
unworthy of Regard. Hence it is that even the
poor Species of *Fops* and *Beaux* have a right to

be

be placed among Enthufiafts, tho' capable of
no other Flame than that, which is kindled by
Taylors and *Peruke-Makers*. All *refined Spe-
culatifts*, as fuch, are great Enthufiafts; for
being devoted to the Exercife of their Imaginations, they are fo *heated* into a Love of their
own Ideas, that they feek no other *fummum
bonum*. The *Grammarian*, the *Critick*, the
Poet, the *Connoiſſeur*, the *Antiquary*, the *Philoſopher*, the *Politician*, are all violent Enthufiafts, tho' their Heat is only a Flame from
Straw, and therefore they all agree in *appro-
priating* Enthufiafm to Religion. All *ambitious*, *proud*, *ſelf-conceited* Perſons, eſpecially if
they are *Scholars*, are violent Enthufiafts, and
their Enthufiafm is an *inflamed* Self-Love, Self-
Efteem, and Self-Seeking. This Fire is fo
kindled in them, that every Thing is naufeous
and difguftful to them, that does not offer Incenfe to that Idol, which their Imagination has
fet up in themfelves. All *Atheifts* are dark
Enthufiafts; their Fire is kindled by a Will
and Imagination turn'd from God into a gloomy
Depth of *Nothingnefs*, and therefore their Enthufiafm is a *dull burning* Fire, that goes in
and out, thro' *Hopes* and *Fears* of they know
not what that is to come. All *profeſſed Infidels*
are remarkable Enthufiafts, they have kindled
a *bold*

a *bold* Fire from a *few faint Ideas*, and therefore they are all Zeal, and Courage, and Induſtry to be *conſtantly blowing* it up. A *Tyndal* and a *Collins* are as inflamed with the Notions of Infidelity, as a St. *Bennet* and St. *Francis* with the Doctrines of the Goſpel.

Enthuſiaſts therefore we all are, as certainly as we are Men ; and conſequently, Enthuſiaſm is not a Thing blameable in *itſelf*, but is the common Condition of human Life in *all its States* ; and every man that lives either *well* or *ill*, is that which he is, from that *prevailing Fire* of Life, or *driving* of our Wills and Deſires, which is properly called Enthuſiaſm. You need not then go to a *Cloyſter*, the *Cell* of a *Monk*, or to a *Field Preacher*, to ſee Enthuſiaſts, they are every where, at *Balls* and *Maſquerades*, at *Court* and the *Exchange :* They ſit in all *Coffee-houſes*, and *cant* in all Aſſemblies. The *Beau* and the *Coquet* have no *Magick*, but where they meet Enthuſiaſts. The *Mercer*, the *Taylor*, the *Bookſeller* have all their Wealth from them ; the Works of a *Bayle*, a *Shaftſbury*, and *Cicero*, would loſe *four Fifths* of their aſtoniſhing Beauties, had they not *keen Enthuſiaſts* for their Readers.

That which concerns us therefore, is only to ſee with what Materials our *prevailing Fire* of Life is kindled, and in what *Species* of Enthu-

ſiaſts

fiafts it truly places us. For either the *Flefh* or
the *Spirit*; either the Wifdom from *above*, or
the Wifdom of *this World*, will have *its Fire*
in us; and we muft have a *Life* that governs
us either according to the Senfuality of the
Beaft, the Subtilty of the *Serpent*, or the Holinefs of the *Angel.* Enthufiafm is not blameable in Religion, when it is true Religion that
kindles it. We are created with *Wills* and
Defires for no other End, but to love, adore,
defire, ferve, and co-operate with God; and
therefore the more we are inflam'd in *this Motion* of our Wills and Defires, the more we
have of a God-like, divine Nature, and Perfection in us. Religious Enthufiafm is not
blameable, when it is a *ftrong Perfuafion*, a *firm
Belief* of a continual Operation, Impreffion,
and Influence from above, when it is a total
Refignation to, and Dependance upon the *immediate Infpiration*, and *Guidance* of the holy
Spirit in the whole Courfe of our Lives; this
is as fober, and rational a Belief, as to believe
that we *always* live, and move, and have our
Being in God. Both Nature and Scripture demonftrate this to be the true Spirit of a Religious Man. Nature tells every one, that we
can only be heavenly by a Spirit deriv'd from
Heaven, as plainly as it tells us, that we can
only

only be earthly, by having the Spirit of this
World breathing in us. The Gospel teaches no
Truth so *constantly*, so *universally* as this, that
every good Thought and good Desire is the
Work of the holy Spirit. And therefore both
Nature and Scripture demonstrate, that the
one only Way to Piety, Virtue and Holiness,
is to *prepare*, *expect*, and *resign* ourselves up
wholly to the Influence and Guidance of the
holy Spirit, in every Thing that we think, or
say, or do. The moment any one departs
from *this Faith*, or loses *this Direction* of his
Will and Desire, so far, and so long he goes
out of the one only Element of all Holiness of
Life. There is nothing that so sanctifies the
Heart of Man, that keeps us in such habitual
Love, Prayer, and Delight in God; nothing
that so kills all the Roots of Evil in our Nature,
that so renews and perfects all our Virtues,
that fills us with so much Love, Goodness,
and good Wishes to every Creature, as *this
Faith*, That God is always *present* in us with
his *Light* and *Holy Spirit*. When the Heart
has once learnt thus to find God, and knows
how to live every where, and in all Things in
this immediate Intercourse with him, seeing
him, loving him, and adoring him in every
Thing, trusting in him, depending upon him

X 4   for

for his continual Light and holy Spirit; when it knows that *this Faith* is infallible; that by thus believing, it thus poffeffes all that it believes of God; then it begins to have the Nature of God in it, and can do nothing but flow forth in Love, Benevolence, and good Will towards every Creature; it can have no Wifh towards any Man, but that he might thus know, and love, and find God in himfelf, as the true Beginning of Heaven, and the heavenly Life in the Soul.

On the other hand, no Error fo hurtful to the Soul, fo deftructive of all the Ends of the Gofpel, as to be led from this Faith and *entire Dependance* upon the holy Spirit of God, or to place our Recovery in any Thing elfe, but in the Operation of the Light and holy Spirit of God upon the Soul. It is withdrawing Men not only from the eafieft, the moft natural, the moft fruitful, but the only poffible Source of all Light and Life. For every Man, as fuch, has an open Gate to God in his Soul, he is always in that Temple, where he can worfhip God in Spirit and Truth: Every Chriftian, as fuch, has the *firft Fruits* of the Spirit, a *Seed* of Life, which is his *Call* and *Qualification* to be always in a State of inward Prayer, Faith, and holy Intercourfe with God.

All

All the *Ordinances* of the Gofpel, the daily
facramental Service of the Church, is to keep
up, and exercife, and ftrengthen *this Faith*;
to raife us to fuch an habitual Faith and Dependance upon the Light and holy Spirit of
God, that by thus feeking and finding God in
the *Inftitutions* of the Church, we may be ha-
bituated to feek him and find him; to live in
his Light, and walk by his Spirit in all the
Actions of our ordinary Life. This is the Enthufiafm in which every good Chriftian ought
to endeavour to live and dye.

   I come now to an *Enthufiaft*, which the
Doctor has accidentally met with, from whom,
it feems, *I have borrowed fome of my ftrange
Notions, and would put them off as my own*,
p. 119. The Doctor has this Intelligence from
his *trufty Affiftant*, who fays, *what elfe can be
expected from thofe, Who read* Jacob Behmen,
Dr. Pordage, *and Mrs.* Lead, *with almoft the
fame Veneration and implicit Faith, that other
People read the Scripture*, ibid. Two of thefe
Writers I know very little of, yet as much as
I defire to know; but *J. Behmen*, call'd the
Teutonick Theofopher, I have read much, and
much efteem: But the Defign of putting off
fome of his ftrange Notions, as *my own*, is as
                                        well

well-grounded, as if the Doctor had charged me with a Design of picking his Pocket.

The illustrious Sir *Isaac Newton*, when he wrote his *Principia*, and publish'd to the World his great Doctrine of *Attraction*, and those *Laws of Nature* by which the *Planets* began, and continue to move in their Orbits, could have told the World, that the *true and infallible* Ground of what he there advanced, was to be found in the *Teutonick Theosopher*, in his *three first Properties of Eternal Nature*; he could have told them, that he had been a *diligent Reader* of that wonderful Author, that he had made large Extracts out of him, and could have referred to him for the Ground of what he had observed of the Number *Seven*. Now why did not this great Man do thus? Must we suppose that he was *loth* to have it thought, that he had been *help'd* by any Thing that he had read? No: It is an unworthy Thought. But Sir *Isaac* well knew, that *Prejudice* and *Partiality* had such Power over many People's Judgments, that Doctrines, tho' ever so deeply founded in, and proved by all the Appearances of Nature, would be suspected by some as dangerous, and condemned by others, even as *false* and *Wicked*, had he made any *References*

rences to an Author that was *only called* an Enthufiaft.

Dr. *Trap* may take himfelf for an *eminent* Example and Proof of this. He has here fhewn with what *Speed* Matters may be determined by Prejudice. For here a *Stranger*, a *Layman*, not fo much as known to the Doctor by Name, who, for ought he can tell, may be fome *fmall Retailer* of Infidelity, or *Snuff-Candle* in the Play-houfe, who has gain'd upon the Doctor by no other *Marks* of Ability and Judgment, but his *Compliments* to him, and his *Scurrility* upon me ; from the *Authority* of this Informer, the Doctor immediately puts *J. B.* into his *Lift* of Enthufiafts. Is not this a Proof of what Sir *Ifaac Newton* muft have met with from fome great Scholars, and to what a *fpeedy Confutation* he muft have expofed himfelf, and the plaineft Appearances of Nature, had he ever referred to the *Teutonick Theofopher ?* Now am I here to fuppofe, that this Cenfure of the Doctor's relating to *J. B.* is a *Rafhnefs* that has here *firft* feized upon him by *Chance*, that he never *before* in his Life allowed himfelf to treat any *Man*, or any *Book* in this manner ; that if he took the Judgment of another, it was of fomebody that he knew ; if he condemn'd an Author, he always *ftaid* till he had read *fomething*

thing of him, at leaſt an *Index*, or a *Title Page* or two of his Works ? Or am I to ſuppoſe, that this has been the Doctor's Method *upwards of thirty-ſeven Years* ; calling one Man an Enthuſiaſt, another a Fanatick, this a monſtrous, that the *moſt pernicious Book of the Age*, as raſhly, as haſtily; regarding no more of Right or Wrong in that which he affirms of theſe Matters, than he has here done with regard to *J. B.*? But I hope the Doctor is ſingular in this Spirit; for if it could be ſuppos'd, that it was common amongſt learned Men, to get their Knowledge of antient and modern, foreign and domeſtick Enthuſiaſts, as haſtily and ſlightly as the Doctor here doth ; muſt it not be very dangerous for the *Unlearned* to take any Opinions of this kind from them ? Muſt it not be ſaid, that *one Grain* of Equity, good Senſe, and real Knowledge, is more to be deſired, than an *hundred Weight* of ſuch Learning ?

When I conſidered the *fallen* Soul, as a *Fire-Spirit*, deprived of its *proper Light*, and therefore become of a Diabolical Nature, I could have directed to *J. B.* for the deep and infallible Ground of it ; but what need was there for that, when I could make the plaineſt Principles of *Nature*; the plaineſt Doctrines of

Scripture,

Scripture, every thing that was said of the
Fall, of *Heaven*, of *Hell*, and the like, to be
undeniable Proofs of it? What I said in the
Second Proposition of the Discourse upon *Regeneration*, concerning the Holy Tri-unity of
God *in Man*, stands not in *that Form* of Expreffion any where that I know of; but for the
true Ground and Certainty of it, I could have
referr'd to the *Teutonick Theosopher*, to many
ancient and modern Writers of the greatest
Name, and to a *venerable Record* of Antiquity, ascrib'd even to St. *Peter* himself; where
he afferts, even upon the *fame Ground* as I
have done, that because we were created in
the Image and Likeness of God, therefore
the tri-une Life arises in us, as it does in God,
and we have *in us*, the *Father*, *Son*, and *Holy
Spirit* *.

But what Occasion was there for these References, when I had fo much better Proof, when
I could shew, that all which the Scriptures fay
of the whole *Nature* and *Manner* of our Redemption, of the whole *Nature* and *Form* of
Baptism, all that they fay of the *Necessity* of
the

* Rationalis Homo, factus ad Imaginem, & Similitudinem
Dei, fert in se Symbolicè Factoris fui *Imitationem*. Habet enim
in se Patrem, Filium & Spiritum. Mens quidem *locum* Patris
obtinet, Filii vero, qui ex mente gignitur, Sermo *Interior*, at
quæ auditur Vox *Prolationis*, Spiritum repræfentat, &c. *Co-
teler. S. S. Patr.* p. 595——1719.

the *Word,* and Holy Spirit of God having
again a *Birth in us,* are abſolute, deciſive
Proofs of it? * I knew alſo very well, that the
moſt eſſential, fundamental, and joyful Doctrines of the Goſpel would be *queſtioned,* or
received with *Difficulty,* had I referr'd to a *poor
Shoemaker* for any Proof of them : And it may
well be believed, that the Doctor would have
been amongſt the *firſt* and *loudeſt* of thoſe, who
would have cry'd out at my Folly and Preſumption in directing to an Author, whom all the
World knew to be an *illiterate Enthuſiaſt ;*
and yet, if all the World knows it as the
Doctor knows it, all the World may be ſaid to
know nothing about it.

Dr. *Trap* has a Fling at my Want of Taſte
for his *Virgil's, Horace's,* and *Terence's* : I own,
when I was about *Eighteen,* I was as fond of
theſe Books as the Doctor can well be *now,*
and ſhould then have been glad to have tranſ-
lated the *Sublime Milton,* if I had found myſelf able ; but this *Ardour* ſoon went off, and
I think it as good a Proof of the *Sublime,* to
deſire the Death of all that is Diabolical and
Serpentine in my own Nature, as to be *charm'd*
with thoſe *Speeches* which the *Devils* make in
Milton. Had the Doctor been more conver-
ſant in the Writings of a Set of Men call'd

Myſtical

* See Regeneration, *p.* 22 *to* 33.

Myftical Divines, than he appears to have
been, he had been better able to have charged
me with *humble Plagiary* than he is at present,
and might have done more Service to what he
calls the *Noble Science of Theology,* than by all
that *Light* which he has got from his *Poets,*
which he acknowledges to have *somewhat of
Wantonness in them,* p. 38. Of these Myftical Divines, I thank God, I have been a diligent Reader, through all Ages of the Church,
from the Apoftolical *Dionyfius the Areopagite,*
down to the great *Fenelon* Archbifhop of *Cam-
bray,* the illuminated *Guion,* and M. *Bertot.*
Had the Doctor read St. *Caffian,* a Recorder of
the Lives, Spirit and Doctrine of the Holy Fathers of the *Defarts,* as often as he had read
the *Story* of *Æneas* and *Dido,* he had been
lefs aftonifhed at many Things in my Writings:
But I apprehend the Doctor to be as great a
Stranger to the Writers of this kind, with
which every Age of the Church has been
blefs'd, and to know no more of the divine
*Rufbrochius, Thaulerus, Sufo, Harphius, Jo-
hannes de Cruce,* &c. than he does of *J. B.*
For had he known any Thing of them, he
had known that I am as chargeable with the
Sentiments of all of them, as with thofe of
J. Behmen. For tho' I never wrote upon any
Subject till I could call it *my own,* till I was fo
fully

fully poffeffed of the Truth of it, that I could fufficiently prove it in my *own Way*, without borrowed Arguments; yet, Doctrines of Religion I have none, but what the Scriptures and the *firft-rate* Saints of the Church are my Vouchers for.

Writers, like thofe I have mentioned, there have been in all Ages of the Church, but as they ferved not the Ends of *Popular Learning*, as they helped no People to *Figure* and *Preferment* in the World, and were ufelefs to *fcholaftick, controverfial* Writers, fo they dropt out of publick Ufe, and were only known, or rather *unknown*, under the Name of *Myftical Writers*, till at laft fome People have hardly heard of that very Name. Tho' if a Man was to be told what is meant by a Myftical Divine, he muft be told of fomething as *heavenly*, as *great*, as *defireable*, as if he was told, what is meant by a real, *regenerate, living* Member of the *Myftical* Body of Chrift. For they were thus called, for no other Reafon, than as *Mofes* and the Prophets, and the Saints of the Old Teftament may be called the *Spiritual Ifrael*, or the true *Myftical Jews*. Thefe Writers began their Office of Teaching, as *John* the *Baptift* did, after they had paffed through every kind of Mortification and Self-denial, every kind

kind of Trial and Purification, both inward and outward. They were deeply learned in all the Mysteries of the Kingdom of God, not thro' the Use of *Lexicons*, or meditating upon *Criticks*, but because they had *passed from Death unto Life.* They highly reverence and excellently direct the true Use of every thing that is *outward* in Religion, but like the Psalmist's *King's Daughter*, they are *all glorious within :* They are truly Sons of *Thunder*, and Sons of *Consolation* ; they break open the *whited Sepulchres* ; they awaken the Heart, and shew it its *Filth* and *Rottenness* of Death, but they leave it not, till the Kingdom of Heaven is raised up within it. If a Man have no Desire but to be of the Spirit of the Gospel, to obtain all that Renovation of Life and Spirit, which alone can make him to be in Christ a new Creature, it is a great Unhappiness to him to be unacquainted with these Writers, or to pass a Day without reading something of what they have written. For tho' the Scriptures are an inexhaustible Source of Spiritual Instruction, leading the Heart to the deepest Knowledge of all the Mysteries of the inward, new Life in God, with the greatest Plainness and Openness of Expression, yet a *worldly Spirit*, the *Schools*,

Y   *Criticism*,

Criticism, and *Controversy* have so dry'd, and deadned every Thing into an outward Letter and figurative Expression, that much of their Use is lost, till these Holy Writers, who interpret them by the same Spirit which wrote them, guide us to the true Use and Understanding of them; for in these Writers, the Spirit of God speaks a second Time, and every Thing that can awaken, convert, instruct and inflame the Heart with the Love of God, and all Holiness and Purity of Life, is to be found in the most irresistible Degree of Conviction. You will perhaps say, Do I then call all the World to these Spiritual Books? No, by no means. But I call all those, whom our Saviour called to himself in these Words; *Come unto me all ye that labour, and are heavy laden, and I will refresh you.*

But to return to the Doctor's Enthusiast.

Jacob Behmen, in his natural Capacity and outward Condition of Life, was as *mean* and illiterate as any one that our Lord called to be an Apostle, but as a *chosen Servant* of God, he may be placed amongst those who had received the highest Measures of Light, Wisdom and Knowledge *from Above*. He was no more a *human Writer*, spoke no more from *Opinion, Conjecture,*

Conjecture, or *Reason*, in what he publifhed to the World, than St. *John* did, when he put his *Revelation* into Writing. He has no Right to be placed amongft the infpir'd *Pen-men* of the New Teftament, he was no Meffenger from God of any Thing *new* in Religion, but the Myftery of all that was *old* and *true* both in Religion and Nature was *opened* in him. This is the *Particularity* of his Character, by which he ftands fully diftinguifhed from all the Prophets, Apoftles, and extraordinary Meffengers of God. They were fent with occafional Meffages, or to make fuch Alterations in the Oeconomy of Religion as pleafed God ; but this Man came on no particular Errand, he had nothing to alter, or add, either in the *Form*, or Doctrine of Religion ; he had no new Truths of Religion to propofe to the World, but all that lay in Religion and Nature, as a Myftery unfearchable, was in its deepeft Ground opened in this Inftrument of God. And all his Works are nothing elfe but a deep Manifeftation of the Grounds and Reafons of that which is *done*, that which is *doing*, and is to *be done*, both in the Kingdom of Nature, and the Kingdom of Grace, from the Beginning to the End of Time. His Works therefore,

Y 2

tho'

tho' immediately from God, have not at all the *Nature* of the Holy Scriptures, they are not offered to the World, as *neceffary* to be received, or as a Rule of Faith and Manners? and therefore no one has any Right to complain, either of the *Depths* of his Matter, or the *Peculiarity* of his Stile : They are juft as they fhould be, for thofe that are fit for them ; and he that likes them not, or finds himfelf unqualified for them, has no Obligation to read them.

The whole Syftem of Chriftianity has generally been looked upon as a Myftery of Salvation, folely founded in the Divine Pleafure ; and to be fuch a Scheme of Redemption, as is wholly to be refolved into the Contrivance of the *Will* and Wifdom of God ; and therefore Men can think as differently of it, can fall into as many Opinions about it, as they can of the Will and Wifdom of God. Hence has arifen all the *fpeculative Oppofition* to the Gofpel : It is becaufe Reafon, human Speculation, and Conjecture, is always imagining it can form a Religion more worthy of the Wifdom and Defigns of the Supreme Being than the Chriftian is ; and would be thought to oppofe the Gofpel only

for

for the Honour of God, and the Divine Attributes. This is the great, prevailing *Idolatry* of the present *Heathen World*; or *that* Part of Mankind who are Infidels, or Deists. Hence also is risen another Species of Idolatry, even amongst Christians of *all Denominations*; who, tho' receiving and professing the Religion of the Gospel, yet worship God not in Spirit and in Truth, but either in the Deadness of an outward Form, or in a *Pharisaical*, carnal Trust and Confidence in their own Opinions and Doctrines. This Body of People, whether they be *Clergy* or *Laity*, are but *nominal Christians*; because they have little more than the *Name* of every Mystery of the Gospel: *Historical Christians*, because satisfied with the *History* of Gospel-Salvation: *Literal Christians*, because looking only to, and contending only for, the *Letter* of the Institutions and Mysteries of Jesus Christ. For the Letter, for the federal Rite, and the *figurative* Expression of Regeneration, they are all Zeal and Industry; but the *Reality* of it, the *true-Life* of the New Birth, they *oppose* and *reject* as heartily as the *Deist* does the outward Form and Letter. Now this *two-fold Idolatry* of the present Heathen and

Christian

Christian World has its full Discovery and
Confutation in the Mystery opened in *J. B.*
which, when understood, leaves no Room
for any Man either to disbelieve the Gospel,
or to content himself with the *Letter* of it.
For, in the Revelation made to this Man, the
first *Beginning* of all Things is opened, the *whole
State*, the *Rise*, the *Workings*, and the *Progress*
of all Nature is revealed, and every Doctrine,
Mystery, and Precept of the Gospel is found,
not to have sprung from any *arbitrary Appointment*, but to have its *eternal, unalterable*
Ground and Reason in Nature; and God
appears to save us by the Methods of the
Gospel, because there was *no other* possible
Way to save us in all the Possibility of Nature. And therefore the *idolatrous* Confidence
of the Deist in his *own Reason*, and of the
nominal Christian in the *outward Letter* of
their Religion, have equally their full Confutation.

To those who confine Idolatry to the
Worship of *such Idols* as the old Heathens
and *Jews* worshipped, it may seem a Para-
dox, to talk of the Idolatry of the *present
World*, either amongst *Deists* or *Christians*.
But if we consider Things more than Words,

we

we shall find, that Idolatry is no where, but where the Heart has *set up* Something in the *Place* of God; and therefore is every-where, and in every Thing, where the Heart places that *Repose*, *Trust*, and *Delight*, which should be placed in God alone. For God is only own'd, and confessed to be *our God*, by these Acknowledgments and Dispositions of our Hearts towards Him. It is an infallible Truth, That all Sin has its Beginning and Continuance in and from Idolatry: This alone debauched the former and the later Ages of the World, and is the one Source of all the Corruption of Manners, from the Beginning to the End of Time. You don't make a *Golden Calf*, as the *Jews* did, to worship it; but if *Mammon* is your God, if your Life is devoted to Pride, Ambition, and Sensuality, your Idolatry is not so *sensible*, but it is as *real* as theirs, who danced about a Golden Calf. You fancy that *Venus* is not your *Goddess*, because you are not worshipping a *figur'd Image* of her, in a Temple call'd by her Name; but if you look at the *Odes*, the *Hymns*, the *Songs*, which you love, which Lust has inspir'd, then you may know that *Venus* is the Goddess of your Heart. It is thus with every Object, and in every Course of

Life,

[328]

Life, that which poffeffes and governs our Heart, has ufurp'd the *Right* and *Place* of God in it, and has that *Worſhip*, *Truſt*, and *Devotion* of the Heart, which is due to God alone : And therefore the Idolatry of the pre- fent World, is only of a different Kind from that of the antient, it is lefs feen, and lefs con- feffed, but not lefs real, than when carved Images, and figur'd Idols were ador'd.

Deifm, or the Religion of *human Reafon*, fet up in Oppofition to the Gofpel, is *direct Idolatry*, and has every Groffnefs and Vanity of Image Worſhip. For to put our Truſt in our own Reafon, to be content with its Light, to refign ourfelves up to it, and depend upon it as our Guide, is a Miftake that has every Grof- nefs and Vanity of the Adoration of an Idol. Now this Kind of Idolatry has over-run all the laſt Ages of the World ; it is the laſt Effort of human Vanity ; it is the utmoſt that Idolatry can do, both to hide and propagate itfelf, and is the Devil under the Appearance of an Angel *of Light*. The Gofpel has no Enemy but this Idolatry, and it is as vifible in the Church, as out of it : Hence it is, that the State of the Church is fo fadly defcribed in the *Revelation* of St. *John*, for fo many Ages, as a fpiritual Whore-

Whoredom. When the old *Jews* left off the *Idols* of the Heathens, they fell into an Idolatry of another kind, which was this, they *idolized* the Rites and Ceremonies of their own true Religion ; they placed that *Confidence* in the outward Letter, and expected that Good from their outward Rites, which they should have placed, fought, expected from God alone. This is the Idolatry of the rational Deift, and the nominal Chriftian. But when the Myftery of all Nature and Grace, which by the Mercy of God has open'd itfelf in the Writings of *J. B.* fhall find its Children, every Idolatry, both within and without the Church, will be afham'd to fhew itfelf.

But it may be afk'd by fome, what warrant I have for all that I have faid of *J. B.* or how I can prove to the World, that his Writings are the Work of the holy Spirit ? It is anfwered, I neither intend, nor defire to prove this to the World. And if any one will difpute or deny every Thing that I have faid of him, he will meet with no Oppofition from me. I have given notice of a *Pearl*, if any one takes it to be otherwife, or has neither Skill or Value for Pearls, he is at Liberty to trample it under his Feet. Nothing paffes with the World for Proof of a divinely infpir'd Writer, but Miracles ;

racles; if People can fee no other Proof but
this, it is not in my Power to give them better
Eyes. I fuppofe the Gofpel, and all the Writings of the New Teftament, have *internal
Characters* of their divine Original, for thofe
that can fee them; but if they had been left to
thofe internal Characters, I am apt to think,
that the Sons of *Cicero*, the Difciples of a *Bayle*,
or thofe who ftand the higheft in fuch like Li-
terature, would, of all Men, be the moft in-
difpofed and unwilling to fee and own them.

Had we no Miracles for Proof of the Infpiration of the Scriptures, they would be ftill what
they are, the *true Word*, and *Wifdom* of God,
and there would be the fame Benefit in believing and receiving them as fuch. But to *whom*
could they be prov'd to come from the Spirit
of God? Not to a *Ciceronian*, becaufe it is
the Character, the *Genius*, the *Greatnefs* of
Cicero, to *diffemble* and *perfonate*; and as an O-
rator, a *Statefman*, and a *Philofopher*, to affirm
or deny as he pleafes, without any Regard to
his own Sentiments. And therefore to the
Sons of *Cicero* nothing can be proved, becaufe
they depart from his Character, if they difcover their own Sentiments, and don't either,
as *Philofophers, Orators*, or *Statefmen*, affirm
and

and deny as they pleafe, or as fuits the Character which they chufe to act under.

Again; It cannot be proved to a Difciple
of *Bayle*; becaufe, tho' he was a Man,
" whofe Strength and Clearnefs of Reafoning
" can be equalled only by the Gaiety, Eafi-
" nefs, and Delicacy of his Wit; who, per-
" vading human Nature with a Glance, ftruck
" into the Province of *Paradox*, ———— and
" had not enough of real Greatnefs, to over-
" come the laft Foible of fuperior Geniufes,
" the Temptation of Honour, which the
" *Academick Exercife of Wit* is fuppofed to
" bring to its Profeffors *.

And therefore to a true Difciple of *Bayle*,
nothing that is juft, fober, or true, can be
fufficiently proved; becaufe it is his Genius,
his Honour, his Ambition, to maintain the
Paradox.

The next Queftion is, *How* this can be
proved, *viz.* That the Scriptures have internal
Characters of their Divinity. Now this can
only be, by an honeft Simplicity, and Love of
Truth, by Humility and Prayer, and Conver-
fion of the Heart to God in the reading of
them. Thefe are the only Difpofitions that
could poffibly bring any Man into a Senfe and
Belief

* Divine Legation of *Mofes*, B. I. p. 33.

Belief of their Divine Original : And therefore, all thofe critical Scholars, and rationally wife Men, whofe Enquiries are animated with a Love of Glory and perfonal Diftinction, and who looked into thofe Writings for fuch Ends, and with fuch Views as they read other Books, would be of all Men the moft unable to fee, and unwilling to own the very *beft Truths* of the Holy Scriptures ; becaufe it is the very Nature and End of the Scriptures, to difcover the Vanity and Falfenefs of that Light and Knowledge, which is got from human Reafoning, and to fubdue that Self-fufficiency, which is fo infeparable from certain *Kinds* and *Degrees* of human Learning.

F I N I S.

Figure of a Fault 345 = 1.

Trinity 149

...ne 164

Prayer 180

Shedding of Blood 183

4/
66.

CPSIA information can be obtained
at www.ICGtesting.com
Printed in the USA
LVHW060804111022
730366LV00024B/497